## Praise For Lawrence Kelter And The Stephanie Chalice Mystery Series

“Lawrence Kelter reminds me of an early Robert Ludlum.”

—Nelson DeMille

"Chalice’s acerbic repartee is like an arsenal of nuclear missiles."

—BookWire Review

“Chalice is irresistible; a contemporary tour de force!”

—James Siegel, Author of Derailed

"Edge of the seat tension with a killer on the streets of New York and homicide detective, Stephanie Chalice hot on the trail."

—Coffee & Crime

“Chalice is dangerous and sexy; fast-paced entertainment that left me spent and clamoring for more.”

—Ann Loring, International Women’s Writing Guild

In The Stephanie Chalice Mystery Series

Don't Close Your Eyes

Ransom Beach

The Brain Vault

# The Brain Vault

Lawrence Kelter

For Iris,
All my best

New York

This book is a work of fiction. Names, places, characters, and incidents are the product of the author's imagination or are used fictitiously. Any resemblance to events, locales, or persons living or dead, is coincidental.



First Edition – July 2011

ISBN-13 978-1456572860
ISBN-10 1456572865

Manufactured/Printed in the United States of America

For
Morris, Doris, Salvatore, and Adelina

# Acknowledgments

The author gratefully acknowledges the following special people for their contributions to this book.

First and foremost to my wife, Isabella, for her love, support, and tireless dedication to this book's perfection.

To my children Dawn and Chris, for what they mean to me.

To Dr. Jill Kelter and Dr. Daniel Oakley for their keen insight into the workings of the preseverative mind.

# The
# Brain Vault

Lawrence Kelter

# One

Newest of all moons, the tail of the waxing crescent was visible as I looked up at the cloud riddled sky, a dagger's silver blade against the vast, black heavens.

It was a lovely night for crime.

Now if you knew me, you'd know that a gal like Stephanie Chalice wouldn't normally be caught dead taking a midnight stroll through Central Park (not without an Uzi under each arm anyway). But I'm not alone, I'm with Gus Lido. Gus and I, we're both on the job, two of New York's finest trying to carve a moment's peace out of a day of sheer chaos. He's in a tux and I'm in an evening gown—even so, we're armed and dangerous, trust me.

I was hoping for an altercation free evening, but such seemed destined not to be the case.

"Hey, watch it," Gus said, grabbing my hand and preventing me from putting my foot down where God and Jimmy Choo had not intended for it to go.

"Wow. Look at the size of that."

Gus shook his head in amazement. "Got to be a Labrador."

*Labrador, how about a Clydesdale?*

"The last time I saw a specimen like that was on an episode of Animal Planet—the crew was in the Serengeti, tracking a herd of elephants."

"Anything else you can tell me from your examination of the specimen? What did the beast have for dinner, Iams or Eukanuba?"

Gus snorted.

Hell of a way to start a story, isn't it?

Yeah, I think so too—In any case, my designer pumps had escaped a fate worse than death.

Well, you may have guessed that Lido and I are a team and then some. We both work homicide out of Midtown North, fighting crime and our sexual urges twenty-four/seven. We seem to be a lot better at solving case crimes than keeping our hormones in check, but we're discreet—at least I think we are. Gus and I have one of the highest case-closing percentages on the squad—we get the job done and manage to get a little something, something in on the side. Few people know that we're together, and I intend to keep the list short. I love my job and my partner. Having your cake and eating it too can be a lot of work. No one ever said life was simple.

Gus and I had just broken away from a retirement party at The Boathouse Cafe. Our boss, Chief of Detectives Sonellio had finally put in his papers after thirty-five years on the job. I really and truly love the old guy. He's been part of my life since way back when. He was my dad's friend when he was on the job and has been like a Dutch uncle to me ever since my dad's passing.

I wasn't sure how well retirement would serve a man like him, a man that had spent the best years of his life putting New York City's most heinous animals behind bars. I wondered just how much time an ex-cop could spend fly fishing before he went absolutely bat shit. He was leaving for his lakeside cabin in Maine over the weekend. I guess we'll just have to see how that goes.

Central Park seemed dreamlike as we strolled along. It looked something like a monotone Van Gogh, with lamp lights playing on shadows and tree tips bending to the wind. The stars were large and clear where the clouds gapped. The air was damp enough to enhance the fragrance of the blossoming flowers.

"Hell of a night," Lido said as we walked along.

"Like something out of a dream."

Lido turned to me looking distressed. He always had an involuntary reaction to the D word. It was like a scene from a cartoon, and two anvils had just swung down from above him, colliding with either side of his head. Dream, that sinister D word, it was for Lido a metaphoric iceberg, an enigma that he could just see at the tip. The rest, that invisible ninety percent taunted him mercilessly. You see my life has at times been a tad bizarre. There's just so much going on in my head when I sleep, weird and crazy stuff. My dreams are usually a preamble to adventure, to trouble, and case crime. I think Lido would prefer it if I became an insomniac, but as we all know, that was not about to happen anytime soon.

"So what'd you think about the party?" Lido asked.

"It was fun," I said, but my eyes said differently, and Gus knew it instantly.

"You look like you're hiding something. What's up?"

I stopped and watched the hypnotic pattern of the tree tips as they continued to sway back and forth. It took a moment until I confessed. "Change can be very hard to accept."

"What's changed?"

"Sonellio, retired, growing old, and—"

"Out of your life." Lido put his arms around me. "He's not gone, Stephanie, just retired."

"He has always been there for me and Ma. I always knew where he was, just a stone's throw away at the precinct. In a few days he'll be off fishing for bass of all things. It just seems completely wrong."

"Maybe you're wrong. Who knows what we'll want when we retire."

Gus was such a fabulous guy; every word out of his mouth resounded with commitment. Our relationship was just coming up on a year, and the marriage word had never reared its ugly head. I suppose that's what made us work—we both knew we were there for each other. "I don't know, maybe you're right." I shrugged.

"Still." Lido lifted my chin and looked into my eyes. "There's more to it than that, isn't there?"

I shook my head. Lido knew exactly why I was sad. Sonellio's health had been on a steady decline over the last several months. There was that constant hacking cough that crackled through my brain like gunfire, and the unhealthy pallor of his skin, which had once been rich with the glow of his Sicilian heritage. Was he really going on vacation, or was it just an excuse so that he could slip away quietly to die in peace?

"He's such a private man. I want to—"

"This is the way he wants it, Stephanie. It would be wrong for you to interfere." Lido leaned in to kiss me. "I'm still here."

Our lips had just touched when a frightening, guttural moan filled the air. Adrenaline pumped the melancholy out of my head.

"Christ, what the hell was that?"

We turned and ran in the direction the noise had come from. I heard it again and tried to hone in on the location. Now I've got long legs, but I had trouble keeping up with Lido in my gown and pumps. The paths of Central Park were a maze in the darkness. We ran for moments, searching for activity, but the paths broke off in different directions, never taking us where we had hoped they would lead us. I could hear the telltale sound off in the distance. It was the sound of a human being in intense pain.

“Do you know where we are?” Lido asked.

I stopped and looked around, trying to get my bearings, somehow trying to imagine the park in daylight as I was familiar with it. I was hoping to find something familiar about the landscape, something that would ring that proverbial bell. And then, looking up at the sky, it came to me. Off in the distance were the tall tree tips that had drawn my attention as they swayed back and forth with the wind. “Let me take you down.”

“You’ve lost me,” Gus said.

“Let me take you down.”

“Are you sloshed?”

“No.” I didn’t take the time to elaborate, I just turned and ran. He knew that I was on to something and followed.

# Two

The evening sky was bright enough for me to make out the tips of the three bald cypress trees I knew stood at the northern tip of the main lawns that made up the Strawberry Fields Memorial. I can't tell you how I knew that we were supposed to be there, but I did. Call it a premonition. "Let me take you down, 'cause I'm going to Strawberry Fields." The verse to John Lennon's song looped through my head as I picked up speed. For a moment, Lido had been left flatfooted, shaking his head in wonder, but he had now caught up and was pacing me, shoulder to shoulder.

"Let me take you down?" Lido asked.

"'Cause I'm going to Strawberry Fields. Don't you get it?"

"Stephanie, have you gone entirely insane?"

"Don't ask me what I'm doing, just follow me."

Gus knew better than to argue. In the time we had worked as a team, he had learned that I had a sixth sense about this sort of thing that was absolutely uncanny.

Okay, there comes a time in every woman's life when she has to make some really tough choices, and this was one of those times. The exquisite Jimmy Choos I was wearing had gone from being a fashion statement to a high speed liability. I didn't want to tumble head over heels like an accelerating albatross, so I kicked them off while in full stride so that I could bravely run barefooted where no evening gown clad detective had ever run before. Damn, I think I just stepped on a slug.

We were now on the looped path I knew would take us directly to the mosaic at the center of the Strawberry Fields memorial. I'd walked it so many times before. My dad was a kid when the Beatles first arrived on the scene back in the sixties. My closet was still filled with his old vinyl albums: Meet the Beatles, Introducing the Beatles, The White Album—he had them all. The songs had become a permanent connection between the two of us; one that transcended time and bridged the gap between the physical and metaphysical world. I can still remember him telling me about the Fab Four. He had an Abbey Road tape in the car that he'd play endlessly. I was just a kid when John Lennon died, but I can still remember how the city was stricken by his murder. It was such an awful and senseless tragedy. It hit my dad really hard—he played his Beatle tapes over and over as if trying to hold onto a shred of the passed artist. Eventually we all moved on, but Lennon's music would always flow from him through my dad to me, words and music we would keep forever.

"Let me take you down, 'cause I'm going to Strawberry Fields. Nothing is real..."

At the center of the Strawberry Fields mosaic, partially covering the word IMAGINE, was a man, barely covered by a tattered bed sheet, lying unconscious. Most of his body was visible. Even in the dark, I could see a strange mosaic pattern on his skin. As I got closer, I could see that he was covered with scars over most of his body. My mind jumped to a conclusion, perhaps unsubstantiated, but it looked like a sadistic montage, a pattern that memorialized the torture I suspected this poor soul must have endured. He had sustained a rather large gash on his ankle near the Achilles tendon where blood was still pooling. Even in the out of doors, the man reeked of cigarette smoke.

"He's still alive," I shouted. I pressed my ear against his chest to confirm my initial diagnosis. I knew that he was alive because bleeding quickly stops after the heart arrests. His heartbeat was weak and slow, nonetheless it was present. "He's still with us, but going fast—call for a bus."

Lido was on his cell phone instantly, requesting help.

I tore the hem off my silk crepe gown and quickly tied a tourniquet around John Doe's leg, desecrating forever the design genius of Donna Karan. My lifesaving triage technique seemed to do the trick, the bleeding stopped. With God's help and a well trained EMT driver, Doe would get to the hospital in time and stay alive. At the same time, tearing away the hem, had transformed my elegant Donna Karan gown into a micro dress, leaving me visible up to the—" The gown was ruined, but I knew a couple of call girls that could make good use of it still—I'm so thrifty.

Lido placed his dinner jacked over Doe's upper body to keep him warm.

"How does he look?"

"Too close to call. He's very weak."

Lido's eyes were traveling up and down my legs. He whispered in my ear. "Promise you'll never throw this dress away." Now, I had a modest collection of hooker skirts and Joan Crawford pumps in the closet that I trotted out when the occasion called for it, but from the reaction I was getting from Lido, I figured one more couldn't hurt. Lido looked feverish. I could see the carotid artery bulge on his neck. We'd be riding with Doe to the hospital in a few minutes. I didn't know where we'd find the opportunity, but while a surgical team was patching Doe, we would likely find ourselves entwined in one of the hospital's on-call rooms—one could only hope.

Time was running out for Doe. While waiting, I continued to scan the portion of his body that Lido's jacket didn't cover. There were scars and burn marks over almost every inch of exposed skin. *Thank God you escaped.* I could only imagine what this poor soul had been through. How long had this poor man been imprisoned?

Off in the distance I could hear an ambulance's electronic yelp drawing closer. I pressed my hand against Doe's chest. "He's still with us. Gus, I think you should meet the bus at the park entrance and lead them here. We don't want to lose any time."

"Agreed. I'll be right back."

I watched Gus as he disappeared into the darkness; his crisp white shirt reflecting moonlight—for a moment, it looked like a ghostly torso disappearing into the tree lined park.

With Gus gone, the park felt eerily silent. I checked Doe again. His heart sounded weak, so I pushed aside Lido's jacket and examined Doe for other wounds I may have missed, wounds that might prove fatal. I rocked him upward a bit to examine his back. As I did, I noticed a bright white object lying nearby under a shrub. I strained to see it more clearly. As I was doing so, I felt something embedded in Doe's back. My senses were racing, sight and touch competing, to identify the two objects.

Sight won out. The object lying at the base of the shrub was nothing other than a pure, white human skull. *What in God's name?* I was still reeling from the first discovery when it dawned on me that the object embedded in Doe's back was a Taser dart. A wire running from the object confirmed my suspicion. My heart rate spiked. I spun around quickly to survey my surroundings, and the hairs on the back of my neck snapped to attention. I was not alone.

And then it hit me. I felt an excruciating pain in

the small of my back, as if I had been hit by an electric power line. I began to shake as the Taser blast racked my body. I tightened my fists to fight it but it was too strong. I had to place my palms against the ground to steady myself. As I did, I heard menacing, adenoid laughter nearby, and the sound of someone approaching from behind me. I was on my hands and knees fighting to stay conscious, trying to keep the muscular spasm from knocking me onto my back. All the time, I heard him drawing closer.

The Taser was still frying my nervous system when I felt his hot breath on my neck dampening my skin with his evil. The sound of his mocking laughter grew louder—it was as if he were in my ears. As I turned to see his face, I heard the sound of others approaching. "Gus." I cried out his name. Somehow I knew it was him. My stricken voice cried out for my other half, my partner and friend.

"Stephanie?" I heard his voice boom back from somewhere in the park.

*Thank God.* "Gus!"

I heard my assailant gasp. Panic set into his labored breathing. He turned and was about to run. I wanted to grab him, do anything to slow him down until Lido arrived.

"Stephanie!" Lido's voice sounded closer.

"Gus," my voice was now nothing more than a whisper.

I tried to pull my hand off the ground, but my muscles were unresponsive. They felt rubbery and disconnected. I finally jerked my hand free, but I couldn't keep my balance and fell over, smacking my head on the rock hard ceramic ground. My assailant was already yards away, slipping into the darkness. I wanted to know him. My eyes drilled through the darkness, but he was already too far away. My brain was struggling to fit the pieces together, but my thoughts just kept bouncing around my head and not making sense. Looking up at the night sky, I saw that dagger moon, hanging low enough to slice through me. It seemed to be falling out of the sky.

"Stephanie!"

Lido sounded just yards away. I couldn't wait to see his face and know that I was safe. Somewhere, somehow, I must have known it already, and knew that I could drop my guard because the moon began to dim, and then everything went black.

# Three

"No showboating, Stephanie—get a good strong grip and hold onto the wing strut with both hands."

"Wing strut? Showboating? What the hell is going on here?" And then the darkness opened up around me and I saw where I was. "Oh, Jesus!" I was thousands of feet up in the air, holding on for dear life, under the wing of a single engine plane with miles of absolutely nothing beneath me. I made the mistake of looking down. "Oh dear God."

"Huge mistake, Stephanie, focus straight ahead; don't let your nerves get the better of you."

"That's easy for you to say."

"Think of something that will distract you—Scotsmen playing bagpipes for instance."

"Scotsmen playing bagpipes; are you insane?" Wait a minute, who am I talking to anyway? I turned my head. "Bear Grylls?" This guy was everywhere. "What in the name of The British Special Forces are we doing here?"

"We're flying over the African Savanna, Stephanie. Not to worry, I'm going to talk you down, but until we're over the drop zone, I want you to hold on firmly with both hands."

"Both hands...*right.*" I grabbed hold of the strut with my free hand just as the plane banked hard to the right. "Better?"

"Much. You wouldn't want turbulence to shake you loose at the wrong time—God knows where you'd land. You might end up in a jagged ravine or in a crocodile infested river. I once broke my back in three places making a routine jump. I must say, holding on with one hand was awfully cavalier of you. You must have ice water in your veins. Most first timers would be absolutely petrified."

"Trust me, I'm paralyzed with fear. I don't think I can do this. I'm going to climb back into the plane."

"Wrong choice."

"Why?"

Grylls threw a glance in the direction of the pilot's chair. It was empty.

"Where's the—?" The plane nosed down just as the words were coming out of my mouth.

"That's our cue, Stephanie. Ready to go?"

"No!" I was shaking my head frantically.

"Right then—on my count: one, two, three, drop."

Grylls let go and began freefalling. As he did, the plane began to plummet. "Oh Christ...*Geronimo.*" Now, I admit the first few seconds were terrifying, but then the adrenaline spike leveled off and I realized that falling through the air was kind of cool. I mean I was still alive and I did have a parachute. "I have a parachute, right?" Grylls was next to me, his face fluttering violently against the wind. "You look like your face is going to fly off."

"Never has before."

The British; so droll. "So what about the parachute, have I got one or am I destined to become a street pizza?"

"Packed it myself." With that, Grylls reached over and pulled my ripcord. "Enjoy the ride, Stephanie. The view's spectacular."

I bounced hard in my harness as the parachute filled with wind. Grylls on the other hand was dropping fast, and growing tinier and tinier by the second. Oh God, there it goes—I finally saw his parachute open. I was hoping he'd wait for me down there. The African Savanna didn't sound like the type of place I'd want to navigate on my own. The ground was growing large as I looked downward, coming at me fast.

"Stephanie, Stephanie?"

I heard Lido's voice. It sounded distant, too distant to pay attention to. I almost didn't hear it. I just knew he was calling me. And then I was back.

"Stephanie, you scared the hell out of me."

I saw Lido through narrow slits. My head ached like hell as I opened my eyes. It took a second before I realized that I was in the hospital. "What am I doing here?"

"You smacked your head pretty good. You've got a concussion."

Gus hugged me. His warm skin felt good against my cheek, but I only gave myself a second to savor his embrace. The light outside told me it was morning. "Doe, did he make it?"

Lido nodded.

"I was out all night?"

"Uh huh. I found you flat on your back, lying next to Doe. What the hell happened?"

"I was—" I was only minimally miserable, until I felt the bile rise toward my mouth. I looked around frantically for something to hurl into. I grabbed a plastic water pitcher and let go. It took a moment before I came up for air. Lido looked as if he had just seen me eviscerated. He was pounding the hell out of the nurse's call button and looking like he needed a hit of oxygen himself.

"Are you okay?"

I nodded but remained silent. I wasn't exactly feeling my oats and needed a moment to regroup. Hospital staff's great when they know they're taking care of a cop. A nurse came flying through the door.

"She's awake," Lido announced.

The nurse took in the scene before her. "Relax, I've got it," she said to Lido, "Go get some air—you look worse than she does."

I smiled in spite of the way I was feeling.

"I'm Greta," the nurse said. She ripped open a pack of wipes and started cleaning my face like I was a baby. "Sorry I wasn't in the room when you woke up." She took the smelly pitcher of spew from me. "Do you still feel like vomiting? How do you feel?"

"Like I've been run over by a truck."

"You may be nauseous for a while. You've got a huge lump on your noggin." She turned to Lido. "Seriously, handsome, am-scray. I'll take care of the lady cop. Why don't you get yourself a cup of New York's worst coffee. Anything will taste good in the condition you're in."

Greta looked to be in her late fifties. She was thin, blond, and looked like she had been on the victorious side of many a bar brawl.

"I'll be back in a couple of minutes," Gus said.

"I seem to be in good hands. Take your time."

We both watched until Gus was out the door. Greta cleaned me up a bit more and then checked my blood pressure.

"He's a good man," she said. "Stayed up all night running back and forth between here and the ICU. Tell me, where do you find a man like that? I've been married three times—never latched onto a man worth keeping."

Greta's comment warmed my heart, but I kept my mouth shut. I wasn't up to snuff and didn't want to say anything I'd end up regretting. Greta glanced at me over the top of her glasses as she pumped the blood pressure cuff. Her look indicated that she was waiting for me to fess up.

"Not talking?"

I shook my head.

"No need to."

"Excuse me?"

"Look, Honey, I've been nursing for thirty years. I've seen couples married for decades where the husbands weren't as concerned about their spouses as Detective Lido is about you. Your blood pressure's fine. If you don't mind me asking, you came in here wearing one of the shortest gowns I've ever seen—you working some kind of decoy detail?"

"You asking if I was dressed as a hooker?"

"Yeah, I see that on TV all the time."

"No, I tore the hem off my dress to make a tourniquet for John Doe."

"Oh, that was pretty quick thinking."

"Thank you."

"You had a busy night."

"I did indeed."

I waited patiently while Greta checked my pulse. "You look like you're strong as a horse, Honey. How'd you hit your head?"

"I'm not sure but I think I was Tasered. The last thing I remember was lying on my back in the middle of Central Park, staring up at the moon."

"No crap? Did they get the son of a bitch that did it?"

"Beats me, I've been asleep. I think he got away. Do you know how John Doe's doing?"

"Not a clue, Honey. I only know what Detective Handsome told me. I think the poor SOB's in a coma. I'm gonna check your temperature." She slipped the thermometer probe into a sanitary plastic sleeve. "Open wide."

I guess I had about thirty seconds of peace and quiet before Greta started prying into my private life again. I still felt light-headed and it took a special effort to put my thoughts together.

I tried to reconstruct the sequence of events that took place the night before, the sprint through Central Park and finding Doe sprawled out in the middle of the Strawberry Fields Mosaic. I pictured myself checking Doe's vitals, just before Lido left to direct the EMS team. Doe's pulse was getting weaker. I rolled him sideways to see if he had a back wound, when... I spit the thermometer out of my mouth.

"Hey, you're not finished."

"There's no time for that now. Get Gus, I need him now." I threw back the sheets and started to get out of bed. Greta tried to stop me, but she saw the look on my face and backed away in a hurry. My heart and my stomach had discrepant ideas. The pitcher wasn't handy enough—I lost it on the linoleum, missing Greta by mere inches."

"Are you nuts, Honey? Get back into bed. I'll find your partner right after I clean up the mess."

"No, I need him now."

"Okay, okay, just let me get the floor—"

"Leave the floor. I need him now."

"Okay."

"Now!"

I think I scared Greta out of the room. She took off running.

I tried to assess my physical condition, my state of readiness, because I'd be leaving the hospital shortly if Lido answered the sixty-four thousand dollar question incorrectly. What I really needed to know was if Lido had seen the skull, the one that was lying under the bushes last night. I had seen it for a split second just before noticing the Taser plug in Doe's back. I'm sure Lido and the EMS team had other things on their mind, like saving Doe's life and mine. All the same, there was a crucial bit of evidence that I needed to get my hands on, and get my hands on it I would, even if I had to carry a barf bag every step of the way.

# Four

Lenox Hill Hospital was just a stone's throw from Central Park. I was sitting next to Lido in the back of an RMP as we were escorted back to the scene of the crime. Okay, so this was the first time I'd ever taken a tour of duty wearing borrowed hospital scrubs, but as I said, there was a human skull in the park last night and I needed to recover it now. There was a perp in the park with us last night. He had likely followed the escaped John Doe and Tasered him moments before Lido and I arrived on the scene. He must've been there, waiting in the shadows, when we found Doe, hiding and waiting for his opportunity to recover the skull. I gave him that opportunity when I sent Lido to guide the EMS team. I was praying that he hadn't circled back later last night to recover his lost treasure.

I was forced to sign releases up the wazoo before they'd let me out of Lenox Hill.

The truth be told, I felt like death warmed over, but

there's something to be said for an adrenaline rush that pushes all concerns about physical wellbeing into the background. Officially, I'd have to undergo a department physical exam before I could return to active duty, but I'm not the kind of gal that sits on the sidelines

It was almost ten AM when we arrived at the park. I felt terribly uneasy. Whoever had Tasered me last night, had ample opportunity to revisit the park in the wee hours and make off with the skull. My heart was pounding in my chest as we arrived.

Lido had forced me to swear that I'd do no more than point out the spot where I'd seen it. If it wasn't still there, I was supposed to wait like a good little girl while the boys in blue conducted their search.

I have to admit, I was feeling awfully woozy as I got out of the RMP, but I had to put on a brave face because Lido was hovering around me like a mother hen. The park looked so completely different in the clear morning sunlight, but it only took a second for me to orient myself once I stepped foot on the memorial's ceramic tiles.

"I don't see it." I flashed back to the prior evening. I could picture the skull lying at the base of a shrub. I walked directly over to where I thought it should be. "It was right here." My heart sunk—I was damn sure the perp had come back and taken it.

"Are you sure?" Lido asked.

"Yeah, right here."

We had a small detail of patrolmen with us. Lido gave them instructions and they began searching for the skull.

"Alright, you sit down in the car and wait," Lido said. "We'll find it if it's still here."

"No, I'm okay. I can help."

"Don't make me get rough."

I gave Gus a weak smile. "Really, I can—"

"First of all, you promised me. Secondly, you look like hell." Gus took my arm and escorted me back to the patrol car. It wasn't like me to give in, but my legs were beginning to feel like rubber and cold sweat was breaking out across my forehead and upper lip.

"Now don't get pissed," Lido said, "but I have to ask...are you sure you saw a human skull last night? It was late, you were Tasered, and you smacked your head. Human skulls aren't lily white anyway. They're more of a creamy color."

"I know what I saw."

"It couldn't have been a white plastic bag? I mean in all the commotion. On the way over here you told me you had dreamt that you were skydiving with Bear Grylls. You sure you didn't dream up this skull?"

"You're pressing your luck."

Lido threw his hands up in defeat and closed the door to the car, leaving me alone with my thoughts—dangerous company. I watched from the car as Lido and the patrolman searched the park. For the moment, there was nothing else I could do. I needed to get my act together, but my body and my will to proceed were not on the same schedule.

I noticed a group of school kids, chaperoned by adults, probably a class trip to the park. Two of the boys in the group were giving me and the patrol car an odd, concerned stare. I thought it strange that the police elicited a response like that from a couple of school kids, but I was tired, too tired to play detective, and the spring air was exquisite. It was warm and smelled from freshly cut grass and lavender. I put my head back and closed my eyes to gather strength. Within a moment, I was floating through the air, tethered to a parachute as I had been before.

"Stephanie."

"Who said that?" The voice I heard did not belong to Bear Grylls. It was a woman's voice.

"I did."

The ethereal form of a woman wearing tribal robes materialized before me. She was floating lithely in the air. I had to do a double take. "Madonna?"

"It ain't the blessed virgin, Sweetheart."

"You don't have a parachute."

"That's for mortals."

"You're amazing." Her hair and makeup were perfect. Her face wasn't fluttering. She was just sitting aloft in the sky with her legs crossed in the lotus position, looking serene and confident. "So, you're just hanging around?"

"I'm here to accompany you on your spiritual journey."

"Don't look now, but the ground's coming up pretty goddamn fast."

Madonna's voice sounded otherworldly. "You don't have to close your eyes, Stephanie. Take my hand and we'll float down together."

"You can do that?"

I reached out and took her extended hands. "I think so. I know I can walk on water. Anyway, what are you worried about? I'm the one without a parachute."

We were below the mountain peaks. I'd be on the ground soon. I braced, not knowing how hard an impact to expect. I said the Our Father—who knew if I'd ever have the chance to commune with The Almighty again.

And then we were down.

We were in the middle of vast rolling grasslands. My parachute and harness were gone. Somehow, my jumpsuit had transformed into a white gauze robe. I was wearing psychedelic flip-flops on my feet.

I heard a rustle in the elephant grass—Madonna was walking toward me through the thicket.

"Well here we are."

"Yes, here we are," Madonna said, "By the way, love your flip-flops...Steve Madden?"

"I haven't got a clue. Your tribal gown is just darling."

"I love these. They look warm, but they're actually very light and airy." She leaned forward to whisper. "And you can get away without wearing underwear."

"That's a big plus," I said in a soft voice.

She winked. "You have no idea."

"Pleasantries aside, why am I here?"

"This is why." The tall elephant grass parted next to her and an adorable little girl strolled out. She was a tiny little thing, dressed in a delicate white blouse and a red tartan plaid skirt.

"She's gorgeous."

"This is why you're here. Stephanie, this is Naponu. Naponu is alone in the world. She has no family."

I felt such a pang. I could feel my heart melting, leaving a desolate cavity within my chest. "Who takes care of her?"

"The Maasai villagers."

"Is she well cared for?"

"The villagers care for her as best they can, but there's no substitute for a mother's love."

"This is why you brought me here; to become her mother?"

"That's right, Stephanie, are you ready to become this little one's mother, her protector and spiritual light?"

Naponu was beautiful and innocent. I doubted she understood a word we were saying, but in her eyes as she looked up at me, I saw such intense need and such boundless hope. I felt so terribly torn. "I don't know. I know that I'll be ready someday, but now? I just don't know."

"Sometimes you have to accept the challenges life throws at you as they come along. Besides, you can be a mother to this special child without doing an ounce of damage to that rockin' bod of yours."

"You had two of your own. You sacrificed your body."

"Yes, that's completely true, but have you ever had an episiotomy?"

"No."

"Trust me, this way's easier. You get the same results and no one has to stitch up your va-jay-jay."

Madonna's words and that precious little face were tugging on my heartstrings. I didn't know what to do. "I'm sorry, I'm just not—"

"You're not sure?"

"I don't know. I want to be sure, but I'm not. Am I a terrible person?"

Madonna smiled. "You're not terrible, you're just feeling intimidated. You want to do the right thing, but you don't want to feel like you're being pushed into something you're not ready for. I have that effect on most people." She glanced up at the sky and spoke to the heavens. "I need the closer," she said, and then a bolt of lightning flashed in the sky.

I heard the grass rustling again. The stalks spread apart from the tips down to the base, parting as I imagined the Red Sea had parted before Moses. Angelina Jolie strode purposely through the clearing, dressed as Lara Croft, head to toe wearing form fitting white Lycra. She was carrying a Glock automatic in a cross-draw shoulder holster, and yes, as if the package wasn't complete enough, the earth mother was holding a baby. "Don't you want to be a mother, Stephanie?"

"This is too much."

"No it's not," Angelina said. "This is how we save the world; one small act of kindness at a time."

"I'm not sure I can do this. There's Ma and my brother Ricky, Gus and my job—I have so much responsibility."

Madonna turned to Angelina. "I thought you said she was tough?"

Angelina shrugged. "You listened to me? What do I know about character? I spent years married to Billy Bob Thornton, didn't I?"

Madonna smiled. "Yes, but you turned it around rather nicely—Pitt's a bit of alright. Anyway, what about Chalice?"

Angelina shrugged. "Word is she kicks ass."

"Christ, this is getting old." Madonna snapped her fingers. Naponu and Angelina's baby disappeared. The music icon and film goddess glared at me fiercely. Fire encircled the ground at their feet. They pointed just behind me. I could swear that I saw fire in their eyes. "Maybe this is what you want."

Dr. Nigel Twain was suddenly standing behind me. Twain has, on many occasions, been the object of my sexual fantasies. He's brilliant, dark, and ever so troubled. All that wrapped up in a package that resembled Tyson Beckford.

"Am I what you want, Stephanie?" Twain had such an incredible voice, the throatiest of British baritones. To make matters worse, he was clad in only a loin cloth, a very immodest loin cloth. Okay, most of his manhood was showing. Dear God, I didn't know whether I was supposed to touch it or feed it peanuts.

How guilty is it possible to feel? There was Gus, the true bluest of boyfriends, and Naponu, the little orphan girl doomed to struggle through life without the love of a family unless I benevolently agreed to become her mother. I had just failed a child in dire need. I couldn't betray my man too.

Twain grinned and laughed roguishly. "Are you kidding, Stephanie, did you see the size of this thing?"

"Nigel, how did you hear my thoughts?"

He gave me a sleazy wink. "How indeed?"

"Gus!" I woke up shouting his name; my heart racing like a thoroughbred's coming down the home stretch at The Kentucky Derby. I looked around and didn't see any of New York's finest. I didn't know how long I had been out and reasoned that they had likely expanded their search to other areas of the park.

The skull—suddenly, it all made sense and I admonished myself for not thinking of it sooner. NYPD had found a decapitated human body in the park just weeks back. To the best of my memory, the case was still unsolved and was being jointly investigated by the FBI.

The victim, Kevin Lee, a thirty-year-old commercial photographer had disappeared along with his friend Paul Liu, the son of R.C Liu, the Chinese Ambassador to the United States, hence the FBI tie in. To date, the whereabouts of Lee's head and the Ambassador's son were still unknown.

From inside the car I searched the vicinity again. Nothing. The catnap had helped a great deal. I was feeling semi-human—well enough to once again resume activity as my headstrong self. I left the security of the patrol car to take matters back into my own hands.

The moment I stepped from the car, my ears filled with the sound of giggling children. It took less than a minute to locate the source of their laughter. It was that group of school kids I had seen before, about twenty kids and four adults. The kids were preteen, and seemed to be having a great time. The hairs stood up on the back of my neck when I saw those two boys, the boys who had stared at me with concern. They were doing their best to hide behind the others. Something was up with those two.

I targeted the adult that seemed to be leading the group and made straight for her. I must have looked bizarre, a detective, with her shield tucked into the waistband of a pair green hospital scrubs. No matter, I approached.

"Detective Stephanie Chalice, how are you?"

The puzzled expression had been anticipated. "Paula Thompson." She extended her hand. "You say you're with the police? Is something wrong?"

I flashed my shield to set her mind at ease. "Everything's fine. It's just that we've been searching the park for evidence and I thought if you didn't mind I'd ask—" Those two boys still looked pretty nervous. It almost looked like they broke out in a cold sweat. "You didn't by any chance visit the Strawberry Fields Memorial this morning, did you?"

Paula smiled. "Loved John Lennon—made it our first stop."

"Would it be okay if I spoke to those two?" I pointed to the two guilty looking boys.

"Corey and Zack, are you sure?"

"If it's okay with you—they look like they want to cooperate with the police."

I could see that Paula needed a moment to think

about it. I backed off so that she'd be comfortable with her own decision. "Wait here, please."

The other adults swarmed around her, no doubt concerned for the children's well being. She seemed to handle them in stride and it only took her a moment to round up the two boys. She did the introductions and we walked a short distance from the others before I spoke. They were just kids and I didn't want to frighten them. It didn't take long. I just smiled at Corey and pointed to his bloated backpack. "Corey," I asked. "What do you have in there?"

# Five

It was midday before I began to feel like myself again. I still had a headache and wasn't going to push myself too hard, but I wasn't going to waste the day, lying on the couch and watching Oprah. Gus took the skull down to the crime lab to get the process started and to fill out the laborious paperwork associated with the proper cataloging of evidence. As I had mentioned, the skull was bright white, Colgate white, fresh as driven snow white, not the creamy, pale yellow color associated with a bone that had gone through normal biological decomposition. My sixth sense was screaming at me, telling me that this was the skull that belonged to Kevin Lee. I couldn't wait to hear the crime lab's results.

Lenox Hill Hospital is a white stone building that occupies an entire city block between Park Avenue and Lexington Avenue—the cross streets are 76th and 77th streets. I don't know if I've adequately conveyed the size and scope of how big the hospital really is.

I'd seen the inside on more occasions than I'd like

to admit; the place was just huge. Imagine Macy's Herald Square filled with hospital beds instead of off-price merchandise. Get the picture?

On my way over to the hospital I thought about the man we'd found unconscious, sprawled out across the Strawberry Fields Memorial mosaic. The man had almost certainly been tortured, his body covered with scars. God only knew what this poor soul had been through and for how long.

A lovely silver haired retiree was manning (for lack of a better word) the reception desk. Her hair had been over-processed, giving it that bluish color we've come to be familiar with. In any case, it went well with her polyester charmeuse blouse. I flashed my badge. "Good morning. A man was admitted through the ER late last night. He's probably listed as John Doe. Can you tell me where I might find him?" She smiled pleasantly, but didn't respond. I gave her a moment. "Can you check your list, please?" I knew that Doe had been in ICU last night, but as I said, the place was enormous and I didn't want to waste any time. Hospital beds, in particular, ICU beds were a precious commodity. Administrators were constantly juggling them for efficiency's sake.

"For what?"

"For the man I brought in last night."

"What's the patient's name?"

"Look under John Doe."

She smiled again and began pecking at the computer's keyboard. "John Doe, oh we have several. Which one are you looking for?" It was a sad reality. New York was full of unidentifiable people: the homeless and the mentally insane. Most of us have no idea how many there really are. They wander the streets, sleeping in the parks when the weather's good and in the subways when it's cold. Most eventually succumb to sickness and end up in the city's hospitals.

"The one that was admitted last night."

She gave me a puzzled look. Apparently we had gone way beyond her technical limitations. I stepped around the counter to look for myself.

"You're not supposed to be here," she said.

"It's alright, dear," I whispered. "I'm with the police."

"You are?"

"Yes, remember I showed you my badge."

"Oh yes, that's right. Please forgive me, I don't sleep well anymore. My mind tends to wander."

The poor thing, unfortunately her mind was too old to be out by itself. Doe, my Doe anyway, was still in ICU on the seventh floor. "Found him, thanks." Was it really going to be that kind of day, the kind that infuriates and exasperates? I had an ache in my head that was hoping not.

As the elevator doors closed, an image came to me. The connection I'd thought of in the park was surfacing again, this time in much greater detail. In the few seconds that it took to reach the seventh floor, my mind filled with thoughts. It was as if my brain had just been the recipient of a huge data dump. I saw newspaper bylines, chronicling a headless body found in Central Park, an unsolved homicide. Thoughts were emerging at a furious rate; details about the investigation and the victim, a commercial photographer living on West End Avenue. I was pulling at the furthest recesses of my brain as the doors opened onto the seventh floor, grasping for every last detail. Every atom of my being was telling me that I was right about the connection, despite yet to have reviewed a solitary shred of evidence.

I was having trouble focusing on John Doe as I approached ICU, which was on the east side of the building. A few more flashes of the tin and I had made it there, standing over the unconscious John Doe. I had hoped that he would have looked better, but he didn't. Things have a way of looking dirty and insidious in the dark. Sometimes our minds see things that aren't really there and they look better in the morning, bathed in cleansing daylight. This time, however, such was not the case.

"And you are?"

A physician was standing behind me. On first impression, he looked to be of Oriental descent, but there was something about his facial features that looked Occidental, and he was tall, probably six feet, taller than most Orientals. He had a wide mustache. My detective's eyes picked up on the edge of a surgical scar, just peeking out from behind the top of his mustache. It was commonplace for men to disguise a cleft lip scar with a mustache. The actor Stacy Keach, television's Mike Hammer, was one of the more famous examples.

My shield was still out. I made sure the doctor made note of it. "Detective Stephanie Chalice." By the by, my name's pronounced *Cha-lee-see*. Have you been reading it as *Chal-lis*? That wouldn't be uncommon. Most seem to gravitate that way, making reference to the cup of Christ. Don't fault yourselves, I should have told you sooner.

"Dr. John Maiguay," the physician said. "Are you the detective that brought this man in last night?"

"Yes, well my partner did." *I was unconscious at the time.* "That was about one in the morning. Did you operate on him?"

"No, I'm just the attending physician." He handed me one of his business cards with his office and beeper numbers on it. I'd enter his information in my Palm Treo as soon as we were finished.

Maiguay had a chart under his arm. I was waiting for him to review it, but he didn't. He was able to recall Doe's information from memory. "He was operated on to repair a jagged gash on his ankle that nicked the anterior tibial artery."

"He lost a lot of blood?"

"Quite a bit—they used three pints in the OR. It was very lucky you found him when you did. Any additional blood loss would probably have proven fatal."

I glanced over at Doe, lying unconscious with scars over his face and body. "I don't think the word lucky quite applies in this case."

"He was also concussed. His hair is long, but—" Maiguay moved Doe's hair aside. When he did, I once again got a strong whiff of cigarette smoke. There was a hefty welt on the back of his head. I was sporting a similar contusion, but you couldn't see it under my long, jet black hair. "See that? There was a modest degree of internal hemorrhaging, nothing fatal, just another factor contributing to his overall depleted condition."

"Will he regain consciousness?"

"Hard to say, he's in a very weakened condition. He's malnourished and dehydrated—his blood chemistry is abysmal. I don't know that he'll ever emerge from his coma. The shock from rapid blood loss and his depleted health may be too large a hurdle for him to overcome."

"In your medical opinion, what's he been through?"

"I'm not a forensics expert, Detective, I can only point out the obvious." Maiguay approached Doe and was about to pull back his blanket. "Are you sure this is something you want to see?"

I nodded. I had seen far worse, the dead, those that I gotten to too late. New York City had far more than its fair share of the criminally violent. "Please tell me what you can."

Maiguay pointed to the abrasions running around Doe's wrists. "He's been bound. I think that you in the trade refer to these as ligature marks. There are several cuts here, many recent, barely healed." He then made reference to the scars on his legs and stomach. "There are more of these on his backside. If you like, I can ask for a consult from someone in dermatology, so they can determine the age of these marks and how they were caused."

"Thank you, that would help." I'd have the department send down someone to make sure the dermatologist wasn't missing anything. If Doe couldn't speak for himself, perhaps the marks on his body could tell us something about the ordeal he had been through and the crimes that had been committed against him. We had brilliant forensic minds on staff, capable of extracting a world of information from even the smallest clues. "We'll send someone over for fingerprints and photographs—with any luck we'll get a quick ID. We can only hope he regains consciousness and is able to identify whoever did this to him."

"I'll pray for him, Detective, because this man will never be able to identify his captor."

"And why is that?"

Maiguay pulled back one of Doe's eyelids. His eye was an opaque white; in appearance similar to that of a hardboiled egg. "My guess is that this is the result of caustic material introduced into the eye."

I felt sullen and nauseous. I placed my hand on Doe's bedrail to support myself. I didn't know if Maiguay picked up on the way I was feeling. In any case, he didn't articulate any concern for my well being.

Who was capable of inflicting such pain on a fellow human being? "Is that all of it?"

"To a layman like me, yes. Unfortunately, Detective, not all scars are visible to the eye."

# Six

My visit to the hospital left me feeling a little out of sorts. Viewing man's inhumanity to man as it had manifested itself in the form of John Doe was just a little too much for me to stomach. My heart filled with dread thinking about the torture the poor man must have endured. How long had he been held captive, and why was it necessary for one human to be so cruel to another? In my line of work, I came across some pretty awful stuff, but this, this was about as bad as it gets. I'm accustomed to getting the call when the body is already cool, but this poor creature—I imagined it was like being caught on an endless loop, circling hell for eternity with no hope of rescue. I was aching for insight. We were at the very beginning of our investigation with so much yet to be determined. Doe's captor was still an enigma to me. I could only hope the clues flowed quickly, because I wanted this one badly.

My thoughts felt muddled. I needed a quick, strong distraction to clear the channels for lucid deliberation. I had been plagued by the store of information that had flooded into my head in the hospital's elevator, pictures of a decapitated body found in Central Park. My plan was to take a quick break and then go right for the research files. Now some choose to lose themselves in a bottle of whiskey, others find the path to distraction with narcotics. I do it a little differently. When I need to escape reality, I visit my mother—to each his own.

Ma, as her loved ones call her, lives close by. She had struggled for a few years, living alone after my dad passed away, not taking much of an interest in life, but now she's got my brother Ricky to fill her days. My big brother is precious.

Now normally, precious would be an odd word choice to describe a fully grown man, but such was not the case. Ricky is an adult in body, but not so mentally. A tragic event in his youth had interrupted his intellectual development. Don't get me wrong, he's not to be pitied. Ricky's tall, winsome, and innocent. I don't know about you, but I don't run across a lot of men with a combination of attributes like that. Okay, he may never win the Nobel Peace Prize, but he's as good a man as God has ever put on this earth. Ma and I love him to death.

Ma lives in a well maintained walk-up; one of the last few bargains left on Manhattan's Upper East Side. It is one of those fabulous eclectic neighborhoods. She knows most of her neighbors and all the local merchants by name, and is in walking distance to everything she needs, the grocers, the cleaners, and her daughter-cum-police detective, me.

I rapped on the door. She opened instantly. Now I wasn't expected and maybe that's good because I caught her red handed. She made a feeble attempt at licking the chocolate off her teeth as she threw her arms around me for a hug.

"Sweetheart, what a nice—"

"Don't hand me that nice surprise bullshit. You're eating chocolate."

"What are you talking about?" She was talking tough, but her eyes were a dead give away.

"You look as guilty as sin. I can smell it on your breath." Ma has a fatal flaw, and I do mean fatal. She's diabetic and loves to misbehave. Now you may think I'm overreacting, but I lost my father to diabetes, so I can't help myself, but to come on a little strong.

"It was only a kiss, a Hershey's Kiss." She opened her hand to corroborate her testimony. "Look, here's the little silver wrapper. I only had one."

"You're sure?"

"Of course I'm sure. You think I'm *stu-nod* (that's Italian for dopey)?"

"Anything but." Okay, it was just one little piece of chocolate, I guess I could cut her some slack. I looked over her shoulder into the apartment. "Where's my darling brother?"

"You don't know his hours yet? Ricky's still at work. He doesn't get home until half past four."

Now this was a new thing. Ricky had begun working part-time for the local hardware store. It wasn't so much about the money, but more to advance his development, teach him responsibility, and give his life a sense of purpose. He had been seeing Dr. Twain for almost a year and making great strides. Yes, this is the same Dr. Nigel Twain that appeared before me in my reverie wearing nothing but a loin cloth. Twain and I go way back, but for the moment, suffice it to say, that in addition to being a hottie, Nigel Twain is one of the most brilliant, albeit controversial, psychiatrists in the world. Okay, New York City, but to those of us residing between the Hudson and East Rivers, New York is the world.

"Right, I forgot. How's that working out?"

"Wonderful. Yesterday he brought home a caulking gun."

"Why?"

"It was on sale." Ma shrugged. "What do you want me to tell you—he wanted to give me a present. He gets a discount too."

"Do you want me to bring it back?"

"Bring it back? Forget about it, I'm going to have it framed. You should see how proud he was."

I started to mist up. I've got so much going on, for the moment I'd forgotten how far he'd come.

"So, you gonna stand out in the hall all day?" Ma grabbed me by the wrist and yanked me inside. "I got stuffed peppers—you hungry?"

I really didn't have much of an appetite, but there's no way to resist Ma's cooking.

Ma gave me the usual mother's once over. "You look thin."

"I'm not thin, I'm wearing black."

"Why, did someone die? It's spring, wear something colorful." Her words were music to my ears. Now, you've probably seen the old Italian women who wear nothing but black and keep their hair in hairnets after they suffer a loss. Well Ma wasn't as bad as that, but for a few years after my father passed away she wore nothing but housecoats. So it was great hearing her address fashion in such an uplifting way.

"Black's fashionable."

She opened my blazer which was unbuttoned, so that she could opine on my weight. "You look skinny, all except for the boobs—you got your period?"

"No, Ma,"

"God bless." She turned and walked into the kitchen. "I got lots of leftovers—sit down." Now Ma loved to cook, and with a hungry man like Ricky around— All I can say is that you couldn't walk through the door of that apartment without getting a meal and a doggie bag to take home with you. She took out the tray of stuffed peppers and a dish of caponata, leftovers from dinner—the tray of peppers was still half full. She whipped out a fresh loaf of semolina bread to seal the deal.

Okay, now I was hungry, salivating on the verge of drooling hunger. Why did I ever move out on my own?

"So what brings you into this neck of the woods?"

God only knew what she was talking about. As I said, I live within walking distance. I work here. I shop here. You'd think I had just flown in from Palermo. "What neck of the woods?"

"Here, to my house."

"What are you talking about? I'm here all the time."

"You're a stranger—I never see you."

"Ma, I was here over the weekend."

"So what, I'm supposed to be impressed by that? Mrs. Peckem's son visits her every day."

"Ma, the man's thirty-five years old and doesn't know how to boil water—he's helpless. I don't know what he'd do without his mother."

"*Whatayamean*, helpless? The man's a podiatrist."

"Honestly, Ma, I'm surprised the man can find his way back from the bathroom. I think she still buys his clothing."

"Ba! Get a dish."

Ma heated my food in a frying pan. I don't think I've ever seen her use the microwave. It took longer, but I couldn't complain. Her food is incredible. I tore off a hunk of bread and wolfed down the entire bowl. I'd have to hit the gym on the way home. I'd have to hit it hard, but the food was truly delicious, and I didn't regret wiping the bowl with my bread to get the last morsel.

Ma was smiling as I finished. "*Madonna,*" she said, "this one can eat. Leave the dishes. I want to show you what I bought."

Being the good daughter, I smiled broadly and followed her into the bedroom. I was hoping that she wasn't going to show me the housecoats she scored at three for twenty at WAL*MART. Alright, NYPD cops don't make that much, but I had a flair for fine clothing. I'm not a snob, but the truth be told, I found mass market body covering a tad icky. "So what'd you get?" I said, sounding excited despite a growing level of apprehension.

Ma took a small box out of her dresser drawer and

handed it to me. “I bought it on the Home Shopping Channel.” The box contained a man’s ring, gold in color with a tiger eye. “I bought it for Ricky.”

“It’s nice.” It really wasn’t half-bad, but I had a strong aversion to the schlock merchandise the television merchants hawked twenty-four/seven.

“Do you think he’ll like it?”

“No doubt.” I gave her a kiss on the cheek. “That was very sweet of you.”

“It’s a genuine tiger eye. It’s very rare.”

This is where I get myself into trouble. Anyone with half a brain would’ve let it slide—fool that I was, I just couldn’t. “Is that what they said on TV?”

Ma nodded. “Three carats.”

“Three carats of wood.”

“What are you talking about, it’s a genuine stone.”

“It’s not a stone, Ma. Tiger eye is wood; polished and coated, but it’s wood. Caveat emptor.”

“Caviar what?”

“Caveat Emptor, buyer beware. Those TV merchants are snake oil salesmen at best. They prey on insomniacs and the uninformed.”

“Ba!” Her Sicilian blood was really flowing now. “All of a sudden you’re a jeweler? They said it was a rare tiger eye.”

“Ma, listen to me.”

“What’s the matter with you?”

Thank God, just then the door bell rang.

“Who’s that?” she said.

“I don’t know—expecting more estate jewelry from QVC? Maybe someone’s here with some rare rhinestones.” Of course I knew who it was—after all, I had extended the invitation myself. Sometimes I just can’t help breaking her chops.

She dismissed me with a wave of her hand.

“I’ll get it.” I rushed to the door. Now a cop should know better than to open the door without checking to see who’s on the other side, but as I said, I’d invited someone. Moreover you tend to be rather self assured with a .45 wedged in under your armpit. The man standing in the doorway was no stranger. It was my dear friend, FBI Agent Herbert Ambler.

# Seven

"Herbert." I threw my arms around my old friend and gave him a hug. I'd asked him to meet me here to discuss the connection in our cases. He hadn't wasted any time.

He sniffed the air. "My keen nose tells me that I'm just in time for a late lunch—sausage and peppers?"

"Stuffed peppers, but that was one hell of a good guess coming from an old Fed like you."

Ambler was no stranger to our home. He and my dad went way back; comrades in arms as it were.

I heard Ma accelerating through the apartment. She was approaching critical velocity when she hit the door. "Herb, is that you?" She gave him a bear hug and a big fat wet one on the cheek."

Ambler had a head as large as a Kodiak bear and a huge smile that stretched from one ear to the other. "I can't remember the last time I got such a reception from two beautiful women."

"Don't let him sweet talk you, Ma. He knows you made stuffed peppers."

Ma glared at me and whacked me on the arm." I

thought you didn't know who it was?" She laughed and turned back to Ambler. "It's so good to see you." Ma took him by the arm and led him into the apartment. "Sit down, sit down. How are you?"

"No complaints, Lisa—and you?"

"Complaints, are you kidding; with my house filled with friends and family? Tell me, you didn't have lunch, did you?"

"Trust me, I know better than to show up at your doorstep unprepared to be plied with food."

"You're a smart man." She pinched his arm. "Good, wait right here, I'll bring you a big dish of stuffed peppers. Stephanie just had some." I could see that Ma was dying to sit down with us, but her instinct to mother one and all wouldn't let her do so until she was sure that Ambler had been stuffed to the gills. "I'll be back in a jiffy. I'm sure you've got business to discuss with my daughter anyway. I'll be right back." Ma was backpedaling toward the kitchen. "I'm so happy you're here. I'll get you something to eat. You look a little thin to me."

I turned to Ambler. Our eyes met and we both grinned. "It's one of life's great mysteries," I said, "Everyone who walks through this door becomes suddenly emaciated—It's on a par with the Bermuda Triangle." Ambler was chuckling behind his vintage aviator glasses. "What the hell is so funny?"

Ambler leaned forward and whispered in my ear. "I already ate. I just don't have the heart to tell her."

"Or the strength to fight with her?"

Ambler nodded. "Amen. Your mother hasn't lost a step, God bless her. Still sneaking the chocolate bars?"

"Nothing's changed." I crossed myself and then the moment of our reunion had passed. Ambler, as we know, had not come for the blue plate special.

I knew that Ambler and I were already on the same page. My veteran FBI friend knew there was a connection as well;
a link between the skull we had recovered and the

murder that took place in Central Park sometime earlier.

"You're familiar with my case?"

"Yes, as a matter of fact I am, but why don't you give me the high profile on it. I'm only familiar with the details as an outsider."

"If you recall, two guys went on a nature walk, neither returned. We identified the decapitated victim from his fingerprints. His name was Kevin Lee, a thirty-year-old commercial photographer, living on West End Avenue. We've conducted a very concentrated investigation, virtually tore apart sections of Central Park and put it back together again when we were done—like I said, we've come up with nothing. If your skull fits our body—It would be a freaking miracle—you say an elementary school kid had it in his backpack?"

"Yes, but probably less than an hour—I'm sure it was Doe that brought the skull with him to Central Park. He would've had it in his grasp if he had stayed conscious."

"And you're so sure of this, why?"

"My John Doe had been badly tortured. Although we still don't have an idea of how long he was incarcerated, I'll bet you dollars to Krispy Kreme donuts that he's been working on his escape for quite a while and was planning on taking the skull with him when he got free. Unfortunately, he was followed to Central Park by his captor. I don't know if he was unconscious from blood loss, the Taser, or a combination of both. We're just lucky that the bastard that Tasered Doe and me didn't risk coming back for it last night. Corey, the school kid, must've stumbled across it that morning on his school trip.

"You're so smart," Ambler said, teasing me.

"I try not to let it go to my head. You know what Einstein said?"

Ambler shook his head. "What, E=mc2?"

"Among other things, yes, but that's not what I was going for."

"Well hell, Stephanie, what did he say?"

"'Before God, we are all equally wise and equally foolish."'

"That's extremely philosophical."

"Hey, you're talking about the scientist who theorized relativity. The man wasn't exactly a chicken plucker."

"No, I guess not. Lee and his companion had a long-standing relationship and were last seen together the morning of Lee's disappearance. His companion was never found, not his skull, nor his body, not anything. We're kind of hoping he's still alive. I'm sure you already know that the missing person is Paul Liu, and that his father is R.C. Liu, the Chinese ambassador to the United States."

Ambler hadn't added much to what I already knew. I did, however, want to get my greedy little hands on his case files ASAP. I'm sure there were details in the records that would contribute to my understanding of the case.

Ma was already on her way out of the kitchen. She had Ambler's second lunch on a serving tray. "Piping hot," she said. "How about a glass of wine?"

"No thank you, Lisa, this will be fine. It looks delicious."

"The bread, oh my God, I forgot the bread." Ma did an about face, rushing back to the kitchen.

Ambler lifted the fork. He paused just before putting the first sumptuous bite into his mouth and looked me in the eye. "So, are we gonna play nice?"

"Ma always taught me to share. How about you?"

# Eight

The ICU nurse wrapped the blood pressure cuff around John Doe's arm and began squeezing the bulb that forced air into the bladder. She looked away as she was doing it in an effort to remain detached. She was a veteran who had seen intense amounts of suffering; the elderly, infants, and small children, victims of terrible accidents, and cancer patients. She had developed a thick skin, but this one, Doe, it hurt for her to look at him. The scars and burns speaking on his behalf, saying to her that which he could no longer express verbally. Somehow his silence bypassed her ears and found a place in her heart. *Who could do such a thing?* She shook her head and then noted his blood pressure on the chart. Despite her best efforts, her gaze drifted, falling upon his face. Her thoughts ran to her son who had just returned from Iraq. He had been injured during his final tour of duty and was now home. He was still in physical therapy, but would be fine. Best of all, he was never going back. He had been honorably discharged.

*Thank God.* She made the sign of the cross and then said a prayer for John Doe, a man she didn't and might never have the opportunity to know. "You poor man," she said, "What happened to you?"

The odor of cigarettes was heavy in the air as the bedroom door was pulled shut. John Doe could hear the metallic thud of the dead bolt as it slammed home. He knew the sound by heart, the terrifying clang he had endured on a daily basis for weeks on end. He was once more alone in his cell.

The room in which Doe was held captive was on the top floor of a brownstone. The room was large, with a high ceiling. A skylight with security bars kept the room bright during the daylight hours. No shadows crossed the light during the daylight hours, and Doe intuited that to mean that no tall trees or large buildings were close in vicinity. All in all, it was a very pleasant room, had it not existed for the express purposes of incarceration and torture.

Doe was naked in the center of the bed—just where he had been left. A wall-mounted surveillance camera was focused on the bed. It had been turned off for some time. Doe had grown into the habit of listening for the hum of the camera's reciprocating motor which would come on at the end of each session. The camera was frozen now, as it had been for weeks. The reason was obvious to Doe—his captor had tired of him or was no longer concerned with his escape, perhaps both. Either explanation reinforced Doe's belief. He was no longer worthy of anyone's attention.

"Maybe I'll feed you today, maybe I won't." The captor's adenoid voice was callous. He abruptly dabbed out his eighteenth cigarette of the day and shut the video camera. "You're fucking useless, you know that?" He said nothing else before leaving the room.

Sound and smell were all that Doe had left. He had been blinded by repeated injections of Drano to his eyes. The room's freshly painted white walls had become a canvas upon which he saw, or imagined only shadows. The muscles in his hands and arms were almost useless from constant restraint with piano wire.

The room was silent now in the aftermath. The captor had satisfied his curiosity and had left Doe to his solitude.

Doe sank back onto the pillow, careful not to allow the piano wires that bound him to cut into his already raw wounds. There was no way for Doe to avoid the pain when the captor was in the room with him. The best he could do was shrink into a corner of his mind and wait for the humiliation to end.

He felt his tears rising up again; tears which followed each encounter. He had been imprisoned a very long time and now accepted the fact that he would never know freedom again. He tried humming but his throat still ached from the needle that had been thrust into his voice box. He swallowed gingerly—it ached as if the needle was still in there, still lodged in his throat, preventing the swallowing mechanism to function normally. He wasn't sure who could hear him, but apparently the captor wanted to safeguard against Doe screaming and being overheard. Drano had been injected into his throat as well, and it had destroyed his vocal cords. But he had taught himself to hum, using only the canals of the nose and throat as resonating chambers.

The windows were open, allowing the warm spring air to wash over him. He had a vague memory of how the room looked, memories from before he had lost his vision. Wrought iron bars were bolted on the inside of the windows over heavy white shades. The floor was composed of tan and brown linoleum squares. The walls were a glossy white. That was how Doe remembered it. He had been heavily sedated in the early days, the days when he still had the strength to resist.

The piano wires were anchored to the ceiling. They allowed him access to a sink and toilet on the north side of the room away from the windows. Not that it mattered. Doe lacked the strength to escape. He no longer fought back when he was tortured. He was fed enough to stay alive, but not enough for adequate nutrition. His muscles were badly atrophied. His will had been crushed.

He no longer thought about escaping. He now truly understood the curse of his vanity. His once youthful body had been scarred and burnt. He had been tortured with cigarettes, leaving scars on his face and body. The more he resisted, the more pain was inflicted on him. His captor would stick needles into his back and face and turn the needle slowly, painfully enlarging the hole. But the most horrible disfigurement had taken place in Doe's mind—he had been turned into a pathetic freak, a blind, mute, deformed gargoyle. He would wake in the middle of the night to his friends' horrified expressions—in his mind, he had become the elephant man, a circus sideshow attraction. He had lived his life striving for physical perfection. Doe no longer hungered for the outside world. His wish was to die in this white room and to be buried anonymously. He hoped that death was not long off.

What Doe did not remember of the room was that the captor kept a cabinet by the door where he maintained the tools he used to incarcerate and torture. The locked cabinet was white Formica with glass doors. There were bottles of sedatives stored on the shelves: alprazolam, diazepam, Versed, morphine, and Triavil. He kept an assortment of hypodermic needles of varying sizes there too; some were used to administer medication, others were used for torture. An unopened bottle of Drano had several small pin holes in the plastic container where the bottle had been pierced with a hypodermic needle to draw out the corrosive material that had been injected into Doe's eyes and throat. And there was the photographic equipment:
Polaroid cameras, packs of film, digital cameras, and video cameras capable of being remotely operated. There was a large assortment of batteries and an unopened

brick of VHS tapes. The drawers were filled with restraints: heavy gauge single-strand piano wire, nylon rope, and bungee cords. One drawer contained cartons of unfiltered cigarettes and matches.

Doe lay silently on the bed, allowing his body to forget the torment it had just endured. The bedding stunk from the embedded odor of cigarette smoke. He focused on the raw flesh on his wrists, convincing himself that the wounds could be magically healed. He remembered a scene from a horror film where a vampire's wounds shrunk and closed before his eyes. Doe pretended that he possessed the same supernatural power—before his mind's eye, the cigarette burns healed, the scars faded, his muscles, once again, swelled and rippled with vitality.

It was easier for him to doze these days. The spring air was intoxicating. He found that blindness acted as a sedative, making his mind less active. He was almost out when he heard the sound of an intense struggle from the room next door.

A bud popped open in Doe's mind, and from it sprang the first glimmer of hope Doe had felt in a very long while. He was not alone.

# Nine

It was after eleven when I got the call from Ambler, putting an abrupt end to my plans for a good night's sleep. He was calling to ask Lido and I down to FBI headquarters in lower Manhattan. Our crime lab had been all over our skull and had then transferred it to the FBI, who was now ready to share its findings, if any, with us. I was hopeful that they had found something before the case went cold again. No information had come from our medical examination of the comatose John Doe. Amazingly, no one had seen a wretched, half-naked man drag his battered body into Central Park. Stuff like that just drives me wild.

We were meeting Ambler at the FBI's crime lab. The night receptionist led Lido and me to the conference room to wait for Ambler and Evans Jack, the department chief. There were still a few technicians working; cases I assumed that could not wait for morning and the next business day.

On our way to the conference room, we passed the skull

preparation unit. I stopped for a moment to watch a heavyset woman working on a small object, meticulously picking away at it with what looked like a dentist's curette. I took a step closer as she placed the object into a small sink which was set into her work station. She began to irrigate with water flowing through a brown rubber tube. The breath caught in my lungs when I saw what she was working on. She used compressed air to dry the moisture from an infant's skull.

I heard Madonna's voice whispering in my ear, "Naponu still needs a mother. That little girl and thousands like her need someone's help, your help." So there I was, Stephanie Chalice, titanium-clad, invulnerable, and cool as a proverbial cucumber, standing on the floor of the FBI's crime lab, pushing back tears.

Lido noticed that I was lagging behind. He stopped and turned. "Hey, what's the matter?"

I turned away from the child's skull and caught up with him.

Lido took my arm. "What's going on?"

"I just needed to catch my breath."

Lido had an incredulous look on his face. "You, the same woman who did a wind sprint in an evening gown the other night? You're out of breath?"

"Just let it go. I'm fine."

"You sure?"

The impenetrable shield was back up. I was no longer Lido's girlfriend. I was no longer a woman with a soul that could be touched. I was back on the job and pushing past Lido before someone else saw the breach in my armor. God knows what kind of insane dream I'd have tonight. Would tonight's reverie see the return of Madonna, Batman, Brad Pitt? Any and all were possible and were among the visitors that frequented my subconscious hallucinations. Only time would tell. For now, though, it was time to get busy. "Time's wasting. Let's see what Ambler's got for us."

Ambler was seated at the head of the conference table. The skull was on the table in front of him, facing us. Absent the white Persian cat, with skull before him, Ambler smacked of Ernst Stavro Blofeld, the head of SPECTRE, and James Bond's number one nemesis. At his side was Evans Jack, the department head. Jack was a huge man with short hair and a full beard. He looked odd wearing a suit. Except for the Gibson SG, he looked a lot like Billy Gibbons, ZZ Top's lead guitarist and longtime oddball; but who am I to judge. He also looked like he could have been Blofeld's, Number One, in any number of James Bond movies. Evans Jack jumped up to welcome us as soon as we entered the room. I shook his huge paw, and then sat down off the corner of the table, close to Ambler.

Ambler turned toward Lido and me, cool as ice, looking at us as if he had never seen us before and didn't care if we'd ever meet again—the man was good.

"Make my day," I said to Ambler. "Give me something we can sink our teeth into."

"It's the skull we've been looking for," Ambler said. "There was a one hundred percent allele match to the remains of Kevin Lee—no question."

"That sounds promising," Lido said.

Ambler picked up a container of Starbucks coffee and sipped. "Promising in so far as we haven't hit the wall, yes. Our unsub isn't perfect. He lost one of his prized possessions, this skull. We had thought that he was meticulous because the trail has gone cold for so long, but by allowing John Doe's escape, he has shown us that he's capable of making mistakes."

"Not to mention that he captures and tortures people. Have you had a chance to look in on our John Doe?"

"Not yet, Chalice." Ambler replied. "I hear he's a mess."

"You have no idea. His body is covered with scars and burns from head to toe. He's been blinded and restrained. God knows what that poor man has been through."

"Any chance he'll regain consciousness?" Ambler asked.

"Slim. We're circulating his photo on the street. We think that's our best chance for determining his identity."

"You'll make his photos available to The Bureau?"

"Already done," Lido said.

"Was there anything found on the skull that will lead us to the unsub?" Unsub was Bureau lingo for unidentified suspect.

"It's clean," Ambler said, with disappointment in his voice. "Jack's people have been over it top to bottom. They found Doe's fingerprints, which unfortunately are not on file. They found common household dust, some cigarette ash...that's about it." "How's that possible?" Lido asked.

Evans Jack picked up the skull. It looked like a baseball cradled in his huge hands. "It's no small job to make a skull look like this. An adult skull articulates with blood, cartilage, membranes, sinew—you know what I'm talking about, yes?"

Lido and I nodded. Ambler pulled out his Blackberry and began scrolling through his emails.

Jack continued, "So now that we understand that human bones are not pure white as found in nature, it begs the question, how and why was this skull cleaned? Typically, a specimen like this has been prepared for anatomical study. You find them at universities, teaching hospitals, museums—you get the picture."

"So you think our unsub is using his victim's skulls to perform anatomical studies? That's a wild one."

"You'd think he'd just take an evening class at NYU," Lido quipped.

"I'm sure the unsub's interest in the human skull goes beyond the ordinary," Ambler said.

"He doesn't want anyone to know what he's doing. This is very private work he's performing," I said. "Why he's doing it, that's the sixty-four thousand dollar question."

“How hard is it to prepare a skull in this way?” Lido asked.

“It really takes a lot of work, but it doesn’t require much training,” Jack said, “All it really requires is a strong stomach and a great deal of determination. I’m sure your unsub has both.”

“So you think he did this himself?” Lido asked.

“Most likely,” Jack replied. “There are signs in the finished product that point to the work of an accomplished amateur. There are several shops out there; some are very advanced and others are just slightly more than butchers. I don’t think this example falls into either category.”

“Butchers, how so?” I asked.

“If you picture Uncle Jed and Granny sitting around the still, the image wouldn’t be too far from wrong. Remember, bone cleaning is a very primitive art form. Professional operations have refined it to a much higher level, but the nitty-gritty is that it was first performed by savages: tribal medicine men, shamans, head hunters—picture a shrunken head. We’re not exactly talking elite company.”

“I’m intrigued, repulsed, but intrigued. Tell me how you know so much about the way this skull was cleaned.”

“There are three ways to clean a bone like this: bug cleaning, boiling, and maceration. Our technicians said that tiny particles of sinew were found on the articulating surfaces of the middle nasal concha, which leads us to believe this specimen was bug cleaned because the beetles were too big to get into those really small crevices.”

“And how did you rule out the other two techniques?”

“Boiling makes a mess, warps the bone, dissolves all the cartilage—shrinks just about everything. Even if you’re very careful, all the articulating fiber is destroyed. No, I’m sure it wasn’t boiled. That leaves bacterial maceration, which is just fancy talk for rotting the meat off the carcass.

It's the equivalent of throwing the specimen in a cesspool. Darn thing usually smells so bad afterward that you can't get rid of the stench." Jack sniffed the skull and winked at us. "Odor free. Another thing, your specimen was chlorine bleached, that's why it's so white. Professionals don't do that. It looks good but there's too much chance the chlorine will damage the bone."

"How should it be whitened?" Lido asked.

I knew where Lido was going with his line of questioning, way back to his adolescence. This was no longer a detective's line of questioning, but more of a twelve-year-old's curiosity. He had an eager partner in Evans Jack. I could tell that at any moment now they'd lay down their pea shooters and start trading baseball cards.

"Mostly peroxide," Jack replied.

"Ordinary household peroxide?" Lido asked.

"Pretty much. It does the job and it doesn't mess with the bones too much. Cheap too—a four percent solution's all you need, and it can be reused two or three times."

*Neat!*

Lido seemed surprised. Apparently he had used peroxide on a booboo before and was surprised that it could be used to bleach something as cool as a human skull. "Really, I didn't think peroxide was strong enough to do that kind of work—I mean if you pour it on a cut, it just sits there and bubbles, kind of like soda pop."

"And after a few seconds, your skin turns white and puffy, doesn't it?" Jack asked.

Lido nodded. "Now that you mention it."

"Well, how do you think your skin would look after a good twenty-four hour soak?"

"I get the picture," Lido said.

"Good old $H_2O_2$ does the trick ninety-five percent of the time. For real tough stains they use Biotex."

"What's that?" Lido asked.

"A product that comes out of the UK," Jack said. "It's not alkaline, so you don't have to worry about it turning your bones to jelly. We maintain a small bug cleaning room on premises. Care to have a look?"

Oh dear God, is he kidding? Ambler looked up from his Blackberry and shot me a stealthy snicker. I had less than no interest in Jack's bug room and was about to tell him so when Lido jumped eagerly out of his chair. What is it with boys? They love all that stuff: dinosaurs, bugs, the Discovery Channel. I have to go celibate once a year when they air Shark Week. I can't get Lido away from the stupid TV.

We went merrily on our way into Evans Jack's bug room. I looked back at Ambler who hadn't budged from his seat.

"Been there," Ambler said. "You enjoy."

No one was looking, so I flipped Ambler the bird. He grinned and turned back to his Blackberry.

You could see how much Evan's Jack loved his work. He was like a tour guide at Disney World. *Stay close together, keep your hands out of the bug boxes—no one under fifty-four inches admitted.* "We keep the bugs separate from everything else because if these critters get hungry enough, they'll eat anything, bones, gristle, your lunch, and your clothes—almost anything. We take added precaution in the bug room. I'll explain as we go along." Jack handed us dust masks. "The beetles produce lots of dust. I'm allergic to it, so I'm gonna do this one, two, three, alright?"

*By all means.*

The room was divided by long tables, Formica tops with metal frames. Glass aquarium tanks resided on the tables. They were of varying sizes. A large air scrubber was mounted on the ceiling. The room was dead silent.

"This is where it happens," Jack said. "The butcher shops use any kind of crap that's handy to house the beetles, but we rely solely on steel reinforced glass aquariums. We visually inspect each colony at least twice a day."

"Different sized tanks for different sized specimens?" Lido asked.

"Exactly right," Jack was glowing with pride as he walked over to a twenty gallon aquarium. "A large bone, like a human tibia might go into a tank this size. We try to make the tanks no bigger than necessary because you've got to keep these hungry bastards fed."

"You're kidding," Lido said.

Lido peered into one of the tanks. He closed his eyes and reared backwards, away from it. "What's going on in there?" I could see that he found the bugs repulsive and yet intriguing at the same time.

Jack walked over to the tank that Lido had asked about. A log sheet was taped to the side of the tank. "Adult male skull, found in the New Jersey Swamp."

"Jimmy Hoffa?"

Jack chuckled, "You never know." He tapped the tank gently, where the beetles could be seen crawling through the eye sockets. "Not for everyone, is it?"

"How long does it take for these things to eat the meat off a skull?" Lido asked.

*Alright, Gus, it's time to go—no more questions, please.* I was starting to get the willies.

"Depends on conditions, Detective. You've got to control their environment. *Dermestes maculatus* like it warm, moist, and dark, about eighty degrees Fahrenheit. There are four stages in the beetle's life cycle: egg, larva, pupae, and adult. A good hot colony of larva could clean a large bone in a couple of days, maybe less."

"How about an entire human body?" Lido asked, showing a macabre interest in all things icky and dorky.

"About a week if prepared properly."

"How much prep work do you have to do?" Lido asked.

I was about to run screaming from the room. I yawned dramatically, hoping Lido would pick up on it. He didn't. Another two minutes and I'd have to start popping buttons off my blouse.

Evans Jack laughed. "It's not like throwing the specimen into a vat of boiling acid, for God's sake; you've got to remove the skin and all the hair. Most of the flesh gets trimmed away before the specimen is ever introduced into the tanks. You've got to take out the eyes, the tongue, and the brain—all the internal organs. As voracious as Dermestes beetles are, they can be very discriminating. For example, they will not eat the flesh off the feet unless you remove all the skin and split the toe pads."

"Such discerning palates. Gus, it's time to go. It's past midnight and I make it a point to only study entomology during the daylight hours."

Evans Jack laughed and then thankfully, he sneezed, signaling that his allergy was kicking in. He sneezed again, this time so loudly that it reverberated through the bug room. "Allergies," Jack reminded us. "What do you say we get some fresh air?"

"My thoughts exactly. Thanks for the tour."

Evans Jack took us back to the conference room. Ambler thanked him for staying so late, and then he left, which thrilled me as Lido looked like he wanted to hang out and talk bugs all night long. I, myself was not up to a stimulating all-nighter on the subject of earthworms and centipedes.

Ambler had finished his coffee and had placed the skull in a brown paper evidence bag.

"I guess we'll take that back with us. Where's the chain of evidence receipt?" I said.

"Not so fast, Chalice," Ambler said. "I've got one more trick up my sleeve. Can I hold onto this a little longer?"

I could see in Ambler's eyes that he had not lost hope. "Yes, sure—let's catch up with each other in the morning. All this bug talk is making my skin crawl. I'm going home to take a shower and incinerate everything I'm wearing." With the building deserted, I leaned over and gave Ambler a peck on the cheek. "Talk to you tomorrow, G-Man."

There was a lot on my mind, but for now it was time to rest and let my premonitions come to me in the form of dreams. I was nodding off in the car as Lido drove home. I was picturing him dressed like a little leaguer, with freckles and tousled hair. There was a huge grin on his face as he rounded third, digging for home. The throw to home was on its way in. The catcher ripped off his mask, revealing Yours Truly. I was crouched to tag him out as he slid feet first into the plate. Then, before I knew it, it was morning. Lido was already awake, smiling at me with a mischievous look on his face. Batter up.

# Ten

Damian Zugg drove along Shore Road to where the tall grass grew in tufts along Long Island Sound's sandy embankment. The windows of his old BMW were rolled down. His vintage 2002 tii was equipped with air conditioning, but Zugg preferred the feel of the wind in his face and The Sound's salty musk filling his nostrils.

Gazing out across the water, Connecticut was sharply in view as he maneuvered his Beemer into the small parking lot the Town of Bayville had recently repaved for the few North Shore residents savvy enough to know the existence of oft deserted Ransom Beach.

He stepped from the car without locking it and walked to the narrow strip of beach.

It was still early morning and Zugg was virtually alone on the beach. Off in the distance, blissfully out of earshot, a solitary Asian family with three small children played in the sand.

Zugg lay down on the sand with his toes just inches from the water's edge. The pain of his migraine headache was intense. He squeezed his eyes shut to cope with the pain. Staring out at the water, he was unable to concentrate. The Sound was already busy with sport boats. A powerful cigarette filled the air with the throaty burble of its powerful engines. The deep bass notes of the boat's thunderous exhaust pounded mercilessly against his temples. *Faster! Hit the throttle and gun that piece of shit!* Zugg counted backwards from ten, watching the cigarette grow small in the distance, ultimately thanking God for the silence. He immediately pulled a small syringe from his shirt pocket, purged the air, and injected himself with six milligrams of Imitrex. He closed his eyes and waited for the blinding migraine to subside. A sharp breeze blew south off the water, cooling his face and filling his ears with its rushing noise. He smiled and wished for the few minutes of sleep the long night had denied him.

He felt the pain begin to ebb, opportunity enough for his fatigue to take hold. His head filled with images. He pictured the small tumors that stretched out across his frontal lobe, throbbing red as he had seen them through the infrared camera. Their pattern was like the island chain that made up the Philippine Archipelago. He imagined them fading from red to a soft pink as more medication migrated through the blood-brain barrier, extinguishing the pain. And then with a merciful wash of serenity, he drifted off.

He was not quite awake when he sensed the presence of someone lying next to him. "How long have you been lying there?" Zugg opened his eyes slowly, squinting against the rising sun. He was immediately aware that his head was for the moment free of pain.

Herbert Ambler folded his newspaper and stowed it under his butt to keep it from flying away. "Maybe twenty minutes. How long were you out?"

Zugg checked his watch. "Something short of a good night's sleep. Didn't have any trouble tracking me down, did you?"

"A man as predictable as you? No… I was careful

not to wake you."

"Well, aren't you just precious." Zugg grinned. "Always happy for your company, my friend." His gaze went immediately to a brown paper bag on the sand beside Ambler. Zugg slapped Ambler on the knee. "What did you bring me for breakfast?"

"No, not breakfast." Ambler smiled and then turned to look across The Sound. "It's like heaven out here, isn't it? Sometimes I wonder how God had the inspiration to create such beauty. I hear the pounding of the surf and it makes me feel like we share the same origin."

"We all arose from the ooze, now didn't we?"

Ambler smiled, still looking out to sea. When he turned back, he noticed the empty syringe lying between them on the sand. "Rough night?"

Zugg followed Ambler's gaze. He nodded. Finding the cap to the syringe, he fitted it over the end of the needle and put it back in his shirt pocket. "So what's in the bag?"

"Are you up for a challenge?"

"Worried you're going to overtax me?"

"Not really, I'm sure you're up to the task."

"You're full of crap, my friend. But don't worry. To quote the irreverent Richard Prior, 'I ain't dead yet.'"

"No you're not, but just for the record, Damien, how are you?"

Zugg turned to look down the beach. The Asian couple that had been playing with their kids was now loading them into a shiny BMW SUV. "How is it that just about everyone can afford a sixty-thousand dollar truck nowadays?"

"Credit to George W."

"Bush—you're kidding, right?"

"He gave us daily affirmation that the American system of capitalism was idiot proof—God love 'em."

Zugg smiled. "You've got a real future in political satire."

"Yeah, I'm a regular Lewis Black."

"Who's more pissed off at the world than you?"

Ambler pried a small mussel out of the sand with his fingertip, examined it, and tossed it into the water. "No more jokes. How are you feeling?"

"I'm three months into what may very well end up being the last year of my life. I'm trying to keep busy."

"Busy is good."

"I've got a friend over at NASA's jet propulsion laboratory in Pasadena. He pulled some strings and got me in for the testing phase of their new thermal imaging system. You can see them clear as day, Herb, over seven thousand microscopic lesions and growing. You can't see them on the MRI, but they're there, real as life…real as death. Hard to get an image like that out of your head."

"What about treatment?"

"You're kidding, right?"

"Does it sound like I'm kidding?"

"Stereotactic radiation of the frontal lobe? I've had fifty good years. I'm not going to spend my last days, deaf, drooling, and wetting my pants." He raised his hand. "It's not open to discussion."

The wind switched direction. Zugg tugged on the brim of his Yankees cap to keep it from blowing off. Ambler could see the trailing end of Zugg's surgical scar where the cap didn't quite cover.

"So what's in the bag?"

Ambler placed the brown paper evidence bag on the sand next to Zugg. He stood and dusted the sand off his slacks.

"I emailed you the case information. The prints have already been lifted." Ambler slipped on a pair of sunglasses.

"That's it? That's all you've got to say?"

Ambler stopped and turned back. "This one's important to me."

"I'll do my best."

"Whatever you can do, my friend—I'll appreciate it."

Zugg read a look of worry on Ambler's face. "Don't worry. What's the worst that could happen, it kills me?"

Ambler shook his head in dismay. "Droll to the last. Call me as soon as you've found something."

"What makes you so sure I'll find something?"

Ambler grinned behind his sunglasses and walked off.

Zugg watched as Ambler climbed into his Volvo and drove away.

Looking around, Zugg confirmed that he was now completely alone on the beach. He quickly pulled open the bag. Within, he saw what appeared to be a sterilized human skull. Zugg took the skull out of the bag and examined it in the bright sunlight. He judged that it was the skull of a young adult male, nineteen to thirty years of age. Turning the skull in his hands, he examined it for abnormalities, but found none that were apparent to the eye.

In the sand, just off his fingertips, the shell of another large mussel protruded up through the sand. Zugg rested the skull on his lap and dug the shell out of the sand. He wiped the moist sand from its shell. *Mytilidae, order mytiloida, bivalve mollusk, Omega-3 rich.* Zugg tore off the beard, pried apart the stubborn shells and chewed down the raw meat. He wiped his mouth clean and then picked the skull up again. Holding it in front of his face, he turned it in his hands, pressing his nose against it as one might sniff a melon at market. With his eyes closed, he paused with his nose almost touching the skull, sniffing hard like a dog trying to extract a scent. In the next instant, he was on his feet, eager and rejuvenated, rushing back to his car.

# Eleven

An *Oxford Inca Energy 400 Spectroscope* running IMQUANT software would normally be the last thing you'd expect to find in someone's home. Nonetheless, there Damien Zugg sat, surrounded by the tens of thousands of small bits he had collected over the years. Forensic pathology: no one living knew more about it. Only the dead were capable of revealing more secrets.

Bordering the basement, metal shelves were lined with boxes filled with the many specimens Zugg had collected over the term of his professional and intellectual career. Each box was clearly labeled and dated. They were of varying sizes, all except for the thirty-inch corrugated boxes stacked under the basement window; each of those contained some two hundred-six bones, roughly the number of bones found in a human skeleton. These were samples he had prepared and catalogued on his own, with hands he could once depend on, with eyes that once saw true. This skull, this pure white skull, it tore at him. He could sense a connection that had been intangible to all else.

The computer screen before him registered in both graphical and digital output, elemental composition—he had found the smallest traces of a substance running horizontally across the temporal bone, barely enough for assay. It had been undetectable in ordinary daylight, but had irradiated under infrared. Data began to fill the screen.

A number counter began to run across the center of the computer screen. When it was done, Zugg would know the specific gravity of the substance.

Zugg glanced at the clock in the lower left corner of the computer screen. It read 7:15 PM. He closed his eyes and rested, face in hand. It had been days since he'd enjoyed a sound night's sleep. His conscious mind was beginning to drift. He glanced at the clock again. It now read 7:40 PM. *Where did the time go?* He was blanking out more and more often, succumbing to weariness, losing little bits of the day, unable to account for the missing time.

He removed his baseball cap. *Time for the seventh inning scratch*, he mused. It had become a part of him, adorning his head at all times, except when he attempted to sleep. The brim was causing irritation where it touched his surgical scar, and his itchy scalp was driving him to the point of distraction. He scratched his shaved head carefully. His scalp prickled constantly, but Zugg had a strong resolve; not wanting to initiate infection, he rarely succumbed to the annoyance.

The counter was now running quickly. He saw that it had finally stopped at 407,979, and then he clicked a tab at the side of the screen. The chemical composition was already there, $C_{25}H_{30}ClN_3$.

Zugg allowed his head to fall limply to the side, his expression, a cross between revelation and disappointment. The scientists at the FBI's forensic lab were capable of identifying the most obscure amounts of almost any substance. What he had found was one of the most common materials used in modern day forensics. The question running through his mind was, had it gotten there by accident? Had someone been clumsy in the lab? Good sense told him that there was no other explanation for gentian violet to be on this otherwise sterile skull, but this was what made Zugg the scientist he was. Somewhere, deep in the recesses of his cancer-riddled brain, a neuron fired telling him not to ignore the clue.

He reached for the phone and dialed Ambler.

# Twelve

Adelaide Tucker rarely strayed from the nurse's station in the middle of the night, except to make necessary rounds. The evening had been quiet and her supervisor was on her meal break for the next thirty minutes. It was time to shut her eyes and take a catnap. It was the only way for her to keep going. No matter how she tried, she had never been able to adjust her sleeping pattern and often ran out of gas at about this hour. She had at first tried ducking into an empty room to get off her feet, but was always being walked in on by randy interns. Nowadays, the chair was good enough. She'd conditioned herself to fall asleep within seconds. Twenty minutes was all it took. It was better than working groggy. God forbid she made a mistake with someone's medication. She felt her eyelids lower and was almost out when she heard the scream. She was used to almost every noise a patient could possibly make: moaning, crying, heaving—she had heard it all and had learned how to ignore or sleep through most of it, but this scream, this one was serious. She had hoped it would be a single outburst, but no, it was followed by another, and yet another. She jumped out of the chair.

It wasn't difficult to follow the screaming to its source. In a moment she was standing over John Doe. "Quiet now, Honey. Calm down." She placed her hand on his shoulder and tried to calm the comatose patient. "I thought you were in a coma. Easy now, it's alright." Doe continued to scream. She could hear the rest of the floor waking up around her. She paged the attending physician and continued her attempt at calming Doe. "What's going on in there?" she said as she stroked his head. "What's got you so worked up?"

John Doe lay motionless in his stark, white room, searching within for the courage to set himself free. Somehow, the spark of life within him had reignited.

He was once again naked upon a bed in the room he had been imprisoned within from the very start.

The surface of his skin, his tapestry of scars was growing in detail and complexity with each passing day—like ancient hieroglyphics, they chronicled his history in the white room. Cigarette burns, needle punctures, electrical burns, and bruises: each a badge of honor, a testament to John Doe's will to survive.

*Still here. I'm still here.* These words that once tormented him had become his mantra. He had once wished for death, but the end never came, and the torture never stopped. "I'm still alive, goddamn it. I'm still here." He was not a brave man, but extreme circumstances had forced him to find courage.

A tab each of Valium and Ambien had been squirreled away in the crevice between his cheek and mandible.

He'd discard them when he was fully awake, but for now, the soft, uncoated pills leached just enough medication into his bloodstream to produce a semiconscious stupor.

A coroner stood over him in his dream. "John Doe is a male Caucasian, approximately twenty-five years old."

"I'm Brian," he mumbled in his sleep. "My name is Brian."

"Height, approximately sixty-eight inches, weight, roughly one-hundred-and-forty pounds, brown hair, brown eyes. Note, the corneas appear to be damaged; more on that to follow. Apparent cause of death—"

"I'm not dead," he said, refuting the coroner's observations. "I'm alive, I'm still alive."

Running his hand over his leg, he noted how loose the flesh had become over his quads, quads that were once taught from competition track and field. They had begun to grow softer after high school, in the years in which he allowed himself to languish—too much dope, too many lazy days—one piled on top of another, years lost in the blink of an eye. His muscles had further atrophied from lying in bed. He knew the exact placement of every scar on his body and could find them with ease; his fingertips reading the raised surfaces on his skin like brail—each conjuring a horrifying memory.

One-by-one, Doe's eyes snapped open to explore the hazy darkness. A small light had been left on to prevent him from tripping. He was now virtually blind, his corneas damaged from caustic applications of Drano. The small light was redundant. Doe knew how to maneuver in the dark using his sense of the room's layout, arms extended forward for precaution—sensory organs adapted for survival like an insect's antennae, searching, sensing, directing.

An electrical generator rested on the floor. It was large and heavy, with sharp metal corners he seemed unable to avoid. He had smashed his leg into it several times before finally growing savvy.

Doe fine tuned his hearing—the house was silent. He'd heard the front door close,

the car starting and pulling away. Still he waited several minutes to be absolutely sure. The threat of more electric shocks had trained him very well. At times it was little more than a pulse. Other times, when he had been "bad", the jumper cables had been clamped on with the current running until he had passed out. As a result, he had learned to stay perfectly still during those occasions when his hair was sheared and his head measured and marked. *How long?* he wondered. How long before they were ready for the next step. How long would they keep him alive? *Not long. I have to do it now.*

Doe counted time until five minutes had elapsed and then pushed the remnants of the two pills from his mouth. They were soft from saliva absorption but they had maintained their integrity. He could distinguish the Valium's small button shape and the Ambien's oblong contour as he ground them into powder between his thumb and forefinger and flicked it away. He was no longer bound to the bed as he had been in the past. His captor was relying solely on sedatives to keep him secure. The reason, he assumed, was because they felt he had been broken, and no longer had the will to escape.

One foot off the bed, then the other—cigarette butts beneath the pads of his feet. He scraped the sole of one foot against the other to remove the butts, and then turned to face the bed. Beneath the frame, stashed by the headboard, a paper grocery bag had remained unnoticed for days. Doe retrieved it. Holding it between his hands, he pressed lightly on the sides of the bag. It was still there, still inside. He placed the treasure on the bed for safekeeping and moved to the opposite wall, the outside wall, where a solitary window was covered with wrought iron bars and a shade.

He tore away the shade. On prior nights, he had opened it cautiously so that his work would go undetected. There was no need for precaution tonight. The bars were secured to the inside of the window, lag bolted into studs.

It was not uncommon for the windows of a ground level dwelling to be covered with security bars, but Doe's prison was three levels up, the top level of a New York brownstone.

Doe's fingers explored the exposed metal threads of the three-inch lag bolts that he had wormed out of the two-by-four studs, one excruciating micron at a time over a period of weeks, twisting the bolts with his raw fingers. The plaster board around the bolts had been ground away. Doe could now feel the hard pulp of the pine studs by pressing his fingertips into the holes. A mere half-inch of the lag bolt's thread remained buried in the wood. Doe took hold of the bars with his two hands. One foot up against the wall and then the other, he positioned himself like a huge spider over the bars and began to tug.

He was amazed by how firmly the last half-inch of the bolts still held. *Push with the legs.* He stiffened his back and squeezed with every ounce of his strength. He felt his runner's legs growing rock hard, his muscles becoming tetanus from the strain. *I'm still strong,* he thought, *I can do it.* Sweat ran into his eyes. A cramp developed in his calf, forcing him to ease up. He took that foot off the wall and waited for the pain to stop and then back on, the moment it disappeared. *Pull, pull, pull, goddamn it, pull.* The shade had been destroyed. It would be impossible to hide his efforts—if he didn't get out now, the torture would be devastating. The bars would be reinforced, making future attempts impossible. It was now or never. His back felt like a bow that had been bent too far and was about to snap. *One last tug.*

The bars came free with a loud creak. They were still in his hands as his back smashed onto the hardwood floor with a thud. Pain seared his spinal cord in waves. He fought to stay conscious. The pain gradually diminished.

Rising, he allowed his fingertips to revel in the exquisite cool of the window's exposed glass, for scant seconds only, and then he picked up the security bars he had just pried free and shattered the window. The sounds of the outside world flooded into his ears for the first time in weeks, the sound of traffic, the even hum of the central air unit, and the patter of rain against tree leaves.

A quick turn and he was back, facing the bed. He pulled the sheet free and wrapped it around his torso. He carefully tucked the treasure filled paper bag under his arm.

He was careful to avoid the shattered glass in the window frame with his face, hands, and shoulders. He was half out the window. *Free, I'm free.* He was almost through when a jagged edge caught his ankle. The warm blood began to run over his heel. He pressed his thumb against the wound, but the blood continued to run. He searched his mind for a remedy but was unsuccessful.

He stepped out into the rain, into the humid night's air—one foot at a time, cautiously onto the asphalt roof. Bracing himself against the building's exterior, he looked out into the night, his first taste of freedom—an opportunity he thought would never come. The world had been reduced to a dark haze. Colors and shapes that he was once able to define, clearly now ran into one another like a somber watercolor painting. He gazed down, beyond the roof's edge. It blended into the darkness; a great dark void he feared would bring the end if he fell. He was intimidated by the challenge but not defeated.

One foot at a time, he slid his feet along the roof's surface, holding the precious paper bag with one hand. The fingertips of his other hand grazed the building's brick, monitoring his distance so as not to come too close to the edge.

For a brief moment, his wounded heart filled with exuberance. He'd thought he'd never again see the outside world, and though it had been reduced to a world of shadows, it filled him with a sense of liberation.

Slip-steps along the roof's edge until he reached the corner of the house, he kneeled and tested the gutter's strength where they were joined, pushing down on the apex. It seemed secure. From below, the central air unit blew hot exhaust into the air—he could feel the rising air current on his face as he looked over the edge. Hanging from the gutter, it would be a short fall onto the air conditioning unit. He centered himself above it by listening for the compressor's hum.

He clenched the paper bag in his teeth and then feeling with his feet got down on his knees and backed toward the edge. He felt the gutter's extruded metal in his left hand. Pushing against it, it now seemed far less sturdy than it had scant moments before. He thought about the jump, the safest way to spring from the roof. He wanted to do it slowly and cautiously but as he inched backwards, the opportunity for caution disappeared as the gutter broke free from the roof. Doe plummeted downward and disappeared into the darkness.

Dr. Maiguay was in the middle of a very busy night. He had just intibated a middle aged woman in respiratory failure when the page came in from ICU. The pager began to vibrate, the LED switching from red to a bright turquoise, just as he was squeezing the breathing tube past the vocal cords. He concentrated to push the distraction out of his mind for the few seconds it took for him to position the apparatus.

He was drenched in sweat when he came off the elevator. He heard the screaming and raced toward the intensive care unit. "What the hell is going on in here, nurse? This man is—"

"Comatose?" Tucker said. "He still is. You ever see a coma patient go off the wall like this?"

"No, but it is possible." Maiguay listened to his heart. "He's extremely rapid. "Push ten milligrams of Valium."

Tucker left the room and quickly returned with the medication. She filled a syringe, purged the air, and administered the IV sedative. The screaming subsided immediately. "That was wild."

Maiguay checked Doe's heart again. "Much better." He pulled the stethoscope out of his ears and draped it around his neck. “I think he’ll stay quiet.”

“So people can scream while they’re in a coma?”

“His brain’s inactive, not dead. Somewhere in his subconscious, he’s dreaming. My guess is that he’s experiencing dream terror as a manifestation of having been tortured. I don’t blame the poor man for screaming, do you? All we can do is keep him comfortable.” Maiguay left the unit.

Tucker looked at Doe’s desecrated face. “Alright, once is okay. Next time, do your crazy ass dreaming on somebody else’s shift.” She checked her watch and yawned. “It’s gonna be a really long night.”

# Thirteen

Dr. Walter Bock was not the kind of physician that inspired confidence. Perhaps that was the reason he was collecting bodily fluids and conducting follow-up checkups instead of pursuing excellence in the field of medicine and actually helping those who needed it. Under no circumstances would he have been my first choice for a physician. For that matter, he wouldn't have been second or third, but the department had demanded that I have a follow up physical to ascertain that I was, in fact, suitably fit for active duty after being Tasered and knocked unconscious. Probably not a bad idea; my head still ached like hell. So, there I was.

Bock was a balding German with a perspiration problem and a severe case of flabby butt. At any rate, he was the doc that was going to give me my mandatory once over. Sometimes, you just have to go with the flow, kick back and say, "What the hell."

If I played my cards right, I'd be out of his office in thirty minutes and officially back on the case.

I was already in an examination gown when Bock entered the room. He walked right past me without looking at me and began flipping through my file. "Good to see you again, Detective. Feeling okay since your injury?" I'd been examined by Bock before and knew that he was playing coy. I knew that he was one of those stealth peekers and would certainly find an opportunity at some point to take a refresher course in female anatomy at my expense.

There was a photo on the wall, with Bock posing alongside a big boned Shepard in front of a G-Class Mercedes truck. A mate of other than the canine persuasion was conspicuously absent. As for the SUV—I thought that Mercedes was turning out some stunning automobiles, but the G-Class truck looked to me like a rolling gas chamber, a carry over from WWII and the days when industrialized Germany focused its efforts on supporting Hitler's mass genocide campaign. Personally, I wouldn't be caught dead in one of them.

He wrapped the pressure cuff around my arm and pumped the bulb until the cuff was full. He twisted the wheel so that air would begin to bleed.

"They gave you a short gown," he said without taking his eyes off the sphygmomanometer dial. Somehow he had managed to check out my legs without making it obvious. Hopefully he hadn't seen more than that.

I hadn't thought the gown short, but I suddenly worried otherwise. I checked myself quickly. All of my feminine apparatus appeared to be concealed.

"Pressure's a bit high, Chalice. You're not drinking are you?"

*No, but now might be a good time to start.* "Of course my pressure's a little high. I'm in the middle of a case and I'm chomping at the bit to get back to it." *Steady girl, stay calm. Get the okay to resume active duty. Don't let this dirty little doctor get the best of you.*

"You have to learn to relax, Detective. You wouldn't want to do permanent damage. A concussion is not a matter to be taken lightly."

Bock was right, but allowing a dangerous perp to continue to wander the streets was unhealthy for Paul Liu and God knew who else. "I don't always do what's good for me."

"So I take it you're not hitting the bottle."

*"No."*

"Just being careful; lot's of cops on the sauce you know. It's an occupational hazard."

"Just wine with dinner."

"Good. Your pulse, I mean. You exercise?"

*Like a fiend.* "Yes, avidly."

Bock turned away from me. He'd put on a ton of weight since the last time I saw him, and his slacks were way too tight. I mean it wasn't pretty. It looked like he was smuggling cottage cheese. I laughed.

"Everything alright, Detective?"

*Sure, maybe you should check my pressure now.* "Yes, fine."

"I'm going to draw some blood—which arm?"

"Take your pick, I'm ambidextrous."

"You're a funny cop. I like that. He swabbed me with alcohol and tied a rubber tourniquet around my arm. He held up a basket full of squish balls. It felt good to squeeze anything, just to release a little tension.

He jabbed me with one of those venipuncture thingies, so that he could spill Chalice blood into multiple collection tubes without breaking stride. It was like tapping a keg of beer so that you could fill every mug in the frat house. He finished and gave me a Betty Boop bandage for my arm. "Can you jump on the scale for me, please?"

"Sure." *Almost done,* I told myself. I couldn't wait to get back into action. I heard my pulse pounding in my ears as I got off the examination table. It reminded me of the ticking clock. Every second lost worsened the chances for us finding the Chinese Ambassador's son alive. I cursed myself for having smacked my head, and having to play doctor with the lame Dr. Bock. Sometimes life doesn't give you a choice.

I stepped up onto the scale. *Christ, I put on three pounds. Where the hell did that come from?* The gym was going to see a lot of me once this case was behind us. *Three pounds, really? Damn those stuffed peppers.*

My mind was miles away as Bock conducted the rest of his tests. Distraction seemed to make the time go more quickly—Bock's quips and leering glances seemed less irritating. He finally finished his exam. I left him a urine sample on the way out.

# Fourteen

My skin was crawling as I answered Ambler's call. My head was spinning, and I was nauseous. I wasn't sure if I was experiencing latent side effects from the concussion or if I needed a clue fix. Surely this was shaping up to be one of the most bizarre cases I had ever worked on. I had chided Lido on his childlike, almost gleeful interest in Evans Jack's bug room. The truth was that I too had an almost macabre interest in the way the case was unfolding. Somewhere in New York City, a deranged monster was abducting young men, torturing them, and decapitating them. If that wasn't bad enough, he was using their bug scrubbed craniums for some kind of anatomical study—to which end I could scarcely hazard a guess. It was just business as usual in The Big Apple.

Evans Jack and his dissertation on the bug cleaning of human remains had sent my appetite for meat and meat-like substances on a long term hiatus. As I mentioned before, my head was dizzy, and I was nauseous, but like most New Yorkers, I find that pizza and beer will go down under almost any circumstances. This time was no exception.

Lido and I did a hit and run on Vincent's, a neighborhood pizzeria my family has been frequenting for thirty years. We ordered a couple of slices and two cold sodas and were back on our way to work in three minutes flat. Thin crust, lots of cheese, and the sauce…it'll drive you out of your mind—that first bite brought all my childhood memories streaming back. Brick oven pizza kicks the crap out of the stuff that comes out of steel ovens. Forget about those mass market brands—Pizza Hut, I don't think so. I'm a city girl for Christ's sake.

My cell phone rang. Ambler's name appeared on the display.

"G-Man, speak to me."

"The doc give you a clean bill of health?"

"Yeah, my scans came over just before I left the office. I'm good to go."

"I have something. It's not much, but it comes from a highly valued source. What say I pick you up in the morning for a quick jaunt out to the Island."

"Long Island?"

"Yes, Long Island. Don't ask questions. I know this won't make a lot of sense until I explain it all in person."

I could never doubt anything Ambler told me. In all matters, he was sincere and professional. He'd been my father's lifelong friend and now mine. If he wanted no questions, there would be none. My faith in the man was iron clad. Besides, I needed some time to pour over the case files the FBI had sent over. Research wasn't always fun, but it was vital. "Okay, where and when?"

"Nine sharp in front of your building. There shouldn't be any traffic at that hour; we're going against traffic… Oh, just one more thing."

"Yeah?'

"Lose the boyfriend."

*What?* I wanted to ask why. Again, I knew Ambler had a solid reason. "Okay," I said, making sure there was no drama in my voice for Lido to pick up on. "Anything else I should know?"

"Yeah, Long Island's beautiful this time of year—the rhododendrons are in bloom."

"Great, I'll wear my Easter bonnet and a calico dress."

Ambler chuckled and then signed off.

"What's up?" Lido asked.

"Ambler wants to show us something." I said *us* because I was still trying to come up with a clever way to finesse Lido out of the transaction. I know I shouldn't have... I mean the guy's solid gold. I should've just told him that Ambler asked him to opt out on the Long Island trip, but I didn't. I wanted to spare his feelings.

Is lying to spare someone's feelings really lying? My thought stream sounded like one of those Sarah Jessica Parker meaning of life questions from Sex and the City. The kind of query she'd raise when she was in a quandary about life, love, and her relationship *du jour*.

"On Long Island?" Lido asked. "What's that all about?"

"I don't know. He was kind of vague. I'm not worried about him wasting our time."

"Nor me. What time does he want to meet us?"

"Nine AM."

"You'll have to go it solo. I'm scheduled to give a court deposition in the morning."

"Oh, that's right." I was so focused on the mission of tactfully ditching my partner that I had completely forgotten that he was due in court in the morning—how fortuitous.

"I'll miss you."

"I'll miss you too."

I breathed a sigh of relief and then we went back to the house and dug into the evidence files.

# Fifteen

I hit the street at nine sharp. Ambler was already there, parked at the curb, eating bacon and eggs off a sheet of aluminum foil and looking happy as a kid in a candy store doing so. His Volvo was covered with dust. It wasn't one of the new sexy models. It was a good twenty years old, dating back to the day when the Swedes were stuffing engines into God ugly sheet metal boxes and pretentiously marketing them under the hoax that Volvo drivers were smart. Well the drivers may have been smart, but the company's marketing executives were dumb as sticks. They didn't sell any of those boxy, ugly cars—go figure. Speaking of smart Swedes, who's smarter than Invar Kamprad, the founder of IKEA. Here's a guy who's amassed a multibillion dollar fortune solely from marketing furniture constructed entirely from sawdust and glue. Volvo should have hired this guy fifty years ago. Had they done so, every car buyer in the free world would today be self-assembling their own cars from cryptic instructions that are wholly undecipherable, and lining up for miles to do so.

Anyway, so much for my attempt at neo-economic satire. I jumped into the passenger seat, rested, fresh as a daisy, and ready for my excursion to Long Island. The Volvo reeked from Ambler's greasy food.

"We could've stopped for breakfast."

"I got here early and got hungry. The guy on the corner makes a great scrambled egg. Want something for the ride?"

I knew the deli Ambler was talking about. The owner was affectionately referred to in the neighborhood as Rat Hair Harry, a bald Persian with tufts growing out of his auditory canals. "I'll pass on breakfast, but if you're hungry, we can grab lunch before we head back."

"Okay." Ambler threw his Swedish halftrack into gear and rolled slowly toward the 59th Street Bridge. "So how'd you dump the Boy Wonder?"

"There was no dumping involved. Gus was scheduled to give a court deposition this morning."

"How fortuitous."

"Those were my thoughts exactly."

"Great minds think alike."

"Don't flatter yourself."

"But you would've dumped him if you had to?"

"You ask me to come alone, I come alone. A girl knows who she can depend on. So what's the deal?"

Ambler sighed as he struggled to maneuver through the dense Manhattan traffic. "I hope it lightens up once we're over the bridge."

"I thought you said there wouldn't be any traffic."

Ambler sneered at me. It was one of his playful sneers. He had a large repertoire. This one was saying, kiss my butt. "I'm a middle aged Fed, not the All Knowing Oz." At that instant, the traffic cleared. It was almost as if it opened up on cue. We were over the bridge in minutes, cruising on the Long Island Expressway. The question still remained, where was Ambler taking me?

Few people were as forthcoming as Ambler, but there was something in his voice that told me he was holding back. He was obviously wrestling with something, so I figured I'd coax him along. "It'll go easier for you if you just come out with it. What have you got me involved in now?"

"What are you talking about?"

"You're being evasive."

"You're only in the car a few minutes; would you stop."

"Okay, I'll just sit here. Take me anywhere you like."

Ambler looked uncomfortable, as if he was squirming in his seat. Still, it took a moment before he said anything. "Damien Zugg."

"Excuse me?"

"Damien Zugg, you wanted to know where we're going, so I told you. We're going to see Damien Zugg."

There was something about that name that I just couldn't quite put my finger on. I was sure that I'd heard it before. My antennae went up. "How exactly do I know that name?"

"He's an ex-department head with The Bureau...forensics to be exact."

"You're dancing all around it. There's something about that name that I should know. Spill it. You know I'll figure it out eventually."

"He was very highly respected."

"So was O. J. Simpson before he traded in a pigskin for sauté knife."

And then it all came rushing back; headlines about a Polish serial killer the FBI tracked down in the Midwest. "Tamar Wald."

"Touché,"

"It's coming back now. Damien Zugg put together the forensics puzzle that led to the capture of Tamar Wald, the serial rapist and murderer."

"You're a veritable compendium of information. While we're at it, you left out that Wald also humped livestock."

"It wasn't germane."

"Remember anything else?"

"He left The Bureau, didn't he? Isn't he the one that went off the proverbial deep end?"

"Those are just rumors, Stephanie. Rumors are the stories people make up when they want to put their own spin on the truth. I've known Damien Zugg many years. He's a very private man working through a very difficult time in his life. He's fighting a battle against cancer. That's why I asked you to come alone. It's not that I have an issue with Lido. I just figure the fewer people Zugg has to interact with the better. He's absolutely brilliant and The Bureau still consults with him. I gave him Kevin Lee's skull to examine and he found something. It's a small something, but something nonetheless, and I'd like to have the police department's support so that he can continue helping us."

"And you thought I'd argue with you?"

"He has his good days and his bad days. Yesterday was one of his better days. He was sleep deprived and a little testy, but on the whole he was the Damien Zugg I've always known. There are times when he's not. There are days when I'm not sure who I'm talking to.

"Is he schizophrenic?"

"No, but the disease he's fighting with... it plays havoc with his mind, with his personality—sometimes he's a real mess."

"What's wrong with him?"

"He's got brain cancer, Stephanie."

"God, I'm sorry. That's so terribly sad."

"It's more than sad, it's tragic. For a man as gifted as Damien Zugg, being unable to count on his mind is—I really don't know how to put it into words. Sometimes you have to wonder about what makes God tick."

"What happens to him when he's off?"

Ambler turned to look me in the eye and then abruptly pulled the car to the side of the road and put on the warning flashers.

We were on a causeway, surrounded on both sides by water. We had already exited the expressway and were somewhere on Long Island's North Shore.

"What's going on?"

"I need some fresh air." Ambler got out, propped himself against the fender and looked off toward the water.

I jumped out of the car and joined him. We were both looking out at the water. "What's up?"

"This is the Robert Graff Causeway. It separates Beaver Lake from Mill Neck Bay. Pretty, isn't it?"

I scanned the lake. The sun cast a sharp glare across the surface of the water. Gnats were dancing in the air in front of me. The tide was low and the water smelled gamey. "It's alright. It's not exactly the Pacific Coast Highway. Tell me what's going on."

"Disease has this way of destroying the mind. I'm not talking about the tumors. People change when they know they're going to die. It becomes a disease of the mind; digesting gray matter in exactly the same manner the cancer cells digest healthy living tissue."

"As a friend, it hurts for you to see him like that—I understand. As cops, though, we need to know his information is reliable. Is he still reliable?"

"He was yesterday. I just never know what I'm going to find the next time I see him."

"Then we'll have to take it one day at a time."

Ambler cuffed me playfully on the chin. "You're pretty wise for someone so young. How'd you learn so much so fast?"

"I had some pretty good teachers."

"Thanks, kid."

What was going on here? Ambler was a no BS kind of guy, and yet he felt it necessary to stop in the middle of nowhere to explain himself to me. How much of a mess was Zugg? All I could think of was that Ambler felt it necessary to set such a low level of expectation that Zugg would seem acceptable no matter how bad he was.

The time for speculation was over. The clock was ticking. Hopefully the Ambassador's son was out there, somewhere, and still alive. "Come on, let's go. I can now check the Robert Graff Causeway off of my bucket list. I want to meet Zugg and find out what kind of mess you've gotten me into this time."

# Sixteen

Ambler overshot the driveway.

"What's the matter, that powerful four cylinder getting away from you?"

"Lay off the Volvo, Chalice. It's a good reliable car." He swung a U-turn and pulled into the driveway.

The gravel driveway was badly overgrown. We rolled over the weeds, snapping yard-high sapling trees until we came upon a large fallen branch blocking the way.

"We'll have to hoof it." Ambler turned off the engine. A moss covered BMW sat facing us on the driveway. He pointed at the vintage sports car through the windshield. "The man's here."

Ambler paused alongside the BMW. "1971 2002tii—at one time, this was one sweet ride."

"Unlike your Swedemobile."

Ambler snarled at me.

"Okay, I'm done; no more knocks on the Volvo." The property was a mess, but there was lots of it. "The place is going to waste. He doesn't have the money for the upkeep?"

"I think the land's been with the family for ages—Bureau pension and disability are more than enough to cover the taxes, even here in Nassau County. Chances are the mortgage is long paid for."

"So then what?"

Ambler shrugged. "I just don't think he cares anymore."

I felt as if I was just beginning to understand why Ambler was filled with so much trepidation. God only knew what we'd find when we knocked on the door. The house was set at the rear of the property, its back porch just yards from a pond.

I scanned the house. Large oak trees towered over the Cape Cod style home, bathing it in shadow. The roof was covered in moss, and the white paint on the soffit was badly worn, leaving the grayed pine exposed and unprotected. The cedar shakes had somehow managed to retain a modicum of their original orange hue. The porch steps creaked as we approached the house. Deciduous pine needles dangled from the overhang. Opening the screen door, Ambler rapped lightly.

A moment passed before he knocked again, a bit more determinedly this time. He listened carefully, hoping to hear footsteps inside; nothing.

I brushed aside a spider web and rubbed a circle in the window which was virtually opaque with grime. I peered in and looked for signs of life. Within, the immediate room was bare, no furnishings of any kind. Barren oak floors were heavy with dust. "Are you sure he's expecting us?"

Ambler nodded. "I'm going around back."

There were dried mud footprints on the back deck and on the burlap mat outside the backdoor. "Someone's been here recently," he said. "It rained a couple of nights ago. These prints would have washed away."

Stepping off the porch, I could see a faint trail of smoke rising above the tall thickets that bordered the pond. A pungent odor was distinct in the air. "You smell that?" I pointed to where a thin trail of smoke rose near the water's edge. "Something's burning over there." We bounded through the thickets to the water's edge. Lying on the ground was a religious censer—a trail of aromatic smoke rose from it.

Ambler looked around uneasily. "This is strange, even for Zugg."

The pond was covered in shadow. Its surface appeared viscose and scummy. I stared at the dark water not knowing what to expect. There was something on the ground near my feet. "What the hell?" A hooded monastic robe lay on the ground.

I pointed to the robe, "What do you make of this?" Suddenly, the hairs on the back of his neck rose. *Something's wrong.*

The shadows across the pond shifted. Looking down at the water I could now see past the surface. At first I doubted my eyes, but then I was sure that I was right. The crown of a bald head was visible just beneath the surface. *He's dead*, I thought. The severity of the disease—he just couldn't take it any more. My eyes enlarged and then focused. I was trying to comprehend what I was seeing, and then the head began to rise out of the water.

Zugg stepped out of the water, his naked white body pale, damp, and lifeless looking, like a wet, shivering dog. My heart jumped into my throat. Zugg seemed bewildered as he looked me squarely in the eye for what was probably no longer than a second, yet seemed like moments. He wearily scooped up his robe, and covered himself. Not a word was spoken as he trudged wearily to his house.

I turned to Ambler, my mouth gaping wide. I didn't need to say anything, nor did he. The message was in our eyes.

# Seventeen

A long moment passed as I attempted to calm down. I was struggling to find every last ounce of control, to keep my emotions even and level, but I couldn't. "What the hell was that?"

"Quiet," Ambler said, a bit more agitated than I'd ever seen him before. Beyond the outright shock of seeing Zugg rise naked from the lake, Ambler was no doubt concerned about his colleague's mental health, not to mention having introduced me into a situation that was out of his control. "He'll hear you."

"That's the least of my problems. What was he doing in the lake?"

"I don't know. I don't know. I don't know. Give me a minute to think. I've never seen him like this before. I've seen him act strangely, but nothing like this. Anyway, you can't say I didn't warn you."

"Are you crazy? Nothing you said could have prepared me for this.

*This* is the lynchpin upon which our investigation hinges? I need a Valium and a couch session with Dr. Twain. Forget Dr. Twain. I need multiple sessions with a psychologist in Vienna. I need Sigmund-fucking-Freud."

"Calm down, you're hysterical."

"You're goddamned right, I'm hysterical. I just saw a naked man breach the lake like Moby Dick and look me straight in the eye. I felt like Captain Ahab at the moment of his demise."

The screen door creaked. I looked up and saw Zugg on the house's rear deck, dressed in sweats and a baseball cap. He beckoned for us to come into the house and then disappeared inside.

"Are you still up for this?" Ambler asked. "I can do this solo if you want to wait out here."

"There's no way I'm dropping this. I want to know what's going on."

"Alright, let's go."

"Just a minute." I felt under my jacket. My Para Ordnance .45 automatic was still there, firmly holstered in its harness. I ran my fingers over the grip for reassurance. "Okay," I said. "Now we can go."

Zugg had arranged three chairs in an otherwise empty living room. Ambler and I took seats. I could see into the kitchen where Zugg was at the stove, pouring tea into two large mugs. He came into the living room and handed me a mug. "Detective Chalice, I presume—chamomile tea for your nerves," Zugg said. He handed a second mug to Ambler. "Yours is spiced with Irish whiskey," he said to Ambler. He took the seat opposite us. "Just a smidge, Herbert; I know you're on duty."

My first instinct was to summon the royal food taster to see if Zugg had slipped poison into our mugs, but I didn't. I sipped the tea, allowing the warm liquid to soothe me. It was hot and strong, and I enjoyed it. Somehow, Zugg now appeared normal as he sat before us.

Ambler broke the ice. "Bad timing?"

Zugg smiled. "Timing-wise, I'd say this is about as

bad as it gets." He turned to me. "Knowing what they say about first impressions, what must you think of me, Detective Chalice?"

*I refuse to answer on the grounds that I may incriminate myself.* "I've got a bunch of years under my belt with NYPD homicide—nothing rattles me anymore. I've seen it all."

"I doubt you ever met anyone else under similar circumstances. Nonetheless, thank you for being polite."

"So tell me, Damien, what the hell were you doing out back?"

"Herbert, I'm surprised you have to ask. You saw the censor and the religious robe. I was submersed in water. Surely you—"

"You were baptizing yourself, Damien?" Ambler asked, making no attempt to conceal his surprise.

"Yes, it's part of my daily routine. My private lifestyle allows me many indulgences."

"Why?" Ambler asked.

"*Happy is he whose fault is taken away,*" Zugg said.

It was a passage I was familiar with. "Psalm 32," I said. "You're afraid of dying with sins?"

"I'm not so much afraid, Detective. I'm just playing by the Almighty's rules. Medicine only offers a brief postponement. I'm hoping to buy myself more time by casting away my transgressions. And yes, you're right, if it's to the Pearly Gates I go, I'd like to go with a clean slate."

"It's not our business to pry into your personal affairs, Dr. Zugg, but I will say a prayer for you."

"Wonderful," Zugg said. "Shall we discuss forensics?"

*By all means.*

"So tell us what you found, Damien," Ambler said.

Zugg rested his chin on thatched fingers. He seemed weary now, his eyelids heavy, as he labored to contribute to the case. "All I found was dye; gentian violet to be specific."

"What's it used for?" I asked. "You don't seem excited about your findings, but surely it was on Kevin Lee's skull for a reason. God knows, all the FBI geniuses with bug boxes and gizmos didn't find it."

"Yes, Detective, it was put there for a reason; but for what reason? Gentian violet is one of the most common and frequently used substances in medicine and forensics. It's used in everything from fingerprinting to the treatment of fungal infections. It's the primary agent used in the Gram stain test, perhaps the single most important bacterial identification test in use today. They even use it in head shops to mark the tongue prior to piercing. So you see, my friends, finding gentian violet on a laboratory specimen may mean everything or it may mean nothing. Someone may have been careless in the forensics lab."

"Or it may be the key to solving this case and rescuing the Chinese ambassador's son."

"Yes," Zugg said, "but which is it?"

"Do you have a theory?" Ambler asked.

"I have several, Herbert, but nothing better than idle speculation. At first I—" Zugg's right eye squeezed abruptly shut. His other eye glossed over and began to tear. He was having an intense migraine or a seizure. I wasn't sure of which, but from the expression on his face, I saw that the pain was severe."

"Are you alright, Damien?" Ambler stood and hovered over him. "Is there something you can take?"

Zugg's eye was twitching. He pointed toward the kitchen. "In the refrigerator…preloaded syringes. Bring me one."

I raced into the kitchen. The syringes Zugg had prepared were in the butter drawer in a sealed plastic bag along with alcohol swabs. I knew my way around a hypodermic; my father had been a severe diabetic and there were times when I helped him with his injections. I had the syringe in my hand, with my thumb on the plunger when I realized that whatever it was in this syringe might not be injected intramuscular like insulin.

I tore open the small packet and handed Zugg the alcohol swab. Zugg's hand was shaking as he swabbed the crease of his arm. I handed him the syringe. He purged it frantically, wasting medication, and then, as if on autopilot, pierced his skin with the needle and guided it into a vein. Zugg went limp in his chair and his eyes rolled back into his head.

# Eighteen

"Do you like clams?"

"How in God's name can you even think of food at a time like this? Did you see the man? He's a friend of yours, for Christ's sake."

Ambler pulled into a head-in parking spot and shut the engine. "I'm sorry, I stress, I eat—you've probably noticed, I'm a pretty big fellow."

"Herbert, come on."

"Look, he threw us out of his house. He obviously wanted to be alone and felt well enough not to need us in attendance."

"Still." It had been less than an hour since Zugg had passed out, only to come around seconds later. He explained to us that it was his body's response to the medication, to the abrupt cessation of pain and that passing out was the psychodynamic equivalent to the rush a junky received from a spike of heroin. The explanation didn't ease my mind one bit.

Despite everything Ambler had told me about the

man's sterling credentials, I couldn't help wondering about how much of the man was truly left. He'd found forensic evidence the all knowing FBI lab had somehow missed. I had known him for the sum total of an hour, during which time he had emerged naked from baptizing himself in a scummy pond, donned a monastic robe, and passed out from his body's response to pain medication—not exactly what I'd call a solid citizen—how about you? What I really wanted to do now, more than anything, was hug a puppy. The only warm blooded creature around was Ambler, and he didn't quite cut it.

"Clams you say?" I couldn't believe that I was responding to Ambler's craving for deep fried sludge.

"Yeah, fried clams, fried calamari, popcorn shrimp; maybe wash it down with a cold one and a huge platter of Cheez Whiz encrusted nachos."

I almost hurled. "Okay, I can see you're in bad shape—order everything. I'll just pick." I was praying they had a decent salad on the menu—what were the chances?

"Atta girl, there's a place right down the street that fries everything in beer batter and bacon grease."

"You really feel like shit, don't you?"

Ambler nodded. "I feel lousy—thanks for indulging me."

"In terms of heartburn, you'll be going where no man has ever dared to go before."

Ambler put his arm over my shoulder and we strolled down the block, our noses sniffing the grease-heavy air.

"It was tough having to see him like that," Ambler said.

"I know. Are you sure it was alright to leave him alone? Maybe we should stop back to check on him before we head back to the city."

Ambler looked pensive. I know he wanted to say that Zugg was fine, that he's tough as a mule and would shake it off. Everything about him wanted to go that route, but he didn't. The expression on his face gave him away. "Maybe that's not a bad idea. I mean, I'm sure he's okay, but—you wouldn't mind?"

"I know that you're worried about damaging his self respect. Under the circumstances though, I'd risk invading his privacy. I'd want a good friend to do the same for me." *God forbid.*

"He was a very vital man. You can see how this is killing him... That came out wrong."

"I understand. We went through the same thing with my dad just a few years ago, you remember."

We were both sullen for a moment and then Ambler nodded. "Your dad was a dynamo."

"Right up until the end, but his body wouldn't follow the game plan."

"Zugg's kind of the same. His body wants to keep going, but his mind won't let him. He can't sleep and sometimes he gets so strange that I don't know who I'm talking to, but then, the next time I see him, he's okay again."

"Where would you place him today? On a scale of one to ten, was he weird or normal?"

Ambler grinned at me. "I'll take the fifth—let's get some chow."

The place Ambler picked had outdoor seating. It was a sunny afternoon and I was glad to get some fresh air. The least I could do was try to dupe my body into feeling healthy while I doused it with fat, free radicals, and toxins.

The restaurant was doing a brisk lunch hour business, so we opted for seats at the bar.

The barmaid looked about eighteen, too young to drink herself, but obviously not too young to mix up all manner of exotic potion. I watched her preparing Long Island Iced Teas for two guys in business suits.
She had the hand-eye coordination of a Ringling Brothers juggler—it looked like she had three bottles in the air simultaneously. Ambler seemed equally enamored as well. "She's good isn't she?"

"Good? That's not quite the adjective I had in mind."

I took a second look at the barmaid and knew where Ambler was going with his comment. She was young and thin, with a midriff top and an ample bosom. Her hair was long, silky, and flowing in the breeze, like a model's in a shampoo commercial. "Herbert Ambler, are you lusting after that young girl?"

"I can look, can't I?"

"You're more than twice her age."

"I'm just looking, Chalice. I'm well aware that I'm off her radar, thank you very much."

I didn't mean to bum him out. The morning had been pretty dreadful already. "I was just busting chops." At that moment, the barmaid turned to us and said that she'd be right over. "See that—she's totally into you."

"Stop it. I'm a Federal agent, not an adolescent school boy."

I didn't have the heart to tell him—what could possibly be less attractive to a pretty teenage girl than a middle aged Fed wearing wingtips and a J C Penney suit with an elasticized waistband? He'd be far better off with a face full of zits, a pocketful of weed, and a pair of Green Day tickets.

The barmaid swung by. She handed us menus and told us that her name was Allison. *If you don't see it on the menu, ask for it* was emblazoned across her perky young breasts.

"I love your blouse."

"Thanks, you should totally get one. It would look great on you. Ready to order? We've got a two-for-one special on Coors."

"So that's why you're so busy."

"Totally—the suits around here like to soak up the suds on their lunch hour."

Ambler didn't need the menu. He ordered all the fried fish he could think of and wrapped it up with sides of onion rings and curly fries. He indulged himself, taking advantage of the Coors special, advising me while ordering that we'd share the two-for-one brews.

"How about you?" Allison asked.

"I'll have a well done Zantac on a Kaiser roll."

Ambler snickered.

Allison seemed confused. "What's a Zantac?"

"It's heartburn medication." I waited a moment to see if she'd get it. She didn't. "We're going to share."

"Whatever."

She grabbed our menus and ducked under the bar to run our order into the kitchen. Ambler watched her make the trip. "I'm getting old, kiddo."

"You're just in a funk. Not that I blame you. The mortality issue, that's pretty heavy stuff. It's not easy to see one of your contemporaries at the end of his days."

"No, I'm serious. I've got twenty-four years with the Bureau. How long can I do this for?"

"You're not ready to retire. What would you do with yourself; fly out to the coast and produce a Mission Impossible sequel?"

He flipped me the most discreet of birds, posting his middle digit just below his eye. "You know, I haven't got a clue, but I know I won't be able to chase psychopaths forever."

"What would you like to do?"

"Honestly, I'd like to curl up on a bearskin rug with Anne Hathaway, but I don't see that happening anytime soon."

This was a serious admission for someone as private as Herbert Ambler. I had always known him to be a lifelong bachelor, and though I had long wondered about his dating habits, I had never asked. I saw him more as an uncle than a colleague and wanted to respect his privacy. Clearly he wanted to talk. "Anne Hathaway, the Devil Wears Prada girl?"

"There's a certain someone for everyone."

"Well, ya, but—" Ambler clearly didn't want to face the reality of Zugg. He had never taken me into his confidence on the subject of his romantic interests. I guess I could indulge him in a few minutes of displacement activity.

"Yeah, I know, don't tell me—I'm setting unrealistic expectations for myself."

"Have you been dating?"

"Once in a blue moon, between the Bureau and keeping late nights with Jim Phelps and the Mission Impossible team, I keep pretty busy."

Dear God, what an existence. I felt so guilty. "Why? You're a good looking, hunk of a man. Just haven't found anybody." In truth, Ambler didn't exactly fit the matinee idol mold, but he was funny, intelligent, and could be damn charming when he wasn't munching down a handful of beer nuts.

Ambler shrugged. I need something easy. You know, casual, no strings attached—something I don't have to work at."

*Uh, that's why they have hookers.* "That kind of relationship doesn't exist, not for long anyway. All relationships take a lot of effort. Let me repeat that, I said *all.* You think Lido and I never argue?"

"You two seem to be pimpin' it."

"I didn't say it wasn't working, but it's not always a walk in the park—we fight, trust me."

"Come on, you two have it made."

"Oh yeah, well last year, just before Christmas, Gus wasn't speaking to me at all."

"You're kidding. What happened?"

"You promise you won't repeat this?"

"Repeat it to whom? Aside from me, Ma, and Ricky, who else knows you're dating?"

"No one, I hope."

"So why weren't the two of you speaking?"

"Gus thought I was having an affair with Dr. Twain."

"Really, were you?"

"*No!* Of course not, but I used to call his name out in my sleep," I said, sounding guilty as hell.

"Yeah, that would piss me off too. So what's the scoop, do you have the dark, brooding shrink on your mind?"

I didn't want to get into it. I only put it out there so he'd realize that Lido and I had to work at our relationship too. Thankfully, the kitchen was fast. I saw that Allison was on her way over with a tray full of goodies. "Wow, look at the size of those onion rings."

That was the last thing I said, and Ambler didn't pursue it further. It's amazing how quiet it can get when you get busy eating, especially when it's your emotional wellbeing that's in need of nourishment. We both knew that there was unfinished business to discuss, but for the moment, we turned our focus to sustenance and Damien Zugg.

# Nineteen

Damien Zugg chased the Imitrex injection with a can of Red Bull to constrict the blood vessels and trigger an adrenaline surge. It was one of the bad days, exhaustion and pain of sufficient intensity to cripple even the most robust spirit. Zugg was not one to go down without a fight.

Almost twenty minutes went by before he found the strength to stand and the will to summit the staircase. And then finally up he went, using the handrail to drag himself up to the attic, one step at a time. If his condition continued to deteriorate, he'd have to move the terrariums downstairs to the main level of the house where it would take less effort to reach.

With the air conditioning switched off, the house's black roof kept the upstairs warm, just the right environment to keep the scorpions happy. The basement would have been a more convenient choice, but it was damp and the scorpions were used to an exceptionally arid climate. Zugg was happy with the heat as well. He'd lost significant weight in the last few months and was always cold. The morning's baptism had chilled him to the bone and his body was having difficulty generating warmth.

He stored the three species separately, in tanks designed to simulate their endemic environment. He checked the tanks before setting up the equipment. The scorpions seemed content, hiding under rocks during the day. He checked the Death Stalkers first, then the Cuban Blues, and finally the Israeli Yellow Tails. Zugg fed them generously. The tanks were crawling with a variety of spiders and centipedes, a veritable smorgasbord of scorpion delicacies.

He set up a fresh collection tube and then put on his gloves to handle them safely. He extracted one from each of the tanks using long forceps and set them into small, but separate holding tanks. He milked the Israeli Yellow first, slipping the stinger into the collection tube and then squeezed firmly about the tail where the poison glands were located.

He'd grown reasonably adept at the process. Working quickly but cautiously, he extracted enough venom to fill the collection tube, and then returned the scorpions to their tanks to rest and dine so that they'd replenish themselves for the next time Zugg needed them.

The task required extreme caution and Zugg found himself spent from the high level concentration that had been demanded of him. He was about to plop into the chair when the doorbell rang. He went to the window and moved the shade just enough to see Ambler and Chalice standing by the front door. His immediate reaction was that of irritation, but it quickly disappeared. They were only there to look in on him, and though their timing was bad, their concern warmed him.

He placed the collected material in the mini-fridge, locked the door to the attic, and carefully negotiated the stairs down to the main level, conserving energy so that he'd appear strong when he answered the door.

"You again." Zugg answered the door with a forced smile and an erect posture, somewhat overcompensating for the temptation to slouch. He knew they'd react to his initial appearance and that it would set their level of concern. He would make the bravest effort possible. "Come in, I was just about to prepare a Scorpion Cocktail. You're just in time."

# Twenty

I looked at Ambler to see if he knew what Zugg was talking about. It was obvious that he didn't. "A Scorpion Cocktail?" I mean someone had to ask.

Zugg bid us entry. He looked much improved since we'd left him, certainly not robust, but healthy enough to get along under his own steam.

"They're delicious, a couple ounces of rum, a little brandy, orange juice, and a twist of lemon—toss it in a blender with ice and serve with one of those adorable little drink umbrellas. They're very refreshing."

*Refreshing, like Seinfeld's notorious Junior Mint?* It struck me odd for Zugg to be offering us a cocktail, or for that matter, that he himself would be contemplating the consumption of alcohol. I wasn't exactly sure of what to make of it, but I let it go.

"You seem much better," Ambler said.

"Well enough," Zugg said, "Come on in, I'll make sure I have all the ingredients."

"No drinks for us. Your friend here just took me to

lunch at the local greasy spoon. I'm stuffed."

"Fried shell fish?" Zugg asked.

I nodded.

"That would've been my choice too. I'm sure you both needed comfort food after you left here. I must have scared the hell out of you."

*How do I admit that he's right without offending him?* "We were just concerned. You looked pretty run down when we left you."

"Not to worry, Detective, the human body is quite resilient. There's no end to the torture it can endure. I myself have seen several at the brink of collapse, who went on to survive for years."

The word torture served as a mental cue. If Zugg was the genius Ambler had so fervently bragged about, then perhaps it would help to see what he had to say on the subject of John Doe. "We didn't get a chance to chat before—did Herbert have a chance to describe the circumstances around which the skull was recovered?"

Zugg looked at Ambler and then shook his head from side to side. "Actually no, I have a feeling that my dear old friend was afraid to overwhelm me with too much information." He scowled at Ambler. "You know, Herbert, this isn't 222b Baker Street. Holmes was one of a kind. As for me, I have trouble piecing things together while puffing on a pipe and engaging in word play with my foil—knowing the facts can actually contribute toward the case's resolution. Had I been up to snuff, I certainly would have asked on my own." Zugg edged slowly into the living room, which, as before was arranged with the three chairs. "Please, fill me in."

We once again took our seats, Zugg in his wooden chair, facing ours. "The skull was found in a brown paper bag at the hand of a man lying unconscious in Central Park. The victim was mostly naked. All he had around him was a tattered bed sheet."

"The word victim usually connotes mortality," Zugg said. "Am I to assume that such is the case?"

"I didn't mean to be vague. Our John Doe is still alive albeit in a deep coma. He was unconscious when we found him and the doctors tell us that he is unlikely to recover."

"Doe had lost a tremendous amount of blood. He apparently severed a small artery," Ambler added.

Zugg rubbed the bristle on his chin. "There must be more contributing toward his condition than simple blood loss. Consciousness usually returns shortly after blood volume is restored and the body is reasonably hydrated."

"Doe was brutally tortured. He appears to have been held captive for quite some time."

"Tortured," Zugg repeated. "I see." He grew quiet, seemingly to withdraw into the annals of his mind. A long moment passed before he returned. "Then lucky for all of us, he escaped. It tells us much about the skull specimen you recovered."

*It does? Tell me, tell me, what does it mean?* I had my own thoughts on the subject, but a credible explanation from Zugg would go a long way toward validating his pedigree.

"The skull was not left behind as a clue for the FBI or for any other law enforcement agency to stumble across. It was discarded. It was discarded because the perpetrator of Kevin Lee's murder, this torturer and connoisseur of the human anatomy was disappointed with what he found. Our unsub went to extraordinary means in order to study this skull. He painstakingly selected his victim. He abducted, murdered, and decapitated Lee. He went through the arduous task of preparing it for study, and when all was said and done, he left his treasure with your John Doe, a living creature he values about as highly as a common moth. Yes, undoubtedly, it was discarded, my friends, because it was imperfect."

I noticed that my mouth was agape. Zugg had left me at a loss for words, a circumstance that was exceedingly uncommon. I examined Zugg's face and could see that he was still ruminating over the facts, but more than this, I could see that he was iron clad in his belief. He was merely running over the details to make sure that he hadn't missed anything. Under better circumstances, he'd probably have been more confident, but such was not the case, his mental state being what it was.

Ambler nudged my elbow and whispered. "Pretty good, huh?" He was grinning proudly.

I was feeling pretty good about Zugg myself. It was more than just his brilliant explanation and profound wisdom. It was a triumph way beyond his ability to reason, assess, and draw a conclusion. It was the fact that he was able to do it now, to reach up from the depths of despair, when most would've thrown in the towel. Zugg had likely accepted that his best moments were forever behind him. To see him at this moment, back at the top of his mental game, was the very definition of uplifting. I could see his spirit glowing from within. "Damien, that was amazing." He looked at me with a warming smile, and then my cell rang. It was an incoming call from Lido. I'll have to do the evasive thing with him. After all, Ambler and I never really told him where we were going. "Hi, Gus."

"Stephanie, you and Ambler still out on the Island?"

"Uh huh. What's up?"

"We caught our first break in the John Doe case."

Gus didn't know it, but he had just missed the first break award by about sixty seconds, coming in just behind Damien Zugg's brilliant revelation. I didn't have the heart to tell him, or the energy to begin telling him about the morning Ambler and I had spent with Zugg. "That's great," I said. "Tell me what you've got."

# Twenty-One

Rediscovering a favorite song is like taking that first deep breath after recovering from a chest cold. It's one of those simple pleasures that can only be described as magic. I was astounded to discover that Ambler's old Volvo had an FM radio. It had an old slide rule dial, but I was able to tune in 104.3 and Led Zeppelin was playing Gallows Pole, a rather obscure tune even for rock radio. Now you're probably saying that my soul is a might old. I mean Zeppelin was breaking the sonic barrier about the time I was learning to walk, but even today, I find kids listening to the artists of the sixties and seventies, Zeppelin, Hendrix, and Cream—it just never got any better than that. Whereas technology seems to take a quantum leap every day, rock music hit the wall after these giants disappeared. So for the moment, I clung to Page's unplugged guitar, to buoy my spirits against the weight of adversity I had been faced with that morning.

We were on our way back to the city to

rendezvous with Lido. This was one of those cases where information was not flowing, and so NYPD had taken to the street in mass, canvassing Manhattan from river to river and tip to tip, with pictures of John Doe. It was sort of a blinders on, nose to the grindstone approach—no magic, no brilliance, just good hard work, but it had paid off. Although we hadn't identified Doe, he had been spotted on the evening he was found in Central Park. Oddly though, the sighting was not in the area surrounding Central Park, but rather in lower Manhattan. A grocery store clerk had seen him stumbling down the steps of a subway entrance. The clerk had seen him from the store checkout counter, through a plate glass window, and across the street. Although the possibility existed for any number of half naked men clad only in a sheet, walking the streets of Manhattan certainly existed, we felt this ID remarkably positive.

"So how do you like the chances of your John Doe taking a subway ride from the steps of City Hall to Central Park?" Ambler asked.

"How do I like them? I like them a lot."

"He wasn't seen? He wasn't stopped?"

"Oh, on the contrary: I'm sure he was seen, and approached, and heckled, and harassed. When's the last time you took a subway ride after midnight in New York City? It's mostly kids partying and homeless folk. What's more, it explains why no one saw him in our target area in and around Central Park. I figure he got on the C train and rode it up to 72$^{nd}$ and Central Park West."

"Why'd he get out there? I mean, why did he get off at the park?"

"Either he thought he was far enough away from his captor to safely emerge from the subway, or he felt consciousness slipping away and figured he'd better hit the street before he took a dirt nap in one of the subway tubes."

"I love it when you're so damn sure of yourself."

"You've got another theory?"

"No, it's just embarrassing. We've been frantically looking for leads on the Paul Liu case only to find his partner's skull in the hands of a torture victim just a stone's throw from Bureau headquarters."

"Yeah, that does look pretty bad. Have to say though, it's not an angle I would have considered. Now if we only knew where Doe had been incarcerated before he escaped. It had to be close to the subway entrance—so far no one other than our observant store clerk has admitted to seeing him on the night we found him."

"Admitted, being the key word. As you pointed out, a man clad in a sheet had to be noticed by someone. Even in the streets of New York City, a sight like that has to jump out at you."

"I'll ask the OIC for more help. We'll concentrate our efforts in the area around the subway entrance. We can go door to door if we have to."

"They still haven't named Sonellio's successor yet?"

"No."

"So who's minding the store?"

"Pamela Shearson."

"Pamela Margaret Shearson?"

"I think so. You obviously know her. I think she's splitting herself between us and her old assignment—hasn't even made an appearance at the house yet."

Ambler rolled his eyes. "Oh, I know her. She's definitely on the fast track. You know they call her PMS, don't you?"

"Oh, that's so flattering for a woman and so clever too. Let me guess, she's moving up the ladder too quickly to win the approval of the Old Boy's Club?"

"At the risk of being politically incorrect, she's a ball buster, Stephanie. She's aligned herself with the force's powerbrokers and associates herself with the right people, but she's never made her bones."

I'd never known Ambler to buy into the majority consensus without a good reason. Never made her bones: that was cop talk for saying she had no street credit, no practical experience. It had taken all of my street smarts to sidestep the landmines that had been placed before me in order to derail my promotion to detective. There are a lot of guys on the job that don't like to see a woman getting ahead too fast, especially guys that are being passed over. In the end, despite all my merits, it was the Frank Chalice pedigree that saw me through—promotion probably would have taken years longer had it not been for dear old dad. So, to set things straight, I just wanted to make sure Shearson wasn't getting a bum rap. The old timers seem to take a dim view of women that are too strong. "Got it, I'll tread lightly. All the same, I'll ask her for more support."

"Atta girl."

"That's the second atta girl you've given me today."

"So?"

"Don't give me a third."

"Why are you so touchy today?"

I didn't have to utter a word. All I had to do was glance over my shoulder toward the back seat where Damien Zugg lay sprawled out, snoring at roughly a hundred decibels—in layman's terms, that's just a whisper below the noise a Boeing 747 generates at takeoff, or the sound level in the good seats at a heavy metal concert.

Ambler got quiet and glued his eyes to the road. "So, I'm thinking a door-to-door search within a ten block radius of the subway station should be our next move…you?"

Ambler nodded as we disappeared into the Queens-Midtown Tunnel on the Queens side. Zugg snored all the way through.

# Twenty Two

We were meeting Lido at FBI headquarters because of its proximity to our hot zone. Lido was already there when we arrived and ready to head up the NYPD portion of the effort. I was just hanging up with Pam Shearson as we walked through the door. Our officer in charge had been most cooperative, and though it served my purpose, I detected in her line of questioning that her interests went far beyond the apprehension of a psychopath and the possible rescue of Paul Liu, the Chinese ambassador's son. It was the bigger picture that she was interested in, the resolution of a high profile case the FBI had stumbled over for months. Media attention would be international in scope, just the kind of attention a mover and shaker sought—subsequent promotion for Ms. Shearson was inevitable, and all she had to do was say yes to my request for reinforcements. She had not been involved in the case at the street level as Sonellio would have been. She was not interested in details. Shearson would simply show up at the arrest, mug for the press, and take the credit. It was a simple formula, one she had obviously mastered.

Shearson had demanded that we use NYPD turf as the site for the command center. Here too the reason was clear. She wanted to downplay the FBI's role in the case. In her eyes, this was now clearly a police matter. The FBI could consult as long as they remained unobtrusive. In the end, if we failed, she'd hang the blame around the Bureau's neck like a neon albatross. The woman was clad in Teflon. There was just one problem, and that was me. Who knows if we would have been able to put two and two together had Ambler not stepped up to request FBI permission to examine the skull found in John Doe's possession? Maybe yes, maybe no—in any case, I was not the kind of cop to crap on my colleague in arms. I had to pull Ambler aside and lay the lowdown on him.

Zugg was another matter all together. His involvement had to be kept on the QT. He was an FBI paid consultant, and though he caused me worry, I felt he had a sizable contribution to make. The question was how to keep him off everyone's radar. Certainly, that was going to be a lot of work.

I felt more like a mediator than a cop as we all filtered into the Bureau's ready room. I had to fill Lido in on Zugg, Ambler in on Shearson, and Zugg in on life as it had to be. Tell me again, why do I like this job?

The nap on the ride in did Zugg a world of good. He was looking...okay. He was wearing his Yankees cap and looking sort of normal. Lido wasn't meeting him under the circumstances that I had, naked and erupting past the surface of a scummy pond like some type of swamp creature. This was going to be easy. Okay, maybe not easy, but easier.

Lido and Zugg shook hands. He picked up on the Yankees cap and immediately began talking about A-Rod, Jeter, Steinbrenner, Godzilla, and— I hadn't a clue if Zugg actually gave a hoot about the Bronx Bombers or if the cap was strictly cosmetic. In any case, he seemed to be engaged by Lido's home team bravado. Thank God Zugg didn't remove his cap and treat Lido to the sight of his post surgical cranium. No one was looking, so I crossed myself for good luck. Of course I'd have to tell Lido about Zugg's state of physical well being, but I'd do so later, perhaps after several bottles of wine and a proper boinking. As they say, timing is everything.

"Who's up for some Bureau swill?" I knew Ambler would want in. "Herbert, I know you want a cup." Lido already had a *vente*-sized cup of Starbucks on the table next to his gear. "Dr, Zugg, how about you?"

"Just water please."

He could have asked for a bottle of Crystal and I would have nodded and said okay. All I really had in mind was getting Ambler alone for a minute. I had him by the sleeve and was already yanking him out the door when Zugg answered. Our eyes connected—Ambler played along.

I still had him in tow when he could no longer control his curiosity. "I love it when you play rough."

I stopped myself from acting on the impulse to flip him off in the middle of the FBI operations center. "We need to talk." I already knew where the kitchen was, having been a frequent guest of Ambler's and the FBI. We walked slowly in the kitchen's direction.

"So what's up? Is it Zugg again? I don't want you to worry because I'll deal with him. I know he creeps you out a little, but he's very good at what he does. Tell me you weren't impressed with him."

"Actually I'm very impressed with Zugg, and he doesn't so much creep me out as worry me. You saw him this morning. I thought we were going to have to call the funeral parlor. I worry that this will kill him."

"That's just something we're going to have to get our arms around. He asked to be here. He feels he can help and we both agree. He's got cancer, Stephanie. He's not going to have a good day everyday. Can you deal with that?"

"Time will tell." That was as far as I wanted to

take it. I didn't want to say how tough I found it dealing with my father's physical and mental decline. Ambler was close enough to the Chalice family to know the intimate details. We were now alone in the kitchen. Ambler was searching for Styrofoam cups. I opened the fridge where they stored the bottled water and those portion sized half & half thingies.

"So what then is on your alleged mind?"

"I love it when you talk cop. It's Shearson. She wants operations housed on NYPD property. She made it perfectly clear that this is a police matter. John Doe is ours, the skull is ours—you catch the drift."

"Jesus, that woman is such a fucking credit whore. I had a bad feeling the moment you told me that she was involved." Ambler handed me a cup of coffee. "That'll be two bucks."

"Excuse me?"

"Well as long as we're not sharing any more. I suppose she wants the Bureau waiting on the sidelines in case she needs her shoes shined."

"You know I would never play it like that."

"I'm glad to hear you say that, Stephanie, because I'm not going to roll over and let Ms. High and Mighty ride roughshod over the FBI. It's true that Doe is an NYPD investigation and technically the skull is your evidence, but this is also a Bureau investigation. Kevin Lee and Paul Liu are linked, and the disappearance of a foreign ambassador's son on US soil is definitely an FBI matter. So, I'll play ball as long as Shearson doesn't get heavy handed, but the moment she does—"

"I know, you'll call the Director."

"In a heartbeat."

"Lighten up, will you. You know how I am. I play fair."

"You'd better," Ambler said with a broad smile on his face.

"Or what? The way I see it, I'm the one with all the power."

"How's that?"

"How'd you like me to tell everyone about your Anne Hathaway fantasy? The two of you would look adorable together on a bearskin rug."

"I wasn't so much thinking adorable as I was incendiary. Anyway, that was told to you in confidence."

"I look like legal or psychiatric counsel to you? You have no protection under the law."

"That would be especially bitchy of you."

We were still alone in the kitchen. I gave Ambler a peck on the cheek and whispered in his ear, "You're so easy."

"And you're such a ball buster."

"Such flattery." I took him by the arm again. "Come on, G-Man, let's go solve us a crime."

# Twenty Three

"Open up, it's us."

I needed no explanation. I had come home for a few minutes and was fresh from the shower when I heard the doorbell. "Just a minute." I threw on a robe and went to the door. Ma and Ricky had stopped by for a visit.

Ricky held forth two enormous bags which I knew at first whiff was Chinese food. "Hungry, Sis?"

"This is a nice surprise. Come in."

"Is Gus home?" Ma asked.

"No. I ran home for a shower and a change of clothes. We're setting up an operation downtown. We'll probably be out all night. Gus and Ambler are holding down the fort until I get back." I gave my brother a kiss on the cheek. He was smiling ear to ear. "How'd you know I'd be home?"

"We took a chance," Ricky said. Ma's mannerisms were beginning to rub off on him.

I gave Ma her obligatory hug and kiss. She walked

in and proceeded to take charge. "Ricky, put those bags on the table. Stephanie, you got paper plates, the coated ones? I don't want the food soaking through."

"Chinese food, huh? I don't know if I should. I had the most fattening lunch imaginable with Ambler. I think Chinese would put me over the—"

"Ba, I told you, you look like a noodle with boobs. You're too friggin' skinny."

Certainly, there was no dissuading Ma from her idea of the perfect female body type. There would be several trips to the gym to atone for this day of sinful eating. Instead of saying a Hail Mary, I'd be doing crunches and a couple of hours on the elliptical machine. "What'd you get?"

"We got tired of Italian food," Ricky said. He looked so grown up as he unpacked the food. I had always thought of him as a kid in a man's body, but all the work with Dr. Twain was paying off. Seeing him now, hungry, tired from a day's work, and thrilled to be breaking bread with his family, he looked like any other guy. It brought a tear to my eye.

"So what's in the bag?" I gave him a playful elbow on his arm. "Holding out on me?"

"We got egg rolls, wonton soup, walnut shrimp, moo shu pork, fried rice—" It sounded like Ricky was only halfway through the menu.

"Okay, okay, I'm in. I'll make a pot of tea." I walked into the kitchen to set up the kettle. "Be right back." I dashed into the bedroom and picked out some clothes appropriate for an all-nighter, going door to door—slacks, a merino sweater, and a comfy pair of shoes. Buttoning my pants, I noticed that I still had a little room. It made me feel a trifle less guilty about gorging myself on noodles and batter covered fried shrimp, which had been sautéed in sugar and corn starch. I combed my hair and sat down at the dinner table without putting on makeup.

The plates were still empty. Ricky was rolling moo shu wraps for the three of us and doing a skillful job at that. Ma was silent. I saw her watching him, her eyes wet, fighting back tears. When I held her hand under the table, she looked at me. She let one tear go and then wiped her eyes dry. "What are we doing here," she said. "Everyone's starving. Give out some food already."

"Here's the moo shu," Ricky said, transferring the wraps from his dish to ours. "I put the plum sauce inside already."

I took a bite. It was really good, sweet, salty, and moist, all at the same time—just the kind of food I normally avoid like the plague. But this was one of those days, when it was easier to go with the flow than fight the world. Did I actually hear Ma say that I looked like a noodle with boobs? And I let it go? I was about to revisit the subject when Ma struck preemptively.

"You look pretty without your makeup on, just simple and clean." She grabbed my hand under the table and squeezed it. "You work too hard." She was misting up again, obviously looking at me and remembering Dad. "Remember, it's only a job. Don't let it take over your life."

"I'm fine, Ma." This was the one thing I couldn't explain to her. It was one thing to be a policeman's wife or mother, and another thing being on the job yourself. This wasn't just a job, this was the job of jobs; NYPD homicide, it's if you're fighting a war for God himself. She would never be able to understand that, looking from the outside in.

"Isn't your sister pretty, Ricky?"

Ricky nodded. He had a huge grin on his face and was stuffing an egg roll into his mouth. He looked up and grinned. The boy had an appetite as big as all outdoors. I know that most men prioritize food above almost all else. Ricky apparently was no exception.

I looked back at Ma. She seemed thoughtful as she ate, as if she was truly appreciative of the time she had with her family and was taking stock in the axiom, life is too short.

Perhaps that was just me, projecting my feeling onto her. Spending the day with Zugg had given me a fresh perspective on life, and how precious it truly was.

# Twenty Four

Five AM. The night's yield had come to nothing: no clues, no suspects, no runs, no hits, no errors. Lido and I were sitting in a coffee shop named the Dugout, hence the baseball analogy—I felt like you were due an explanation.

There's nothing quite as uncomfortable as knocking on someone's door in the middle of the night, waking them from a sound night's sleep, holding photographs in front of their red, watery eyes, while they're yawning, only to leave with a little less hope than you had the moment before you knocked on their door. In law enforcement as in life, anticipation is everything. It's what keeps driving you forward when all seems lost. Lido and I were exhausted and low on hope and life sustaining nutrients.

Breakfast smelled as you'd imagine it would at one of those hole in the wall joints with a bright yellow $1.99 Breakfast Special sign in the window.
My scrambled eggs were served on an oval dish that had

been in and out of the dishwasher so many times that the pattern had worn off the china, and the inside of my coffee mug had a thousand hairline fractures in the surface, stained brown from coffee too deeply imbedded to ever come out. But the eggs were fresh and the coffee was hot—more than that, I couldn't ask for.

"So what's with that guy, Zugg?"

"You mean the FBI's consultant?"

"You know exactly what I mean."

I was hoping that Lido hadn't picked up on Zugg's eccentricities, but Lido was after all a cop, and a good detective to boot. He was certainly capable of reading between the lines, and Zugg read like elementary school paper, the kind with the wide spaces. It seemed like a good time to fill him in on the details before Zugg had another episode. You're nuts though if you think I'm going to give him the gory details. "Zugg's a brilliant forensics specialist. He's retired from the Bureau on permanent disability and Ambler wanted his involvement in the case. He found a chemical on Kevin Lee's skull that the FBI technicians missed." My eggs needed salt and my whole wheat toast needed...well taste. The home fries were frying pan burnt, but they were seasoned with everything imaginable. I put my hand on Lido's. "Zugg's in really poor health, Gus. He's got brain cancer. That's why the baseball cap never comes off. The top of his head looks like a suture roadmap, but it was good of you to engage him in a Yankee's then and now conversation. I'm sure you made him feel right at home."

"I knew something was up. He looked kind of okay when we met, but he crashed within a couple of hours. I think Ambler arranged for him to be driven home."

"That's right. Ambler offered to put Zugg up at a hotel, but he refused. He's got medication at home he probably needs access to—you know how it is."

"Is he strong enough to work?"

"Yes and no. He has his good days and his bad. I guess we'll get to see him both ways. The important thing is that he wants to stay active and assist us with the investigation, and I'm happy to have his help at whatever level he can offer it." There, I had fulfilled my obligation to bring Lido up to speed without divulging too much, giving Lido grave concerns about Zugg's credibility—not that I didn't have concerns of my own, but I was prepared to deal with the setbacks as they arose.

"So, what did Zugg find?"

"A trace amount of gentian violet."

"I know what that is. That's the stuff they use in fingerprint ink."

"Correct, I see you still remember your police academy training. According to Zugg, it's got 1001 uses, and is found in every crime lab in the world. So the real question is whether it was on the skull when we recovered it, or did it accidentally find its way onto the skull somewhere in the FBI crime lab?"

A man was sitting next to me at the counter. His eggs had been prepared sunny side up. He placed his fork under the yolk to lift it off the plate. Then he placed his lips on the eggs and sucked out the yolk—as if I wasn't having enough trouble choking down my breakfast already. "I think it's time to get back out on the street."

"But I haven't finished yet."

I directed Lido to glance at my yolk sucking friend. He had yolk on his nose and was going in for number two. "No, I'm quite sure we're both finished." I grabbed the check and stood. Lido wolfed down as much as he could while I waited to pay the bill, and then met me outside.

"Got grossed out, huh?" he asked.

"I got grossed out—yes."

"Nothing bothers my appetite."

"You ate spam before we started dating. I guess you can choke down almost anything.
Aren't you glad you started dating a nice Italian girl whose mother cooks from dawn to dusk?"

"I'm glad I met you." Gus faked a yawn and grazed my butt as he brought his hand to his mouth. "For everything you bring to the table." He gave me a sexy wink. "Wanna get a room?"

"Just like a man to think about sex at a time like this. It's five AM. We've been up all night and haven't come across a fresh lead. God knows, Shearson's going to come down on us like a ton of bricks if we don't crack this thing wide open soon.

"What can I say? I'm a good healthy boy, with all kinds of appetites. Besides, I just read in Men's Health that a man's testosterone level peaks early in the morning."

"You should've quit while you were ahead. You had a chance before, but bringing up the word testosterone? I can't possibly think of a bigger turnoff. Just so you know for next time, any mention of male specific fluids is a buzz kill for the female libido."

"Sorry. I made a lot of overtime last month—we can get a really nice room."

Gus was teasing me. He was a guy alright, but a guy who knew how to press a woman's buttons. "Sure, take me to the finest hourly rate hotel in the city, someplace where they actually launder the sheets." I whispered in his ear. "We've got work to do. Find me a killer and I'll—" That last part of that sentence was omitted intentionally. I didn't want to embarrass either of us. Back to the conversation of pushing buttons; Gus looked a little flush. He was still leering at me when an RMP screeched to a halt in front of us. The cop leaning out the window looked familiar. I recognized him from the police academy and called out his name, "Lipscomb."

Lido had a queer expression on his face. He pulled me aside. "Did you say lip scum?"

"Lipscomb, Lipscomb, what's the matter with you?"

"I wasn't sure what you said."

"You can be such a jerk." Lip scum, what a visual. I had to pinch myself as I walked over to the car just to keep it in check.

"Chalice," he called back. "Where've you been? We've been looking for you. We found a crime scene."

"How've you been, Lipscomb?" Okay, I'm sorry, this is terrible, but I couldn't say his name with a straight face, and likely would never be able to do so again.

"You're looking good, Chalice—come a long way since we went through the academy together."

Lipscomb was a hunk of sorts; rugged good looks and an overdeveloped body. He was fun to look at but I never saw him as the kind of guy I'd ever want to get close to. He had that cocky macho thing going, twenty-four/seven. He was the kind of guy you'd wake up next to one day, spot a hickie on his neck, chamber a round, and blow his brains out. I winked at him just to be flirtatious and play to his ego so that he wouldn't suspect that Lido and I were a couple. "What'd we find?"

"Courtyard behind a restaurant; broken window, loose gutter—the crime scene guys just got there. They think it may be related to your John Doe case. We've got the area cordoned off—no one's getting in or out until you arrive."

"Let's move." Gus and I jumped into the back of the car. This may not have been the kind of excitement Gus had been looking for, but the news drove any thoughts of sex right out of our minds. Anticipation was high and there would be plenty of the good stuff for Gus when we solved this case. Not that it had ever been bad, but it certainly made a strong argument for solving the case and enjoying a little down time—details to follow.

# Twenty Five

A restaurant named The Nine Circles conjures up many kinds of images, not all of them good. The restaurant whose name bore reference to Dante's Inferno was located on the ground level of a three story brick structure. Apartment dwellings were located above. I took it all in as the RMP pulled up in front of the restaurant. The façade was black with concentric neon rings backlighting the name. I was guessing about the type of food a restaurant with such a name might serve. Well, for the record only, I was spot on—the Nine Circles served Thai. A Zagat's review was framed in the window. The caption read: The Spiciest Thai in Town.

The restaurant's early morning staff was already on site, preparing for the day's trade. NYPD had taken charge; police and specialty teams were moving in and out of the restaurant's doorway.

A second front door which led to the upstairs apartments was likewise NYPD secured.

"Take a quick look," the RMP's driver said. "We

think the upstairs units are abandoned. We didn't want to go in until you arrived."

Likely they were. NYPD and FBI personnel had surrounded the building. Chaos like that would have normally drawn the curiosity of everyone inside, especially at this early hour when the streets were normally quiet.

Lido and I walked straight through the eatery to the rear courtyard.

The yard behind The Nine Circles was a common court, providing access to several buildings, shops, and restaurants. There was also a common access driveway, through which, I imagined the stores took deliveries and had their sanitation removed. There were several technicians already at work, but the only one I noticed was Damien Zugg. Damien Zugg was already back on the job. I saw him kneeling to examine something on the ground. He was picking up a glass fragment with a pair of tweezers and slipping it into a plastic evidence bag.

"Dr. Zugg, back so soon?"

"Couldn't sleep, Chalice." The bags under his eyes corroborated his statement.

"You drove in on your own?"

"Sleep deprivation's not so bad once you get used to it." He stood and held the plastic evidence bag at eye level. "You see?"

The jagged glass fragment was about three inches long. It was red at the very tip. "Blood?"

Zugg nodded and then pointed behind us, back toward the building over the restaurant. The corner window was shattered. Below the window, the gutter was broken away from the building. A crime scene tech was in the process of pulling it free. "This must be the place," Zugg mused. "Dollars to donuts, this is John Doe's blood on the glass. Up yonder is where he was held captive."

"He went out the window and tried to use the gutter to break his fall—pretty brave effort."

"Whatever took place in that room mandated drastic action."

"Care to have a look?"

Zugg followed me to the front of the building where the police had secured the front door. We picked up Lido along the way.

"This the place?" Lido asked.

"Bingo."

Ambler was just getting out of his car. We threw on Kevlar and hit the doorbell. I could hear it chime from out on the street. I counted to five and then pressed on it continually. I doubted we were going to find anyone alive inside. Our perp had likely cleared out after discovering John Doe's escape. I stepped aside and let the strong boys batter the door in. The old wooden door fractured. We cleared away the debris and moved cautiously up the stairs.

Via the staircase, there was access to two apartments, one on each of the second and third levels. I took the top level where we assumed Doe had escaped from. "Open up, NYPD." Lido gave it about two seconds and then kicked in the door. We began going room to room. There was a modest kitchen and a living room, both empty and unremarkable. I moved past the bathroom to where there were two empty bedrooms. They were both stark white.

Nausea hit me in the pit of the stomach. I knew instantly that John Doe had been tortured here.

The picture opened up in my mind—it was like some manner of horrific nightmare. I saw the broken window with Doe's blood dried on the glass and window frame. There were holes in the wall around the window where Doe had freed metal lag bolts from the studs. The security bars that had once contained Doe were on the floor. In the corner of the room, a cabinet in the far corner of the room contained prescription bottles of every size and description. Heavy gauge piano wire had been secured to the ceiling above the single bed and the floor. The floor was covered with cigarette butts and the room stunk of cigarette smoke.

Although I had been trained not to jump to conclusions, I knew in my heart that everything I envisioned about this tragic place was true, and it would be just a short matter of time until the crime lab validated my conclusions.

Ambler, Zugg, and Lido entered the small bedroom. I monitored their expressions. I could see that they were seeing everything exactly as I had, and then Lido must've noticed something I hadn't. I saw the pained expression on his face as he looked back at me and moved to block something from my line of sight.

"What's that, Gus?"

"Um, nothing." Lido shrugged, trying to appear that he didn't know what I was talking about. Pigheaded detective that I was, I just couldn't let it slide. I already knew that we were in the place where John Doe had been incarcerated and tortured. The room was crammed wall to wall with evidence, and I really didn't need to see every God awful item in it...but Stephanie Chalice, bloodhound detective just couldn't leave any stone unturned.

"C'mon, Gus, what's there—I saw your face."

Gus looked at me and sadly shook his head. I wasn't sure if he was registering abject disgust or attempting to communicate that I shouldn't look. I beckoned for him to move aside and he reluctantly complied. Behind him on the floor was a large plastic bottle of drain cleaner pierced by a hypodermic syringe. I turned and walked slowly down the stairs and out to the front of the building to fill my lungs with fresh air.

# Twenty Six

Lido and Ambler followed me downstairs.

"Are you alright?" Gus rubbed my arm. "I tried to warn you."

"I know. Thanks. That bottle of drain cleaner—it just took everything out of me, and the stench of cigarettes, it was as if we were inside a pair of unhealthy lungs."

"Real nice up there," Ambler said. "I wonder if the landlord gets extra for all the B and D stuff."

"I noticed a reciprocating camera on the wall above the bedroom door. Either of you see any tapes while you were up there?"

Lido shook his head. "The perp had enough presence of mind to remove it. Somehow in his warped mind, it's the only truly incriminating piece of evidence."

Ambler looked concerned. "You look a little green, Chalice."

"Must've been all those fried crustaceans you fed me yesterday."

"Curly fries are not crustaceans."

"Don't get cute. You know what I mean."

Ambler offered me a stick of chewing gum. “Peppermint, give it a try, it does wonders for me.”

“Okay, thanks.” I took Ambler’s gum. I had eaten everything I’d been offered in the last twenty-four hours. I made a mental note to stop accepting meal invitations and start planning my own menus. I turned to Lido. “Are our crime scene guys cataloguing the evidence up there?”

Lido nodded.

“Make sure that the chain of evidence begins and ends with NYPD. I don’t mind if Zugg observes, but I don’t want to get any flack from Shearson.”

“Yes, Ma’am,” Ambler said. “Zugg’ll just watch while the boys in blue do the heavy lifting.”

“I’m honestly more concerned with the second bedroom, the empty one. We already know what happened in John Doe’s room. I’d like to know if Paul Liu was the occupant of the other room.”

“Our perp didn’t exactly do a meticulous job of cleaning up before he left,” Lido said. “The lab boys will be at it for days.”

“Our perp got the hell out of there the moment he realized that Doe had escaped. Hard as it is to believe, I will tell you that I’m encouraged by what I saw up there. It looked like the other room was a holding room. I’m hoping that Paul Liu was waiting on deck in the other room until the perp was finished with Doe; never expecting him to escape.”

“He got sloppy,” Ambler said.

“If that’s the case, Liu may still be in decent condition. Let’s hope so.”

“The question is, where has he been moved to?” Lido asked.

Ambler put his big paw on Gus’ shoulder. “This is where the rubber meets the road, my friend. We’ll find him. This case may be among the strangest I’ve come across, but our perp doesn’t strike me as one of the brightest.”

Lip scum, (snicker) Lipscomb clip-clopped down the stairs behind us. “Whoopsie on the second floor—it’s an office and bathroom, leased to the restaurant. Now they need a new door. The restaurant manager arrived just a couple a minutes too late—he's in a really bad mood. You'd think they would've said something in the restaurant before we provided permanent air conditioning."

"Maybe you didn't notice, but the morning staff doesn't speak much English. They're mainly here for set up and deliveries."

"Right," Lipscomb said. "That's why you've got the gold badge and I handle the battering ram." He tipped his cap at me. "Give me a call, Chalice, let's catch up on old times."

*Can't wait.* "I'll do that. Take care."

I waited until Lipscomb was out of earshot. "Hear that," I said to Lido. "He wants to catch up on old times. You know what that means?"

"Sure, the knuckle dragger wants to invite you out for a case of Budweiser, to tearfully reminisce about your days in the academy while he makes a booty call. I don't see how you can resist."

"I hear steroids aren't too good for the old *braciole,*" Ambler quipped.

Lido and I snorted. It wasn't the kind of joke you'd expect from Ambler. He really caught us off guard. I was going to follow up with a comment about Lido's *braciole,* but my off color praise for Lido's manhood was preempted by an irate Oriental man, shouting what I imagined to be obscenities as his little feet scrambled down the stairs. I'm not kidding. He had the smallest feet I'd ever seen.

"What you do?" he ranted, coming toe to toes with the three of us. "You break down door. What you do?"

"We're sorry about that, Mr.—"

"Pakpao, Pakpao, why you break down door?"

"We're sorry, Mr. Pakpao. Are you the manager?"

"Yes, manager. Why you break down door?"

"We believe the upstairs apartments may have been used in the commission of a crime."

"Upstairs? No one live upstairs. Why you break down door?"

The first question I was going to ask my incensed friend was, who lived on the third floor—now I didn't have to. "You say that no one lives on the third floor? You're sure of this?"

"Never see anyone go in or out. You still not answering question—why you break down door?"

"It was part of our investigation," Ambler said. "Your staff didn't indicate that the second floor space was your office. As the detective said, we're very sorry. The City of New York will compensate you for the broken door—save your receipt."

Pakpao seemed to calm down after hearing that he wasn't going to have to eat the cost of replacing his office door. He turned to me and just sort of looked me all up and down. "This lady is cop? *Lawan kanya.* You like Thai food? You come back, Pakpao make you special dish: oysters in fiery rice with long black mushroom."

There was absolutely nothing lost in translation. I didn't need an introduction to Thai cooking to know that Pakpao was offering me the cultural equivalent of Spanish Fly—I'm surprised he didn't intend to enhance the recipe with rhino horn. Part of me wanted to tell him off in no uncertain terms, but the man wasn't worthy of the effort. It was better to ignore his inept attempt at seduction and redirect his thoughts from Yours truly back to the case at hand. "Are you the landlord?"

"Landlord? No."

"Who is the space leased from?" Lido asked.

"Atlas Management."

I was familiar with the name. Atlas was a large commercial real estate management company in the city. They handled hundreds of buildings and likely had never met the party that actually owned the building, nor had any of their current employees met the tenant of the third floor torture chamber—the place had a reputation for being a revolving door. I was hoping that the owner handled the building on his own and knew his tenants personally. Alas, this was a break we were not about to catch. "Mr. Pakpao, do you have any idea how the upstairs window got broken or how the gutter got torn away from the building?"

"Sure I know; kids. The fucking kids do it. American children have no respect. I point them out for you."

I doubted Pakpao was even remotely close to the correct answer. We already knew within reasonable doubt that John Doe had broken the upstairs window in order to escape from his bedroom-cum-torture chamber, and likely tore the gutter away in his attempt to get down onto the ground. The crime lab would likely confirm our suspicions in short order. "I take it you're not the restaurant's owner. You're not the one who established the relationship with Atlas, are you?"

"No, owner live in Bangkok. He not come here much." Pakpao sneezed and pulled a well used handkerchief from his back pocket to wipe his nose. "Excuse, I have running on the nose." Apparently Mr. Pakpao had never been to Berlitz.

Bangkok, the name of the Thai city rang out to me like a position out of the Karma Sutra. From what I understood, it all began back in the sixties, when the Thai government agreed to provide rest and relaxation facilities for American soldiers during the Vietnam War. What was supposed to be R & R, quickly became known as I & I, intercourse and intoxication.
Today, almost ten percent of Bangkok's women are prostitutes. Sadly, life in many Third World countries held little promise for impoverished women. As much as we have to gripe about in the states, we're still head and shoulders above most of the world in terms of rights, liberty, and opportunity. As Dorothy so aptly said in the Wizard of Oz, "There's no place like home."

"So, when you coming back for dinner? You bring your girlfriends. Pakpao make you feast."

Thank God I had taken a mental oath not to accept any more dinner invitations or offers to participate in meaningless group sex, thinly disguised as an invitation to an Oriental buffet. "I'll have to take a rain check, Mr. Pakpao, I'm on a very strict diet." It didn't include long black mushrooms or sleazy Asian men. Lido was snickering and Ambler was fighting to divert his eyes—they knew exactly what was going on.

My refusal must have turned Pakpao off. Just as well, he was about as useful as a rabbi on a pig farm. He shook his head with disappointment. "How Pakpao get money back for door?"

"We'll leave you the information," Lido said. With that, Pakpao threw his hands up in the air and stormed off into the restaurant.

"I thought he'd never give up."

"Don't sweat it, Chalice," Ambler said, wiggling his pinkie. "I hear Asian men aren't much in the *braciole* department either."

We enjoyed a sorely needed laugh, and then I heard an unexpected sound. It started as an odd sounding murmur, but quickly grew into a diffuse and very loud noise. What Asian men may or may not have lacked on an individual basis, they more than made up for in number. Coming towards us was an angry mob of Orientals.

# Twenty Seven

I quickly called for reinforcements. The gathering mob looked to be several hundred strong. For what reason they had assembled was not yet clear. One thing for certain, they were heading directly for us and they did not look happy.

So far, The Nine Circles Restaurant had lived fully to its implied reputation. Nothing good had happened here. It had been the scene of a heinous crime, a place where John Doe had been abused and tortured. It may have been the place where Paul Liu had been held captive and where Kevin Lee may have been murdered and decapitated. All this from a place that was renowned for its Pad Thai noodles and spicy *nam prik*. I'm talking about a dish made with chile sauce, not Mr. Pakpao.

"What the hell is this?" Ambler asked.

Ambler's question was rhetorical. I only hoped that reinforcements arrived in time, with lots of barricades in tow. Lido rushed into the restaurant to redirect the activities of all the available cops inside—they were hitting the street one by one, ready to take on the angry mob.

"You got any idea what we're up against?" Lipscomb asked.

"Haven't got a clue. Have your men form a line in front of the restaurant. Let's try to keep the mob at bay until reinforcements arrive."

"You called it in?" Lipscomb asked.

I nodded. *You bet your steroid pumped up ass I did.*

The mob was about a block away when a Mercedes sedan came around the corner on two wheels and pulled to an abrupt stop in front of us. The windows were tinted, but the diplomatic plates were a giveaway. A well groomed Chinese man sprang from the back seat.

Ambler ID'd him immediately. "That's R. C. Liu, Paul Liu's father." A second oriental man with a goatee and scarred cheek emerged from the rear passenger door and hastened after Liu.

The Chinese ambassador strode briskly up to Ambler, ignoring the forming police line. I wasn't sure how he had learned about this development so quickly. Men with Liu's power enjoy several channels of communication. His accent was British and his diction was impeccable. He had undoubtedly been educated in London. "Ambler, I understand there's finally been a development in my son's case." You could see that the man was full of himself.

God bless Ambler. The man didn't know the meaning of the word intimidation. He glanced at the assembling mob which was already uncomfortably close. "There seems to be an angry mob behind you, Mr. Ambassador. I certainly hope you know nothing about it."

Liu glanced back, regarding the mob as he would a gnat that had landed on his shoulder. He pointed at the crowd. In an instant, the scarred man had turned and was moving toward the crowd, shouting at them in

Chinese. They stopped immediately. It was as if we were watching a film and the director had frozen the frame.

"Thank you, Mr. Ambassador," Ambler continued. "We've found a crime scene, nothing more. It's too early to know if there's a tie in to your son's case."

"I understand that this is where the unidentified man escaped from, the one that was found with Kevin Lee's skull. I'd like to take a look." Without waiting for a response, Liu snapped his fingers. The man with the scarred cheek turned away from the crowd and walked briskly toward the apartment's entrance.

"I'm afraid that won't be possible, Mr. Ambassador." I gave Lipscomb a head nod. In an instant he and two other officers had blocked the man's entrance."

"Who is this?" Liu asked without diverting his gaze from Ambler.

"Detective Stephanie Chalice, Mr. Ambassador. We're in the process of collecting forensic evidence from the crime scene. I'm afraid it's not possible for you or your colleague to go inside."

Ambler grinned, happy to see that I could stand up for myself.

I had heard that women are thought of as subservient in the Far East. Liu turned to me with a forced smile on his face. He was, however, unable to disguise his sentiment. He was looking at me in the same manner that he had regarded the crowd, as if I were an insect, barely worthy of his attention. "Detective Chalice, I have been quite patient up to now. Certainly you would not expect a father to stand idly by when he is perfectly capable of assisting in his son's rescue."

I had no doubt that Liu had access to New York's Chinese underworld and not been as patient as he implied.

The fact that he had not interfered until now made me reasonably certain that his sources had thus far come up empty. "We're on the same page, Mr. Ambassador. Allowing your men to trample our crime scene would only hinder our investigation and possibly invalidate evidence. With all due respect, I ask you not to interfere at this important juncture. We'll report to you immediately, the moment we have news."

"I have to agree with the detective, Mr. Ambassador. Please give us the opportunity to do our job. Your son's safe return is our first and only priority." Ambler's voice was a controlled blend of authority and humility. "We have our very best men investigating the crime scene right now—interfering will only delay the resolution of this very important case."

Liu was momentarily silent. I could almost see him counting in his head as if making a conscious effort to make a patient and wise decision. He turned to me. "I have only one son, Detective Chalice. He is everything to me. I will give you this singular opportunity to follow protocol in the hope that you will have good news for me shortly. I trust you will not disappoint me." He didn't wait for a response. He turned back toward the car. His associate raced back, closed the door for Liu and then hurried to the other side of the car and got in himself.

The Ambassador's car turned and rolled slowly toward the crowd, which was silent, waiting for instructions. Liu rolled his window down and spoke to the crowd in Chinese. His car screeched away. Within seconds, the crowd began to disperse.

"You did well," Ambler said. "He spoke to you directly."

"Forgive me if I'm not impressed."

"Chinese men at his level rarely recognize or have respect for women. The fact that he recognized you and accepted your advice is huge."

"He played ball because we've got the power. Despite his lofty position and access to information of every variety, he's been unable to find his son on his own. Trust me, he did what he did out of need."

"It's all the same to me. Who do you think tipped him off about this place?" Ambler said.

"I wouldn't hazard a guess at this point. A man with that kind of influence can find out just about anything he wants to."

"I just hope Zugg finds something useful in that pile of crap upstairs," Ambler said.

"Me too, my friend. Me too."

# Twenty Eight

I checked my watch. It was a Bulgari by the way, a very extravagant present from Gus. It was nearly eight AM and I was quickly running out of steam. We had survived a very interesting night. Although inconclusive, we had likely found our perp's lair, and if we were lucky, clues that would lead us to Paul Liu before he followed the same grisly path out of this world taken by his friend Kevin Lee.

Ambler had gone back to Bureau headquarters and Lido was taking a short break. I was sipping on a Starbuck's double espresso. Don't ask—you know the reason why. I was making a notation in my notebook when Zugg emerged from the building. "Got a minute?" He looked worn, but I could see on his face that he was on to something. I gulped down the espresso and tossed the cup in the trash—we all have to do our bit to keep the Big Apple bright and shiny.

"Sure. What's up?" It was a clear morning with a light breeze. We began to stroll—I think we both needed the fresh air.

"We checked the apartment from top to bottom. There's no doubt in my mind that the lab will confirm our beliefs about the case. Everything's on its way back to the NYPD crime lab now."

"Super job, Dr. Zugg. How are you holding up?"

"I'm exhausted, but exhaustion is good. With any luck, I'll be too tired and too distracted to do anything but pass out when my head hits the pillow tonight."

Zugg gave me a weary smile. *Please God,* I prayed, *give this man a reprieve.* I had become quite a spontaneous prayer during my father's fight against diabetes and often rattled off a quick blessing—it couldn't hurt. "I really hope so."

Zugg pulled a plastic vial from his pocket. It contained a bug. I knew exactly what it was. "Have you ever seen Dermestes Maculatus in the flesh?"

Zugg's double entendre didn't go unappreciated. "I've seen them eating through flesh, rotted flesh to be exact. Those are the critters they use to clean bones. I got a crash course at the FBI crime lab."

"I see they've left an impression. I found about a dozen of them in the upstairs apartment."

"So you think it's possible that Kevin Lee's skull was cleaned in the upstairs apartment?"

"I'm not sure. It's a small apartment, and I don't know where they'd house the bug cleaning tank. They're very adept at escape. I think I'd have found a great many more had they been physically housed in that apartment. Moreover, Dermestes Maculates need to eat all the time. If they're not busy cleaning bones, you have to feed them scraps of rotten flesh or they'll die. I didn't find any evidence of rotted flesh in the upstairs apartment."

"So where does that leave us?"

"The skull may have been cleaned nearby or the beetles might simply have been transported back to the apartment on someone's clothing. Dermestes love wool, cotton, and hemp. They're worse than moths."

I made a mental note to strip in the hall before I returned home to my apartment. God forbid they got into my closet and made a meal out of my Roberto Cavalli jeans—suicide would not be out of the question. "Not to mention the Thai restaurant downstairs. Who knows what they're cooking in that kitchen."

Zugg smiled. "You joke, but the point's a good one. All restaurants have garbage and scraps; enough I'm sure to maintain a small population of carrion feeders. Aside from which, insects are a staple of the Thai diet. I've been all over the Far East. The first time I was in Chiang Mai, I was served what I thought was a dish of French fries. I ate a few before I realized my French fries had eyes."

"Christ, what were they?"

"Caterpillars. All bugs are a great source of protein. Frying them in oil destroys any poisonous acids."

"Lovely, can't wait to try some." I had the sense that we had just struck the tip of the iceberg and that we would uncover clues of all varieties as we continued to dig. I was cautiously optimistic. "I guess we'll just keep searching."

We continued to walk. The blocks in lower Manhattan pass very quickly. It wasn't long before we were standing in front of City Hall. We were just steps away from the city's main man. I could have thrown a stone and hit his window. Zugg looked like he needed to rest. I spotted a café with outside tables not far from a subway grating, so I sat down without asking. Zugg followed my lead. "Let me get you a snack."

"You're very considerate, Detective." I could see Zugg's body settle wearily onto his chair.

"No biggie, I'm pretty tired too. I'd say you've done really well."

"For a man with cancer."

"For anyone. You're an amazing guy."

I looked up and let the morning's sun warm my face. "That feels good."

"Come to think of it, I am hungry."

After the fried fish, the Chinese food, the putrid eggs, and the conversation on bug munching, I was not planning to go anywhere near food, but I figured the least I could do was keep Zugg company while he nourished himself. "You never really explained this the other day; why do you think our perp discarded Kevin Lee's skull? You said that it was discarded because it was imperfect—imperfect for what?"

"I haven't quite gotten that far. Perhaps today's evidence will shed additional light. What would you like?"

"Just coffee for me, thanks." I had just finished a double espresso, but felt my body crying out for more caffeine. Zugg didn't listen to me. He ordered pastries for two. Despite all of my complaining, I began picking the moment the pastries arrived. *Where is my willpower these days?*

The pastry was filled with chocolate. I wouldn't have gone near it in the old days, but the new Chalice was an endorphin fiend, and chocolate had become one of my favorite vices. "I can't believe I'm eating this, but it's amazing."

"I know I don't know you very well, so don't take offense, but you worry too much about your figure. I wouldn't say anything if you were one of those nutrition freaks and were worried to death about your intake of free radicals and toxins. My sense is that you worry about food for all the wrong reasons. I'm a sick man, so I can get away with saying this, you have a beautiful figure. With genes like yours, you can afford a few indulgences. Life's too short, live a little."

I didn't know how to respond to Zugg, so I repaid the compliment by finishing every crumb on my plate.

Despite the early hour, the location was very tranquil. I felt my body relaxing—exhaustion and endorphins in just the right combination can make you feel a little light headed.

It felt as if I was a step out of pace with the world, as if we were in different time zones. I was awake, but my mind was drifting away. Pedestrians seemed to walk by in slow motion and the sound of the street's traffic seemed miles away. I found myself staring at the subway grating. I had seen them everyday, lining the street, but never thought about them much before except to make sure I didn't catch my heel in one. For some reason, I couldn't take my eyes off this grating. The crossed metal construction seemed to hypnotize me, the contrast of silver metal above a darkened pit. And then the world shifted and I was back. I saw something moving on the subway grating. I really wasn't sure what I had seen, but I had to satisfy my curiosity. I had a feeling in my gut about the case that quickly mushroomed into an overwhelming, half-baked idea I knew I had to pursue.

Zugg seemed to be enjoying his pastry.

"Say, Dr, Zugg, do you have another one of those vials?"

Perception had changed hands. This time it was Zugg that was looking at me as if I was crazy instead of the other way around. He shrugged, reached into his jacket pocket and handed me one. "Any special reason why you need one?"

"Enjoy your breakfast, Dr. Zugg, I'll be right back."

# Twenty Nine

"I tell you, I'm not crazy."

Lido and Ambler looked at each other. Reading their expressions, I could see that they were trying to decide whether I had had a really sensational premonition or had gone completely off the deep end. Honestly, I wasn't sure myself, but as I've said in the past, my gut feelings usually panned out, and I was hoping that I had hit pay dirt again.

Ambler's phone rang. He spoke for a moment before shutting down. "MTA is sending someone down."

"How long?"

"Just be patient. I told them it was one of Detective Chalice's hot hunches and they said they'd send someone down by rocket sled." He winked at me. "Just kidding, it won't be long."

Ambler was busting chops, but I could sense that deep down he was as eager as I was to see if something turned up.

Zugg was still at hand. He was looking at the two

vials, comparing the beetle he had found in the apartment to the one I had procured as it walked merrily across the subway grating. "To the naked eye they're the same, Dermestes Maculatus. You've got a very sharp eye, Detective. What made you look so closely? This is New York after all. Water bugs aren't exactly uncommon. How did you know this wasn't just another common roach?"

"I can't tell you how I knew. Bugs and I aren't exactly simpatico. Something just told me to check it out."

"Bully for you. I was next to you and I didn't see it."

"I was sitting there, enjoying breakfast and it was so peaceful and quiet. And then I realized that it was just too quiet. I mean it's the height of rush hour. I was sitting a few feet from a subway vent and it was dead quiet. At that hour, trains should have gone ripping through every few minutes."

"That's what made you curious?" Zugg asked.

"She's a witch," Lido said. "She's got a sixth sense." He gave me a playful punch on the shoulder. "Still, you want to look around down there? What do you think we'll find?"

*Isn't it every girl's dream?* "Sure, I can't wait to crawl around in the subway tunnels—it's on my list of the ten things I have to do before I die."

"No, really," Lido said.

"Dr. Zugg found beetles in the apartment and they're crawling out of the subway just a few blocks away. Maybe they came from the same place—I don't know. It's worth a shot."

"They've got twenty-foot alligators crawling around down there too," Lido said in a silly voice.

"That's the sewer system."

"No difference as far as I'm concerned."

I knew where Lido was coming from. I certainly wasn't looking forward to a subterranean excursion through the New York City subway tunnels, but sometimes you just have to do what you have to do. "Alligators you say?" I was smiling. Still, it wasn't as if Steve Irwin could come to our rescue. The poor Crocodile Hunter was wrestling alligators in heaven.

We didn't wait very long. An MTA car pulled up in front of us and two transit cops got out. The guy that got out of the passenger seat held rank. He introduced himself as Sam Doyle. He looked like I imagine Dennis Leary would look like with a beer belly and a triple chin. The other transit cop was a brother. His name was Beaks. Beaks didn't look quite awake. We made our introductions and got straight to it.

"What's the hot interest in the subway tunnels?" Doyle asked.

"We want to pull the grating and have a look down here," Ambler said.

"Whoa, whoa, whoa," Doyle said. "Not so fast. What's down there?"

Zugg held the two vials up to Doyle's face. "Dermestes beetles. They're carrion feeders."

Doyle jumped back. "Hey, Joe DiMaggio, put the bugs away."

Zugg stuffed the vials back into his pocket. We were all a bit surprised at the way Doyle overreacted.

"You're kidding, right? You find a couple of cockroaches and you want to deploy valuable city resources to take a tour of the subway's underground? Beaks, get back in the car. We've got real work to do."

"As the man said, they're carrion feeders. They eat rotting flesh and we have reason to believe this subway tunnel is linked to an important investigation."

"Trust me, Jimmy Hoffa's not down there." Doyle looked around. No one was smiling. "Look, I'm not arguing with you, lady.
Personally, I'd like nothing more than to give you a private subway tour, but you're wasting everyone's time. I'm sure there's all kinds of rotting carcasses down there: rats, cats, children...just kidding, but you get my point. The last thing a fine dame like you wants to do is

crawl around in that sludge. Trust me, you don't want to go down there. I don't even know where that shaft leads to. Some of these fucking things lead nowhere."

"Nowhere?"

"Yes, really, nowhere—some of the tunnels are abandoned. Some have been sealed off. Some of the tunnels in this end of Manhattan are over a hundred years old. They're fucking dangerous and that's no joke."

"Listen, Doyle, I appreciate your concern, I really do. I'm not gonna lease space down there. I just want to take a look around. So please get on the horn and call someone who can yank this grating."

"Not on your authority, girlie."

"Girlie?" I raised an incensed eyebrow.

"Don't get bent out of shape." He turned to his partner. "Get back in the car, Beaks." Beaks still didn't look sure of anything. He held his spot. "I said get back in the car." Doyle walked back toward the car. "I'll pull the tunnel maps to see what's down there, Detective. Meanwhile, you want to look around where you got no business? Fine, call your CO and have him make an official request." He turned to Beaks who had finally gotten behind the wheel, but was still looking confused. "Go," he said impatiently. "It's a fucking car, drive it."

I watched them drive off.

"Shit, you need Shearson again," Ambler said. "Too bad."

I wasn't worried about Shearson. I had learned how to motivate her from our prior conversation. I knew what it took to push her buttons. She had lots of interest in this case and with the potential promotion she saw coming along with its successful resolve. All I had to do was keep her in the loop, salt the mine as it were, until she was sure it was going to make her rich. "Not a problem."

In my years on the job, I'd learned that it was a blessing to have a sixth sense, that ability to sense aspects of the case and reach for conclusions mere mortals could not. I'd also learned that it was a mistake to go off half cocked and make commitments in the name of the New York Police Department and your commanding officer that might prove fruitless and utterly embarrassing. I wasn't going to take a chance on wasting time and resources. Furthermore, I needed to prove that Doyle was wrong. I hate that guy. Now usually, this being modern times, a cop's first move would be to hit the computer and Google your way to the answer, but I knew of a resource that might prove more valuable at a time like this, a resource that might very well hold the answer I wouldn't find on a modern day computer. So while my colleagues waited for the MTA to arrive, I set off to confirm my suspicions.

# Thirty

It was a little past six PM when I met Zugg, Lido, and Ambler back on the corner of Broadway and Warren Street, the site of my infamous subway grating. Lido looked refreshed and Ambler...well what can I say, he looked like business as usual. Zugg looked pretty good—perhaps it was the fading light of day that masked his appearance.

"I assume you got Shearson's buy in on this?" Ambler said. "You know there's no way the MTA is letting us down there without her request, especially after making such a warm impression on MTA dickhead, Doyle."

"We're good to go, my friend. Shearson's behind this operation one hundred percent. She's already contacted the MTA. They should be here as soon as they can round up the equipment and personnel."

"She must smell promotion in the air," Ambler quipped.

"What'd you find?" Lido asked.

I had a stack of photocopies in a folder under my arm. "You are going to love this."

"Look at the expression on her face," Ambler said. "Why you cocky broad, you think you've got this all figured out, don't you?"

"I prefer to remain humble."

Ambler couldn't hold back any longer. He flipped me the bird.

Lido looked smug and happy, ready to share in my excitement. I sensed Ambler was withholding judgment.

"It all starts at 260 Broadway."

"The crime scene?" Zugg said.

"Right, it all starts at The Nine Circles Restaurant and what's beneath it."

Ambler looked a bit impatient. "Come on, Chalice, spill it. What's beneath the restaurant, and don't give us some riddle with a reference to Dante's Inferno—I'm not getting any younger."

The Municipal Archives contained some surprisingly good period photographs and detailed records. I made copies of every one of them. The top page of the stack was an official authorization from the New York State Legislature. It was dated 1868. "Gentlemen, I give you Beach Pneumatic Transit."

"The hell is that, Chalice?" Ambler asked.

"1868, Alfred Ely Beach received permission and funding to build pneumatic tubes beneath the city to transport mail and packages from the city's main post office over on Broadway and Cedar Street."

"So?"

"Beach didn't build mail tubes, he built a subway, and used Devlin's Clothing Store at 260 Broadway as a secret vantage point to access the tunnel. He worked at night, removing rocks and debris and bringing in construction materials. Today Devlin's is The Nine Circles Restaurant, the home of our horny little friend, Mr. Pakpao."

"Why did he have to work on the QT, Chalice?" Lido asked.

"Because, Gus, he didn't have permission to build a subway. Beach was following his own agenda and had to keep his activities secret from Boss Tweed and the political power barons of Tammany Hall. He built a fan-propelled pneumatic subway that ran three hundred feet." I had to go to my notes in order to continue. "Says here that the tunnel started at Warren and Broadway, directly across from City Hall. It ran under the south side of Warren Street to Broadway before curving south to Broadway and Murray Streets. It goes on to say that Beach decorated the lobby with frescoes, fine paintings, and a goldfish fountain, in order to gain popular support after it opened—the man had style."

Zugg was beaming. "You're an intelligent and persistent young woman. So what you're saying is that the Beach Subway tunnel runs from our crime scene to the ventilation grating just inches from where we're standing now?"

"It's a fact."

Ambler looked dubious. "And you think the tunnel's still down there? That was almost a hundred and fifty years ago. It's certainly been destroyed by now."

"Maybe not. The last account which was written in 1912, states that they found remnants of Beach's wooden train while they were building the BMT subway lines."

"This is too much." Ambler walked over to a parked car and shifted his bulk onto its fender. It took a moment and then I could see acceptance winning him over. "I think the whole thing's crazy, but Chalice's been right about crazier shit than this. I say we go for it."

"We already are." I saw an MTA truck with a winch rolling toward us. It was time to take our act south of the border.

# Thirty-One

Bennett was meeting his date for the first time and had chosen The Nine Circles Restaurant for the rendezvous. “So, what convinced you to register at sugardaddy.com?”

“You’ve got money, I don’t—It’s just easier to be up front about these things—we’re both adults, aren’t we?”

Bennett was a personal injury attorney and Paola was an aspiring pop star, emphasis on the word aspiring. They, as so many before them, had been brought together via the magic and mayhem of the internet. Bennett was fifty, but warranted in his online profile that he was only forty-five. He was a Sephardic Jew with a tanning salon tan from Rockland County. She was a twenty-three year old Latina, hoping to be the next Shakira. It was a match made in heaven, or perhaps and more appropriately, the island resort of Hedonism.

Sugardaddy.com was a website that existed

to…well, I'm sure you can figure it out.

"Are you married?"

"Do you care?" Bennett had a wife, three kids, three dogs, and a mortgage payment large enough to choke a horse, but he had just settled a three million dollar lawsuit, the largest of his career, and was now flush with coin of the realm, flush enough to add a little long sought spice to his life.

Paola liked sex and didn't mind putting out for money so long as she didn't get labeled a whore for doing so. "No, not really, I'm struggling and you seem nice. Let's have dinner and see if we enjoy each other's company." Paola had worn her Miracle Bra and a low cut tee to make sure Bennett enjoyed her company.

Enjoy each other's company, for Bennett, it was a euphemism for private fuck buddy. "So you're a dancer. You'll have to dance for me."

Paola winked at him. "If you play your cards right."

"Great, let's order. You like oysters?" Bennett signaled for the waiter to come over.

The restaurant was crowded despite the police barricade in front of the next door apartment. The house drink was the Grey Goose Blue Elephant, which Pakpao had premixed with Puerto Rican vodka—yes, it actually exists. At twelve dollars a pop, he was cleaning up; more than enough money to replace the upstairs office door the boys in blue had reduced to toothpicks. Yes of course the city would go through the motions of paying the tab, but as we all know, the records would most likely be lost by an underpaid clerk and Pakpao would never see a nickel of remuneration—such is life.

The walls were painted an indigo blue, and with the lights dim, you could hardly notice the large black air vent in the far wall. The vent was ornate, constructed of iron and intricately fashioned in an oriental pattern; a reproduction from the Han Dynasty, but as I said, it rarely got the attention it deserved from the restaurant patrons or anyone else, and certainly not from Bennett and Paola who were already holding hands.

Behind the vent he waited, patiently and quietly, watching normal everyday folks who had come to dine and socialize. He was a stranger to this world and completely envious of all that shunned him. Air whistled through his occluded nasal passages; heavy breathing, adenoid breath, his to listen to for a lifetime. He opened his mouth to gather sufficient air to fill his deprived lungs.

He sat on the ground hugging his knees, focusing through the spaces in the vent at the people sitting close by, smelling their food and perfume, and listening to their conversations. He had unobstructed vision in one eye, which was trained on a young man with crew cut hair doing a poor job of eating Pad Thai noodles with chop sticks. Pakpao kept them in supply for the tourists, despite the fact that the Thai people eat their noodles with a fork. The man he was watching had a cleft chin and sharp features. His hair was so short that the suture line between the occipital and temporal bones were clearly visible on the back of his head. He focused there, at the perfectly formed skull. His pulse jumped to a hundred and forty beats per minute and sweat began to trickle down his temple.

The restaurant's air conditioning cycled off, and the intake of air through the large vent quit immediately.

Paola subconsciously heard a few seconds of heavy breathing,
but was uncertain of what she heard or where it had come from. She pulled her hand from Bennet's so that she could take a look around, but there was no one close enough to have been the source.

"Is everything alright?" Bennett asked.

She no longer heard it and chalked it off to the loud noise level in the restaurant and the bad acoustics. "Yeah, I'm fine." She put her hand back in his. "I hope they bring out our food soon. My stomach is growling."

# Thirty Two

"How long is it going to take to get that truck into place?" I was holding my safety helmet under my arm and waiting impatiently for the MTA to yank the ventilation grating out of the sidewalk.

"Patience, Chalice," Ambler said. "They're almost ready."

The MTA truck seemed to be moving in slow motion as it backed up, positioning its winch over the ventilation shaft. Doyle was there, looking on unhappily, no doubt worried that his wife wouldn't keep his dinner warm and his beer cold while I wasted his time looking for cooties in the ventilation shaft. A workman stood behind the truck directing the truck as daylight faded in the sky above us.

"I didn't want to go down there in the dark," Lido said.

"You? I'm a girl, how do you think I feel?"

"You're the toughest girl I know."

"No doubt," Ambler quipped.

We had set up a mobile command post. Zugg was within, conserving his energy while we waited for all the fireworks to go off.

Doyle could hold his tongue no longer. I could see him building up a good head of steam as he approached me. “You couldn’t wait until morning? What do you think you’re going to find down there in the dark? Waste everyone’s time. Someone could get hurt down there.”

“That’s what they have lights for, Doyle. No one asked you to stick around. Go home, we’ve got it covered. Something good comes of it, you’ll get credit. Trust me, we above ground cops are good that way.”

“You just don’t want to listen. You haven’t been underground in the dark—accidents happen, especially in old tunnels like that.”

“According to you, there’s nothing down there. If that’s the case, we’ll be in and out in ten minutes.”

I’d been so focused on Doyle that I didn’t see that the MTA crew had the grating hooked. The winch tightened and the grating came free with a loud creak. The truck rolled forward and laid it down on the roadway where it was out of the way. The MTA guys moved cautiously setting up the ladder and emergency lighting. It took some time until they were satisfied that the vent could be explored safely and then the safety engineer descended into the vent. We stood around anxiously waiting for the okay to proceed. And then it came, the all clear. Lido, Ambler, and I put on our safety helmets and began climbing down into the earth.

# Thirty Three

We're never truly sure at which moment sleep takes us. It's in the moment we return to consciousness that we determine how well we slept. Did we sleep soundly? Did we awaken refreshed? Did we dream or toss and turn? It's at that instant of awakening that we judge our night's work. For John Doe, the night had lasted several days, but when consciousness finally returned, he was immediately aware that he was out of danger.

*How long have I been asleep?* He laid silently for a long moment and then a thought formed in his mind, *I'm back.* He was immediately aware of his physical condition. He was aware that his mouth was parched and that his shoulders ached, but he was otherwise free of pain. His wrists were unrestrained and although his vision had been reduced to no more than shadows of light and dark, he knew that he was no longer in the cube-like white room in which he had been imprisoned for so long. *I'm free.*

He was still motionless as he began to recall the events of the evening on which he had escaped, and replayed them all in his mind, beginning with the squirreling of the pills in the pouch of his cheek to his emerging from the subway and entering Central Park. He remembered lying on his bed for a great while playing possum, until he was sure that he was alone and could attempt to pull the bars free of the window before his captor returned. He was lying just so now, awake in his hospital bed playing possum, looking no different than while he was in his coma, except for the small amount of light he allowed to enter through the slits that formed under his eyelids. *No more darkness. No more darkness.*

He was aware that he was in a large room and could sense others around him, moving and performing tasks. He heard the clatter of small metallic objects and was aware of the room's smell, a clean, antiseptic smell, and of low level voices around him. His mind was struggling to piece it all together. *Lie quiet. Lie quiet until you're sure.* His mind went back to the park, the last place he could remember. He remembered the warm blood running from his ankle where he had cut it on the window's jagged glass, and the feeling that life was evaporating from his body, leaving him with every labored breath. The sounds of the night, darkness and shadows, and the cool breeze playing against his skin, were all he remembered from his night of liberation. He could still feel the air playing against his skin, and the feeling of freedom it had given him.

He was still terribly disoriented when he felt a light pressure on his wrist and then understanding broke through the barrier. *I'm in a hospital. Someone's taking my pulse.*

"Welcome back."

He felt a light pressure on the apex of his arm, and then a warm sensation coursing throughout his body. He tried to speak and made a hoarse whisper before remembering that his vocal cords had been destroyed. And then, once again, he was gone.

# Thirty Four

God bless Lido, I could feel his eyes on me, safeguarding my every step as I climbed the ladder down to the bottom of the ventilation shaft. Doyle may not have been justified in trying to postpone the tunnel's exploration until morning, but he had been right about the darkness and the dilapidated condition of the old structure. Despite the helmet lights and the strong beacons we carried, I was very aware that we were out of our element and that our visit here could prove treacherous with as little as a single misplaced step in any direction.

Sal, the MTA safety engineer began to lead us as we advanced into the darkness. There was much less space here than I had imagined. The tunnel's ceiling was low and added to the feeling of claustrophobia. I took a deep breath and followed directly behind him. The air was damp and I could feel it sticking to my skin. The ground beneath my feet was covered with debris, pieces of wood, and bits of brick that had come free from the tunnel walls. I panned the darkness before me with my beacon, checking the floor for anything I might trip on and of course for clues. The walls around me looked unsafe, as if the bricks had grown tired from the century long burden of holding their brethren in place and were exhausted and were ready to give up their struggle. I scanned the wall before me with my searchlight and immediately felt something run over my boot. *Don't think about it. Move forward.* I hesitated and slowly moved on. Odd noises surrounded me, the hissing of steam through underground pipes and the movement of rodents lurking beneath the debris. More worrisome still was the sound of the tunnel settling around us, a tunnel that had not entertained visitors in nearly one hundred years.

Water dripped from a dozen spots in front of us. Searching the tunnel's roof, I could see where the water had compromised the tunnel's skin—a fissure in the mortar between the bricks had developed as a result of the leak. Cracks had spread across the tunnel's arched roof.

Progress was slow. The engineer advanced with caution. I was hoping to see more beetles down here, but spotting them in the darkness was impossible.

After several minutes, we came upon a large air exchanger.

"Wait here," Sal said, as he climbed up a rubble embankment to get a closer look. I could see him as he advanced cautiously toward it, shining his light through. He studied it for some minutes before returning. Surprisingly, he had a smile on his face. "You'll want to see this."

"Beach's subway station?"

He nodded. "It's not in great shape, but yeah—I can't believe it. The vent is an air exchanger for the subway station—pretty cool stuff."

"Jesus Christ, Chalice, you're a goddamn witch," Ambler said. "I can't fucking believe it."

Lido smiled at me. His expression read, *way to go!*

"I want to get a look in there."

"That should be okay if we go one at a time. That pile of rubble is pretty unsteady. I don't think it'll support much more than that."

I carefully navigated over the debris to the vent. The engineer was right, as it felt unsteady beneath my feet. The vent was a crossed grill of iron bars approximately four feet square, set into the tunnel's old brick wall. I pressed my face and my beacon to the iron. Beyond it was the subway track and the platform. It was completely black in there and I could only see the small area that my beacon illuminated, but there was no doubt that this was Alfred Beach's pneumatic subway station. The far wall was covered with ages of soot, but I could just distinguish on it, a small area of a fresco. I was hungry for more detail, but my vantage point was poor. Nonetheless, I lingered for several moments hoping to stumble across something, anything. "We've got to get in there." I began carefully back toward the others.

I could see that Sal was deep in thought. "That's a tall order, Detective. We pull that vent and there's a good chance the tunnel could collapse around it."

I had no desire to be buried alive, but there was no way that I was going to leave empty handed after coming this far. "There's got to be a way."

"Gotta be done," Ambler said. "Find a way."

Sal pulled out his radio. He held it under his chin for a moment. I could see that he was solidifying his thought process. He finally pressed the talk button. "Tommy, you there? I need lumber and an oxy-acetylene torch."

I smiled at Lido—we were going in.

# Thirty Five

“So you’re a singer?” Bennett asked. “What kind of stuff do you do?”

“Crossover Latin pop. I did the Warped Tour, two years ago,” Paola said, in an effort to establish credibility as an entertainer.

“Crossover Latin, what’s that like?”

“A little like J-Lo…more like Shakira.”

“Shakira—can you dance like her? She’s hot.”

“Exactly like her.” Paola played with Bennett’s fingers.

“I have a colleague who’s an entertainment attorney. You should meet him.” Bennett’s only connection to the aforementioned entertainment attorney was as an adversary in a legal suit. It was his lawyer’s spin on, I’m a movie producer and you’d be perfect for a spot in my next film—all he needed was a casting couch.

“Really? That would be so cool.” She smiled and then leaned across the table. “Come here,” she said, beckoning with her finger. “You’re a good guy.” Bennett had never kissed a Latina before. She was much more accomplished at the art of persuasion than he. While their lips were still together, Paola picked up on the sound of wheezing coming through the air vent and pulled away momentarily. “Do you have a cold?”

“Me? No, why do you ask?”

“I thought you were wheezing.”

“Excited, yeah, but no wheezing. Give me another.” He leaned back across the table, tongue breaching lips before he renewed contact.

Paola listened for the wheezing noise, but it was gone.  Satisfied that Bennett was not going to infect her with the plague, she put her hand under the table and rested it on his leg.

# Thirty Six

We had to clear out of the tunnel while they worked on the vent. As I mentioned, the tunnel was narrow with a low roof and didn't permit more than a few people at a time. Sal had measured the vent and was in the process of having lumber cut topside to support the vent's enclosure before he cut through the metal.

I watched as the precut two-by-fours and planks were fed into the tunnel.

"Sal's a good man," Lido said. "I think he wants to get through that vent as badly as you do. Thank God they're not all like Doyle."

"Amen."

Ambler was in the mobile command post grabbing a little R & R with Zugg while the MTA did their thing. "I'm worried about Zugg. He looks weak. I hope he's not overdoing it."

"I know, he looks pale."

"Ambler asked him if he wanted a ride home, but

he wouldn't hear of it. The man has a serious level of commitment."

My cell phone rang. I pulled it from my pocket and checked the incoming number. I didn't recognize the number, but it was a 212 area code with an uptown exchange. "Detective Chalice, who am I speaking with?" It was a night nurse at Lenox Hill.

Lido must've seen my unhappy expression and began prodding me for information before I hung up. "What's going on?"

"It's not good," I whispered. I was off the phone shortly afterward.

"Doe?"

I nodded. "That was a nurse at Lenox Hill—Doe's breathing is very weak. They don't expect him to make it through the night."

"Shit." Lido rubbed his chin. "There's no point running down there now."

"Too bad we never found out who he is. At least he could've had family and friends with him."

Lido nodded. "Maybe it's for the best. I mean the poor guy's been through so much. What kind of life would he have?"

I shrugged. "The human spirit can be pretty strong. Look at Zugg. It's too bad he's not going to be around long enough to see his captor brought to justice. I wish we could've at least done that for him."

"Maybe he'll hold on a little longer."

Lido noticed something and was motioning for me to turn around. Sal was on the ladder, his head and shoulders peeking out of the tunnel and he was smiling. "We're ready for the torch," he said, and gave me a big thumb's up.

# Thirty Seven

When I got back into the tunnel, I could see that Sal had reinforced the area around the vent with lumber to support the weight of the brick tunnel that surrounded it. The vent itself had been cut out with an oxy-acetylene torch and had been propped up against the wall alongside the newly created passageway. Sal and his crew had cleared the debris from the floor in front of the vent.

"I don't know what we're going to find on the other side, so be very careful. I would try to be as unobtrusive as possible," Sal said.

"Got it, I won't touch anything." At least I said that I wouldn't. "You're a good man. I really appreciate it."

"No sweat, Detective. I wouldn't have missed this for anything. A discovery like this—I wouldn't be surprised if they film a documentary down here. Most fun I've had in years."

"I know, it's really cool, isn't it?" *Once you learn to*

*ignore the rats and stench and stuff.* "I think we're ready to go in." Lido and Ambler were onboard, Zugg too. He had taken advantage of a little down time in the command center and was now back on the job—God only knew, he needed the rest.

"Okay," Sal said. "There's a short drop onto the tracks on the other side. There wasn't enough time to clear away the mess in there, so be careful."

"Right, will do."

Sal checked his searchlight and went through first. He was waiting for me on the other side and took my hand as I stepped onto the tracks. Beach's subway had been propelled with the air from giant fans and so the tracks were only there to guide the train. They were not electrified. They were black from creosote and covered with ages and ages of filth. Aside from that, it looked as if the train could still run on them if the debris was cleared away.

I boosted myself up onto the subway platform and immediately had a sense of how grand and spectacular Beach's subway station must have been. I envisioned it in operation before the turn of the century. The broken remnants of what must have been the goldfish fountain were still there, and the frescoes that had been painted on the wall were still somewhat visible. I had read an archived article from the New York Herald, a long defunct newspaper, which had reviewed the subway's opening. It had been entitled "Fashionable Reception Held In The Bowels Of The Earth." Beach had gone to tremendous lengths to ensure public support for his project. I had read that the waiting room had been decorated with fine paintings and a grand piano, and that Beach himself conducted tours for notables and dignitaries. I could almost imagine it filled with New

Yorkers eagerly waiting for their chance to take a ride.

I raised my searchlight and read a sign above what I assumed was the original entrance.
It read, Exit – Warren Street.

The exit itself was buried in rocks and cement and must have been sealed off decades ago when the modern subway was built.

"This place is a gas," Lido said.

"I say we go nuts and hold the next Policeman's Halloween party down here—could you imagine?"

"Only a psycho like you would think of something like that at a time like this. I still can't believe you found it."

"Just dumb luck. What were the chances I'd be munching pastry just as one of Zugg's beetles came up for a breather."

"Go ahead, play the modesty card. In my book, you're too cool for school."

My mind flashed back to a rainy afternoon. Lido was dressed like a nerd and I was in a cheerleader's skirt. As I recall, Lido took great pleasure in caressing my pompoms, but I digress. "Thanks, Babe, I know we just made the Discovery Channel—let's see if this place has any significance to our case."

We split up again, searching the platform. I found a door marked, *Utility Closet*, and tried the doorknob. It stuck, but came open after a few attempts. The smell of the damp tunnel paled in comparison to the horrible smell that hit me when I opened the door. My searchlight beam immediately fell on a reflective object. It took a moment until my brain sorted it out—I was looking at a large glass fish tank. The lid was askew and the closet was filled with beetles. Now, I've seen a lot, and had self control up the yin yang, nonetheless, I couldn't help but shriek. I mean goddamn, it looked like the entire closet was alive. The walls were completely covered and crawling with bugs. I heard footsteps racing toward me. It was Ambler.

"What the hell happened? You scared the shit out of me." I stepped aside so that he had a clear view of the inside of the closet. His mouth dropped. "I understand," he said. "I'll get Zugg."

# Thirty Eight

Lido had just joined us. “Are you alright?”

“Take a look inside the closet. It’s really creepy.”

Lido took a look for himself, returning quickly. “That’s a hell of a lot of bugs.”

“Don’t say I didn’t warn you.”

“You didn’t warn me. You just said it was creepy.”

“Don’t be so technical; creepy is creepy. Bugs are creepy; connect the dots.” Lido knew that he was being teased. Still, my skin was beginning to crawl. It was time to get Zugg’s assessment and move on.

Zugg put on protective gloves that covered him up to the elbow and immediately drove his hand into the tank of beetles, exploring to see if anything was in there with the colony. What he found was not a surprise. He withdrew his hand, holding onto a section of a spine.

He studied the specimen for a moment before speaking, doing his best to assess with insufficient light. “These are the first five spinal vertebrae, the uppermost portion of the cervical spine, beginning with the atlas and running through C5. The atlas is fractured at the point where it articulates with the skull, and C5 is scored. It was most likely sawed through between C5 and C6."

"The Medical Examiner's report on Kevin Lee stated that his spine was severed just above the sixth cervical vertebra."

"That's right, Chalice," Zugg said. "There's little chance that this section of spine belongs to anyone but the late Kevin Lee."

"Can you tell us anything else?" Lido asked.

"Yes," Zugg replied. "This beetle colony is cool. They've had nothing to eat for quite some time. Most have left the tank in search of a new source of food."

"Explain what you mean by cool," Ambler said.

"We speak of beetle colonies in terms of temperature as it relates to their activity. If this tank had a large supply of rotting meat, the colony would be 'hot', highly active and consuming the meat. This colony is cool, you understand."

Ambler nodded.

"We can draw a correlation between the colony's temperature and the time it will take them to consume the specimen that's been introduced into the tank," Zugg said.

"It's been deserted, like the apartment where John Doe was held captive."

"Very reasonable conclusion," Zugg said. "I'll snoop around in here. I suggest that the rest of you push on."

Zugg's suggestion was music to my ears. I couldn't wait to put as much distance between me and those disgusting bugs as possible. We left him in the utility closet to collect any forensic evidence that might have been left behind, while the rest of us continued to search the subway platform.

We'd found the perp's bone cleaning tank. We'd found his torture chamber as well—smart money would say that our perp was long gone. Still, we had to investigate the subway thoroughly to find a clue that might lead us to his new location. What else was down here?

I continued to explore the platform, but didn't find very much of anything, so I turned my attention to the tracks. There was a huge heap of debris at the far end of the tracks, so I moved in for a closer look. "Oh my God, come look at this." Sitting on the tracks were the remnants of Beach's original subway car. It had been constructed of wood and had not held up very well. Still, it was an amazing find. I looked within. The upholstered seats were still in tact. It was like taking a step back in time. I got down onto the tracks to find a better vantage point as Sal, Ambler, and Lido hurried over.

I heard them ooh and ah as they examined the small subway car. I was now behind the train at the very end of the tracks. I turned my searchlight, expecting to see a brick wall. What I found was completely unexpected. "Sal, over here." Before me was a metal door.

Sal was next to me in an instant. "Why I'll be damned. Where the hell do you think that leads to?" He tried the doorknob. "Locked."

I had a good idea of what was on the other side. Much of the tunnel was excavated using Devlin's Clothing Store at 260 Broadway to secretly move materials in and out. Devlin's site was now home to the Nine Circles Restaurant. Got the picture? "We've got to get in there."

Sal looked at the door and the surrounding area. "It's embedded in bedrock. We'll knock it down."

I got on my radio and called for the battering ram.

# Thirty Nine

The air conditioning cycled back on. He drew a deep breath as a fresh supply of cool, dehumidified air began to move past the air vent into the tiny space he occupied in the sealed off staircase.

He had grown quite fond of his tiny hiding space. There was barely enough room for him to sit comfortably, but he did not find it claustrophobic. To the contrary, he found it comforting, in the same manner that an infant enjoys the security of its crib. His only light was that which had migrated through the spaces in the air vent. He came here on most nights, to ogle the diners, listen to their conversations, and encroach upon their privacy. It is a world in which he had never found acceptance, a world he would give anything to be a part of. He took keen interest in the handsome men, especially those that dined with enticing partners. He imagined himself in their place and used them for his vicarious fantasies.

He still had a keen interest in the good looking

man that was eating his noodles with chopsticks. The man's hair was so short that it resembled sandpaper. His dining partner was exotic looking, with dark almond shaped eyes and teal eye makeup. He found her quite fetching, just the kind of woman he had longed for, the kind he had never known.

He stared again at the man's perfectly smooth skull, and then bravely ran his fingertips over his own forehead, noting each and every imperfection. Frustrated, he quickly ended the comparison, his adenoid breathing grew heavy.

Thirty feet away from him, the abandoned staircase he sat within ended somewhere beneath the ground. A riveting thud echoed through the old stairwell. He clutched his chest and turned to look down into the darkness.

Paola jumped. "What the hell was that?"

Bennett was busy sucking an oyster off its shell. "Maybe something wrong with the air conditioning—they probably need a new compressor."

"I know what a bad compressor sounds like. My father repairs cooling systems for a living. Trust me that was no compressor."

"Maybe it's one of those old steam pipes. You know the old part of the city. Those things go all the time."

"Steam pipe, my ass."

Bennett picked up the bottle of white Chablis that Pakpao had recommended to them and refilled her glass. "Drink up. Don't let some silly little noises ruin our evening. If you don't like it here, we can go someplace else for drinks afterward—maybe your place." He smiled pathetically.

Paola leaned across the table and gave him another long kiss. Their lips were still together when a second loud thud hit their ears, this one several decibels louder than the first. "*Fuck*, what was that? Look me in the eye and tell me you think that was the air conditioning."

"No, I don't know what that was."

The sound of wheezing and frightened breathing began to penetrate the restaurant.

Paola jumped from her chair. "Holy shit, what the hell was that? We have to get out of here."

"I'll get the check."

Pakpao saw them from his usual spot by the bar, the spot where he kept an eye on the cash register, and raced over to them. "Everything okay?"

"No, everything is not okay," Paola said. "I heard a really disturbing noise coming from that air vent."

"Yeah, we want the check," Bennett said.

"That's nothing," Pakpao said. "It's just the old building. I move your table. You stay. I bring you a round of drinks on the house."

"I don't think so," Paola said.

Bennett took out his wallet.

Another loud thud reverberated through the air vent, followed by another, drawing the attention of most of the diners. The sound of distressed moaning was now impossible to deny.

"We are so out of here," Paola said. "Tell me that's the fucking air conditioning. It sounds like there's an animal trapped back there."

Pakpao chuckled to make light of the disturbance. "Animal, you say animal? There no animal behind the wall—you very funny."

A loud crashing sound filled the restaurant. Bennett stuffed his wallet back into his back pocket and turned to Pakpao. "Dinner's on you. We're leaving." Ah, the advantages of knowing the law. Bennett knew exactly what he could get away with.

Just a few feet away, just on the other side of the vent, he grew into a panic. He would normally have escaped through the upstairs air vent in the hallway of his apartment, but the police were still there, collecting evidence. His breathing became labored and his heart began to pound. He heard voices coming from below ground, and the sound of people approaching, ascending the stairs. He looked through the air vent at the altercation taking place. "Trapped," he said in his adenoid voice. "I'm trapped."

The restaurant filled with the sound of a jarring thud, sending the diners to their feet. Pakpao approached the vent just as a second jarring thud sounded. This time plaster dust flew from around the large air vent and the wall cracked around it. He got closer to the vent, trying to see within. A third thud sent him reeling backwards, away from the wall. He turned to face his patrons, just as frenzied screams filled the air, emanating from the air vent. "Beautiful night for outdoor dining—we bring tables outside." Pakpao approached a large table of diners. "Complimentary desserts—no reason to leave."

The sound of loud footsteps climbing the stairs filled the restaurant. The diners began to move toward the exit just as the wall fractured and the large air vent fell to the ground.

# Forty

We were on our way up the stairs when I heard a pounding noise above us. "Something's going on here—hurry." We began racing up the stairs. They were old and rickety, so I could only move so fast, but I was certain that something important was happening just in front of us. The air in the stairwell was stale. It was damp and had a heavy odor of cigarette smoke.

I heard a crash and then light filtered into the stairwell. A small man was standing at the top of the stairs, looking out through a large opening in the stairwell wall. He was facing away from me, but I could tell from his body language that he was about to flee. "Stop, NYPD." He turned back to look at me. What I saw turned my blood to ice. The man's face, it honestly frightened me.

In the next instant, he was gone, ducking and squeezing through the hole in the wall. I needed a moment to mentally regroup. The man's appearance was terribly disturbing. I tried to convince myself that it was just the shadows playing tricks on my eyes, but I knew better.

"Did you see that?"

Lido was just behind me. "Someone just ran out." It didn't sound like Lido had seen the man's face—now was not the time to tell him.

"Right, hurry."

I heard several people screaming as I approached the top of the stairs. I dove through the opening in the wall and found myself in the Nine Circles Restaurant. The restaurant was in chaos. Women were screaming, the crowd parting to permit the exit of the man I had seen, frantically racing to the exit. He turned back toward me to check, and my heart froze again. The restaurant's lighting was more than adequate and I was able to see this man's disfigurement in all its horrible detail. I could see that he was Asian in appearance, but his forehead was grossly deformed, with a large bulbous protrusion that drooped down and covered his left eye. Other smaller protrusions were visible through his hair. His upper lip and nose were severely disfigured. He tried to cover his face as he turned away from me, but that split second's exposure to him was enough. His image would remain etched in my mind forever.

"Oh my God." This time Lido had seen him as well.

The man was pushing his way toward the door. I could hear him wheezing from where I stood, his severe heavy wheezing—it was haunting. And his odor, it was stale, stale like the underground tunnel, and heavily laden with cigarette smoke.

I was just scant steps behind him when he hit the restaurant's door. "Stop," I repeated, "police."

He pushed through the door and was out on the street. I was the first to reach him. I got my hand on his shoulder. He looked back at me with severe panic on his face, as if he were a wild animal that had never before faced captivity. He began screaming, loud indecipherable noises, more beastly than human.

Lido and Ambler had him now. They were looking at one another as they attempted to subdue him without causing him harm. Their expressions needed no translation. The man continued to struggle, his wheezing growing louder and louder, his struggling becoming more desperate. Lido and Ambler were attempting to calm him down when I heard a buzzing noise that I had heard many times before. The man shuddered and collapsed into Lido's arms.

Doyle was standing behind them, holding a Taser.

# Forty One

Saint Vincent's was the closest hospital, but Shearson was able to pull a few strings and so we were able to redirect and take the disfigured man to Lenox Hill under police supervision. Lenox Hill was in our primary jurisdiction; Saint Vincent's was not. We felt a lot more comfortable having our suspect on our own turf.

Speaking of our suspect; what the hell was he doing in that sealed off stairwell, and was he the man responsible for Kevin Lee's murder, Paul Liu's disappearance, and the torture of John Doe? He certainly didn't look capable. He was quite small, almost frail, and of course, his vision was occluded. His fists had been clenched during the apprehension, something I would have thought of as normal, but they were still clenched in the hospital under sedation. He didn't seem like he had the wherewithal to take three men prisoner, but hey, you never know what anyone is capable of when they get truly desperate. I wasn't about to pass judgment—not for now anyway.

He had already been swabbed for DNA and his specimens were on their way to the crime lab for comparison to the forensic evidence found in the apartment above The Nine Circles Restaurant.

I was standing at the doorway, looking in on him when Dr. Maiguay stepped out of the elevator. “You bring us the oddest patients, Detective. I understand that you found this man living in an underground tunnel.”

“Strange but true.”

“Merciful Jesus, what is going on in this city?”

“The same thing that’s always been going on—there’s an entire world out there that someone like you is unaware of and never has exposure to: criminals, the indigent, victims, homeless people—more than you want to know about. How’s my other John Doe?”

“Hanging on by a thread. The priest has already given last rights. You never identified him?”

“I’m afraid not.”

Zugg came off the next elevator. I introduced him to Maiguay. Zugg had been studying the subway’s utility closet when our suspect had been apprehended. He had not seen him until now. He was squinting from the doorway. “May I take a closer look?” he asked.

“By all means, Dr. Zugg. He’s sedated and taking nutrients through the IV. He’ll be out for quite a while.”

Zugg moved slowly into the room. I could see that Zugg, despite all he had seen over the years, was taken aback by the man’s appearance. He took some time studying the suspect before returning.

“His appearance is alarming, isn’t it, Dr. Zugg?” Maiguay said.

“You’re a master of the obvious, Doctor. It’s a shame he’s never had the benefit of reconstructive surgery,” Zugg said.

“Even so, he’d never be normal,” Maiguay said.

“No, not normal, but certainly better,” Zugg replied. “Maybe he wouldn’t have spent his life lurking around defunct subway tunnels like some kind of lab animal."

"I wonder how long he's been down there."

"A great while, I would think." Zugg looked again at the suspect. "Look at his skin, so pale. It takes great courage to leave the shadows."

"I pity him," Maiguay said, "People recoiling in disgust at the very sight of him—an outcast since birth. I wonder if his own mother had the courage to love him. I doubt he's ever known a moment of true happiness."

Maiguay sounded quite prophetic. "You seem to know his pain very well, Doctor."

"I see a lot of unfortunates in my line of work," Maiguay said. "You can't help but become absorbed in their lives, their anguish. I honestly don't know how they make it through—I don't think I'd have the strength." Maiguay's pager went off. I could hear it vibrating on his belt and saw the LED change from a red to bright turquoise. "Excuse me, I have to run."

Maiguay jumped back in the elevator, leaving me alone with Zugg. "This creature certainly explains a lot," Zugg said.

"I was hoping you'd say that." The elevator chimed again. The ward was starting to sound like a pinball arcade. Lido and Ambler stepped off and joined us. "Good timing. The brilliant Dr. Zugg was just about to enlighten me with his revelations on the case and other manner of prestidigitation."

Zugg smiled. "No slight of hand, Chalice, just my observations."

"Why's he still sedated," Ambler asked. "We should have him up and answering questions. What exactly are we waiting for?"

"The doctor has him sedated and I have to say I agree," Zugg said. "This man's been through a terrible ordeal. We found him neglected and frightened. It's the middle of the night. Let's give him the benefit of a sound night's sleep."

Ambler was not in an agreeable mood. Like the rest of us, he was exhausted, and he knew that R. C. Liu and the Director of the FBI would be breathing down his neck at any minute. “Are you crazy, Damien? Paul Liu’s been MIA way too long. If our perp has any information, I want it now, before the Chinese Ambassador’s kid becomes a statistic.”

Zugg spoke with great confidence. “Paul Liu is fine, I assure you.”

“How can you know that, Dr. Zugg?”

“He’s fine and being well cared for—of this I’ve no question.”

“Enlighten us please—the rest of us aren’t quite up to speed.”

“I know that Paul Liu is fine because the top of his skull has not been sheared off and bolted to the top of our suspect’s head.”

# Forty Two

An explanation like Zugg's can not be rendered while loitering around in a hospital corridor. It required a table and chairs and enough cafeteria coffee to force our sleeping neurons to fire.

It was now about two AM. The only coffee available came by way of a vending machine. It was tasteless and watery. I could only hope that it contained a reasonable level of stimulant.

Ambler was at wit's end. This was his second night without sleep and I had just dragged him through one of the city's long lost subterranean cavities. He was facing the wrath of God if he didn't quickly produce the missing Paul Liu. On top of that, he was getting Silence of the Lambs answers from the forensic genius he had personally hand picked and dragged out of retirement to assist us with the case. He was screwed. At least he was very close to it unless we pulled this thing together quickly.

"Alright, Damien, could you please explain in

layman's terms, just how you're so sure no harm has come to Paul Liu."

I didn't know how Zugg was holding on. He looked close to death. God only knew how he was holding it together. "It was clumsy of me to be so blunt."

"It's alright, Dr. Zugg," I said. "We're all just very tired and confused."

Zugg unbuttoned the cuffs of his shirt and rolled up his sleeves. "Well, it goes something like this. It's my guess that the man we found would like to replace the top of his skull with Paul Liu's."

Ambler almost choked. "Are you crazy?"

Those were the words forming on the tip of my tongue, but knowing what I did about Zugg, I refrained from uttering that response. "Now hold on, Herbert, I'm sure the good doctor will elaborate." God, I was hoping he was going to say something that made sense. Lido was looking at him like he was crazy also.

"I think that our unsub has been hiding behind that air vent for years, waiting for the right person with the right skull to come along. I'll bet if you go back and check Paul Liu's charge records, you'll find that he's dined at The Nine Circles Restaurant often—at the very least, he ate there just before he went missing."

"Easy enough to check out," Lido said. "It doesn't explain why Kevin Lee was abducted and murdered."

I already knew the answer to this one, Zugg had told me at the time of our first meeting. "They used Kevin Lee for practice, Gus. They studied his skull, marked it up, and threw it away when they were done."

Lido looked at me as if I had grown a second head, which wouldn't exactly have been weird in a case like this one. "Dr. Zugg told me before. I'm not all that clever."

Lido sighed. "Thank God."

"So you think Paul Liu's skull is a good replacement for his? You're talking about some manner of skull transplant?"

"I am, Detective. They've made incredible advances in the art and science of reconstructive

medicine.
The suspect has severe cleft palate disfigurement, but that is repairable, and small defects in the skull can be fixed with synthetic patches. This man's skull, however, is so terribly deformed that it would require replacing the entire brain vault and we're just not that advanced yet. There must be blood flow to the bone of the skull and the underlying tissues. We haven't developed the synthetic materials or process to do it."

"So this is possible?" Ambler asked. "They can cut off the top of the perp's head and replace it with the top of Liu's?"

"Our suspect and Liu both share a common Asian bone structure. They are both young male adults, and from what I remember of Liu's photo, his hat size was about the same as our suspect's. Our suspect had likely examined Liu from a distance and decided that he was a good fit."

"It explains why you found Gentian violet on Kevin Lee's skull," I said. "It was being marked with suture lines."

Zugg grinned. "I see you're way ahead of me, Chalice. If that's so, our suspect would simply have to peel back the skin, saw away the defective section of skull, and cover it with a healthy replacement. The healthy skull would be prepared in advance, like a puzzle piece, to fit exactly as the one it's replacing. The same medications that are used to prevent organ rejection and infection should work in this application as well."

"What are all those protrusions and knobs on the suspect's head?" Lido asked.

"Our dysmorphic friend likely suffers from a congenital disease known as V-Holoprosencephaly. The plates of his skull did not fuse together as they normally should have. By God's infinite wisdom, the skull starts off in separate pieces and then fuses together as we mature."

"To facilitate passage through the birth canal."

"Partially correct. You no doubt learned about the bregmatic junction in your high school biology class. At the center of the forehead and at other suture junctions, the bones unite over time. At birth, the coronal and sagital sutures have yet to form—it gives the brain room to grow, and as Chalice pointed out, it makes it easier on Mom to deliver. The protrusions you asked about, Lido, are areas where the plates of the skull never fused together. Those bulges are tissue and brain filled cysts."

"This sounds incredible," Ambler said.

"So, what do you do with those protruding cysts?" Lido asked. "You can't just cut them off and throw them away."

"There are many surgical procedures in which portions of the brain are removed without a marked loss in function." Zugg adjusted his cap so that we could see his surgical scar. "No one knows this as well as me." He tugged his cap until it again covered most of the scar. "One of the cures for epilepsy involves the separation of the brain's left and right hemisphere."

"So this is real?" Ambler asked.

"Sadly, yes. Children are still born with birth defects everyday; especially in Third World countries where the quality of nutrition is poor and medicine is a century behind the rest of the civilized world."

As satisfying as Zugg's explanation was, there was one problem we hadn't covered. "A surgery like this would require a skilled surgeon and assistants, yes?"

"Undoubtedly."

"So someone else is involved; a surgeon and perhaps others."

"Why is that a problem, Detective?"

Zugg had stopped making sense. He was solid right up to the very end, but his last comment had me completely baffled. I turned my head to the side. Zugg must've seen that I was perplexed. He smiled and filled in the blanks. "Nothing is a problem, Detective, for those who are insane."

# Forty Three

Doe was fighting his way back. Deep in the womb of unconscious bliss, all of his disfigurements were gone. His skin was taught and smooth, his vision was sharp, and he had every reason to live. Weaving in and out of consciousness, he was vaguely aware that he was not alone. He wanted to open his eyes, but couldn't. Perhaps somewhere, deep down in his psyche, he understood that he was blind, and it prevented his eyes from opening. He would never again be able to see more than shadows, but the conscious mind was unaware of this defect or any other.

The oxygen flowing to his nostrils slowed to a deathly hiss, and then stopped.

He felt a soft caress against his cheeks and envisioned a white angel, buoyant in the air before him, its soft down-like wings stroking his face. His perfect, unfettered spirit rose just as the pillow was forced down over his face.

"Goodbye, Brian."

Brian Wainscot, the man generically known to the police as John Doe, did not struggle as he left his earthly confines, and his murderer behind.

# Forty Four

I went out hard and slept like a rock from three AM until seven. It wasn't a lot of sleep, but the quality was there. I felt like I was ready to take on the world when the alarm went off.

Ambler had his expert, and I had one of my own. Before breaking up, we agreed that a psychiatrist should be present at our suspect's questioning, and so it was that I was showered, dressed, and present at the home of Dr. Nigel Twain at ten-thirty on a quiet Saturday morning. Twain had privileges at Lenox Hill and had assisted me on a few of my cases. His methods may have been a tad unconventional, but he had proved that he had a cop's sense about things, and there just weren't too many headshrinkers that brought credentials like that to the table. Aside from that, he was easy on the eyes.

Twain lived at 172 Bleecker in the apartment once occupied by James Agee, a novelist and film critic, who had won the Pulitzer Prize posthumously. Twain and

Greenwich Village went together like hand and glove. He, like many of New York's nontraditional citizens migrated here, a melting pot for bohemians, artists, musicians, not to mention a slew of New York University's horny coeds.

I'd called to apprise him of the situation and had given him roughly an hour to get his handsome self together. He seemed eager to be involved, so I was surprised to find him in his robe when I arrived. Not that I'm complaining, mind you. He was showered and shaved, just not dressed. He smelled like soap and looked like a hearty breakfast—but I had already eaten.

"Nigel." I hugged him and walked into his apartment. "Throw some clothes on. We have a case that needs breaking." His eyes were a little bloodshot, so I didn't know if he was sporting a hangover or had shampoo in his eyes.

"Right-o, I'll be with you in a shake. You look lovely, Darling."

Twain had that throaty British baritone voice that could drive me and just about any red-blooded American girl crazy. He looked a little wobbly and not quite under his own power as he lumbered off toward his bedroom.

I plopped down on his sofa where a bottle of liquor was set out with some ice. The ice was fresh, so Twain was not hung over as I originally suspected. He was sporting a fresh buzz. Pre-noon is a little bit early for Yours truly to be hitting the bottle, but who am I to judge? It was a tall thin bottle. The label read Alandia Strong 68. I was unfamiliar with it, so I pulled the stopper and had a sniff. It smelled a lot like anisette.

Twain returned quickly, dressed in wool slacks and a cotton pullover. "I see you've uncorked the green fairy. Join me for a glass, won't you?"

"It's a little early, isn't it? What is this stuff anyway?"

"Absinthe, darling lady. I smuggled a supply home when I came back from Europe."

"Smuggled, why smuggled? You never heard of

the duty free shop?"

"Stephanie, the green fairy's just become legal here in the states but I've had a contraband stash here for a while. I used to think of it like Cuban cigars."

"Cuban cigars are banned for political reasons. Something tells me that's not the case with your private stock of hooch."

"Absinthe was banned in the states in the early 1920's because some of the distillers used low grade alcohol."

"And?"

"And as a result, some unfortunate people went blind."

"You know your eyes are a little bloodshot."

"That's not from the alcohol. I munched down a mescal button with last night's supper."

"Jesus, Nigel, why didn't you tell me—I thought you were toasted. You're mixing alcohol with hallucinogens and you expect to help me with a high profile investigation? Are you nuts?"

"Never say die, my lovely, I'm coming down as we speak."

"Forget about it, you're in no shape to diagnose the criminally insane."

Twain poured a sip of his green fairy into an odd glass and then added a splash of ice water. The green stuff turned a fuzzy white. Nigel swirled the liquid in its glass and drank it.

"Oh, that's beautiful. That'll help."

Nigel had the silliest expression on his face that I had ever seen. "I only do this for the religious experience—you know that. I use mescal for its entheogenic qualities."

That much was true. Nigel was devoutly religious. His nearness to God began when he was a child growing up in London. He had lived through much ridicule for his use of psychoactive substances in the treating of his patients. For him, popping a peyote button was about the same as you or I dropping aspirin.

I needed a little time to assess Twain's state of mind, so I quizzed him to see if he had presence of mind. "So tell me about this green liquid you just chugged."

"My dear girl, absinthe has been around since the nineteenth century. It's said to have hallucinogenic qualities, but I can assure you it does not—if anyone should know, it's me. It was a very popular drink in most of Europe, Paris in particular, where it was enjoyed by many of the day's most highly regarded artistes and creative minds: Baudelaire, Lautrec, van Gogh, Gauguin, and Picasso, were all fond of the drink."

Now Picasso, I understood; he'd have had to have been blitzed to paint some of the stuff he did. Go to the museum and check out Guernica, you'll know exactly what I mean.

"It's made from wormwood."

I didn't need to know that. As far as I was concerned, I'd spent too much time in the insect world already. I mean I know there are no actual bugs in wormwood, but a girl's got to draw the line somewhere.

So a few minutes had passed and Twain was still looking silly, but as far as I could tell, he was completely lucid. "Nigel, I'll ask you one last time. Are you in touch with reality? Are you going to be able to analyze my tunnel rat and tell me what's going on in his crazy head?"

"Like no one else can."

Good enough for me. I put Twain in the car and drove to Lenox Hill. Nigel Twain had never led me astray.

# Forty Five

Zugg had gotten a lift back home. I sincerely hoped that he was enjoying some rest. The man had a good soul—what he was going through, it just wasn't fair. I felt as if I needed to thank him daily for his help, as if each time I saw him might be the last. I didn't for his sake—to help him stay strong and hopeful. I did include him in my prayers at the end of each day. As a matter of routine, I prayed each night for my father's eternal spirit, my family and friends, and of course for Gus. I had recently included my old boss, Sonellio, and now Zugg. The list was growing: the names of those I implored God to safeguard, the ones I couldn't protect on my own. Who would be next?

Ambler and Lido both looked like they had benefited from some well needed shuteye. They were at the hospital and waiting for us when we arrived. Lido was cordial to Twain, despite his nagging suspicions that Twain was a frequent visitor in my dreams, a demonic tempter with an animal magnetism I could not resist. Was that in Lido's mind or mine? Ambler had his doubts about Twain, but kept his mouth shut, and would continue to do so as long as Twain continued to come through for us. As I mentioned, the man was a bit eccentric, but he had the right stuff.

"Your John Doe died last night," Ambler said.

"The tortured man?" Twain asked. I'd given him a high level briefing on the drive uptown. The fact that he had retained some of it was good news—it just confirmed for me that he wasn't totally sloshed.

"That's too bad. It would've been nice if he had seen his assailant brought to justice."

"He might be able to do that yet." Twain was hinting at the afterlife. I wasn't saying his beliefs didn't have merit, but I didn't want to get into it.

"I hope they're sending him for an autopsy."

"They are," Lido replied. "I made the call myself."

"Nigel is here to do a preliminary psychological evaluation on our tunnel boy."

Ambler turned to Twain. "Lido and I already looked in on him. He's awake and the nurses have him cleaned up. I don't want to waste any more time. We have to get over this poor little urchin thing and treat him like the suspect he is; one that may be responsible for torture, homicide, and kidnapping. We can't allow his disfigurement to play on our sympathies a moment longer."

"Agreed," Twain said. "So long as he's able to communicate—based on Chalice's description, withdrawal is the least of our worries. I won't know until I see him. In any case, I'm ready."

Maiguay was waiting in attendance when we arrived at the psychiatric wing. "I'm sorry your John Doe didn't make it, Detective. I know you were counting on his coming around."

"Life doesn't always go the right way. Thanks for everything you did." Maiguay was familiar with Lido and

Ambler. I introduced him to Twain. “Dr. Twain is here on behalf of NYPD to do a psychological assessment.”

They shook hands. “You have privileges with Lenox Hill?” Maiguay asked.

“For many years. You did the initial intake on our suspect?”

“I did. He had tremendous levels of anxiety, so I put him on two milligrams of Xanax and he still jumps out of his skin at the slightest start. Frankly, Dr. Twain, I think he’s frightened to death. The good Lord only knows how long he’s been roaming around those subway tunnels. He’s been plucked from his native environment, chased by the police, Tasared—”

Ambler interrupted. “That poor man you’re so damn worried about may be guilty of torture and murder. If he has any information that might lead us to Paul Liu, we need to get it out of him now.”

“Torture, murder...him? I wouldn’t think so. I’m no psychologist, but he has very limited executive functioning.”

“What does that mean?” Lido asked.

Twain answered as the resident psychological expert in the group. “It means he couldn’t possibly plan anything as complex as abduction or carrying out any of those horrible deeds that befell Kevin Lee. Did you attempt any rudimentary testing, Dr. Maiguay?”

“Yes, just the basics of course.”

“How did he do with the Tower of Hanoi Test?”

“He was distracted by it as one would expect from a patient with frontal lobe damage. He was unable to complete the test. I attempted the Wisconsin Card Sorting Task with similar poor results.”

“I see,” Twain said. “Does he respond to a name?”

“Yes, he responds to the name Rat.”

“Rat? He responds to the name, Rat?”

Maiguay nodded. “As I said, his level of executive functioning is almost nil.”

“He sounds preseverative,” Twain said.

“Before we go all soft and gooey again, how do we

know he's not a malingerer?" Ambler asked. "I've seen plenty of good fakers in my day."

"That's not for me to determine," Maiguay said. "I suggest we let Dr. Twain evaluate for himself."

"Then what are we waiting for," I said. "Let's roll."

# Forty Six

Lenox Hill had a monitoring room in the psychiatric ward, with a one way mirror similar to the setup NYPD used for lineup identification. Ambler, Lido, and I filed into the observation room.

“That Maiguay is a bleeding heart,” Ambler said, his temperature still running on high.”

“He’s a doctor, not a cop. What would you expect of him or anyone like him?” Lido said.

They were both right, but for now I was more interested in Twain’s assessment of our suspect. We watched as he entered the room, the one occupied by the man that responded to the name, Rat.

Twain entered the room in a very unassuming manner. Nonetheless, our suspect was startled by the opening door and looked nervous as he watched Twain enter the room. Twain’s posture was relaxed and his facial expression was pleasant. He pulled a chair alongside Rat’s bed. Just for the record, Rat was restrained. He was after all a murder suspect.

"Hello," Nigel said.

Rat did not respond. He continued to monitor his new visitor with extreme caution.

"You've been through quite an ordeal. I do hope you're feeling a little bit better after a good night's sleep and some tender loving care." Twain had studied Rat through the door's glass viewing panel prior to entering the room so as not to be shocked by the man's appearance. Even so, I could see him fighting the temptation to stare at the man's gross facial deformities.

Though retrained, Rat did his best to put a few additional inches between himself and Twain, but he did not speak.

"I mean you no harm. I merely need to ask you a few questions, will that be alright?" Twain's British voice was peaceful and soothing to the point of sending us all off for a catnap.

I could see Rat turn his wrists within his leather restraints. As I noticed the other day, his fists were still clenched. "Hurt," his voice was very nasal, barely decipherable, not uncommon for someone with such a severely damaged palate.

Twain picked up on his movements. "Are your restraints too tight?"

"Hurt, hurt."

"I'm going to loosen your wrist restraints, just a notch. Do I have your word that you will remain calm and in your bed?"

Rat did not respond. Twain waited a moment, likely making a mental assessment of whether to proceed or not. He finally adjusted the restraints, loosening each a single notch and no more.

"Is that better?"

As before, Rat was unresponsive. The Tower of Hanoi Test was on the bed with him. It looked like a common children's toy, a circular base with a pole in the middle; brightly colored rings were stacked on the pole, their size diminishing as they got to the top. Rat turned back to the toy and began to stare at it.

"How are you feeling?"

"Hungry."

"The doctor is feeding you intravenously. Do you understand what that means?"

"Hungry." Rat switched gears. He grinned and began to kick his feet playfully. Twain watched attentively.

"I'll see that you're brought some food. Is there something special you might like?"

"Hot dog, ketchup...hot dog, ketchup."

"Okay, I'll see about getting you something you like... Can you tell me your name?"

"Rat." He was getting more and more excited. The Tower of Hanoi toy fell off the bed.

Twain made no attempt to retrieve the toy or calm him down. "Is that the only name you have?"

"Rat."

"I'm sure that's not the name you were born with. Don't you have another name, a name you like better?"

Rat looked off the side of the bed, searching for his toy. He continued to kick his legs.

"Who gave you that name?"

"Sir."

"Who is Sir?"

Rat did not respond.

"I'm going to ask you some important questions. I hope you'll answer them as best you can." Twain paused momentarily, and then continued. "A friend of mine is lost, and I was wondering if you might know where he is. His name is Paul and I'm very concerned about him."

"Paul." Rat began to smile.

"Paul is a very good friend of mine. Can you tell me something about Paul? Is he alright?"

"Like Paul."

"Why do you like Paul?"

"Paul perfect."

"Do you know where I can find him? I miss him very much and I worry about him."

"Where Paul?"

"When was the last time you saw Paul?"

Rat's smile faded. He began to pout.

"Did someone take Paul?"

"Gone." He was on the verge of tears.

"Is Paul with someone you know?"

"Sir."

"How can I find Sir?"

Rat stopped kicking but did not respond verbally. He turned away from Twain and intensified his search for the Tower of Hanoi toy.

"Thank you. You've been very helpful. I'll see that you're brought something to eat." Twain stood and walked to the door. He turned back before exiting. "Why is Paul perfect?"

Rat grinned, but didn't respond.

Within a moment, Twain had joined us in the monitoring room.

"What do you think, Nigel?"

"On one hand, he appears to have extremely limited executive functioning, as Dr. Maiguay suggested. He lacks the ability to organize, so the idea of his masterminding an elaborate crime seems well beyond his intellectual capability. His mannerisms, speech, and of course his moniker, all relate to someone who has lived his life in subservience. He may have been abused by this Sir character he referenced. The lesions on his forehead, the large one in particular may be responsible for his limited intellect. The areas of the brain that deal with speech and cognition are located in the frontal lobe."

"So you buy the whole thing?"

"I didn't say that—ten minutes does not an evaluation make."

"So it's possible he's full of shit?" Ambler said.

"Yes," Twain replied. I could see he was still mulling over the facts. "There's always that."

# Forty Seven

The camping trip had been her idea, breaking early for lunch and a quickie had been his. They were in the Ford pickup with the windows rolled down. It was after the act, and Randy was ready for his post coital nap. He wanted to pass out and stay passed out until there wasn't enough daylight left for anything but finding their way out of The Pine Barrens.

"Let's get moving," Angela said. "It's a gorgeous day."

"Let me close my eyes. Five minutes, that's all."

"No way. I know what you're thinking," She leaned over and kissed him. It was a prelude to après sex smooching, something she knew he wanted no part of. "Ready?"

*Damn, she's got dick breath.* Randy pushed open the door and jumped out. "I gotta take a pee. Be right back." Randy walked around to the back of the pickup, pulled a Budweiser out of the cooler and popped the top. "That's better."

They were parked just a few yards from one of the many swamps that were found in The Pine Barrens—

Randy still had the Budweiser to his lips while hanging hog. "You're right, sure is a nice day." He found a large rock to pee on, and began to give it a good shower. The large stone was brown—Randy was tickled to see that it was white beneath where his stream had washed away the mud. He tried to clean off the entire surface. It wasn't until he had zipped, that a small frog sprang from an indentation in the rock, and Randy realized that the rock he had peed on wasn't a rock at all.

# Forty Eight

"The pellet with the poison's in the flagon with the dragon. The vessel with the pestle has the brew that is true."

"What?"

Twain and I were alone for a moment, away from the others, sitting in the waiting area. That silly grin was back on his face. God only knew what he was blabbering about now.

"The pellet with the poison's in the vessel with the pestle. The chalice from the palace has the brew that is true."

I could only assume that the mescal he had consumed was still in his system and was taking him on another ride.

"The chalice from the palace has the brew that is true—you sound really silly, Nigel. That's an exchange from an old movie, isn't it?"

Twain was still grinning. The Court Jester, I saw it last night."

"And that's funny, why?"

"Because, dear girl, because the chalice holds the brew that is true."

"I'm not chalice, Nigel. I'm *Cha-lee-see*. Snap out of it before someone hears you."

"I absolutely adore Danny Kaye. He was bloody hysterical."

"I loved Dean Martin, but you don't hear me crooning, 'That's Amore', do you?" It's a good thing you didn't lose it while you were with our suspect, you could have compromised the entire case."

"Oh settle down, Missy, I'm very much under control."

I didn't know if it would help, but those coffee vending machines were all over the place, so I procured a cup of steaming hot swill for Twain. It had the opposite effect of that intended.

He began laughing uncontrollably. "Is the pellet with the poison in there?"

Judging by the last cup of hospital joe I'd had, it certainly could have been. "Settle down, we need to talk."

Twain dragged his hand across his face, using it as a prop to dramatically transform his expression to a serious one. He took a sip of the coffee and pretended to wretch. "That's bad enough to sober anyone. What's on your mind?"

"I want to know what you really think about our suspect."

"I've already told you."

"I know, but is he for real? Is he capable of kidnap and murder?"

"Everyone's capable, Stephanie, you just have to push them hard enough. That man certainly has reason enough to commit a heinous act. Is it possible that somewhere in his warped mind he plays with the delusion that he can switch skulls with someone else? The answer is probably yes. Does he fancy Paul Liu's skull? Maybe, but on the basis of his mental attributes, he doesn't have the wherewithal to pull off anything that elaborate, not nearly so."

"So you'd say no."

"I'm saying I don't know. I need considerably more time with him to make an intellectual assessment. At this moment, I'd have to say that all options are possible. He may be a child or he may be a monster—I'm not yet sure of which."

I heard the elevator ding behind me and caught R.C Liu's profile as he emerged. I did my best to slink down in my seat and hide my face. Ambler, Lido, and a small army of cops were just outside our suspect's room. Surely they could deal with the annoying R. C. Liu without me.

"Who's that?" Twain asked.

"That's R.C. Liu," I whispered. "He's the Chinese ambassador."

"Ah, the missing lad's father."

"That's right."

"Why are you trying to avoid him?"

"He's not a pleasant man. He wants to take control of the investigation and he wants answers I don't have yet."

"How could he take over? He has no jurisdiction over police matters."

"Jurisdiction, no, power, influence, and high level connections, yes—a word in the wrong ear and I'll have the brass telling me to take a hike. Besides, who knows what kind of connections he has. Just because he dresses like royalty doesn't mean he can't get down and dirty if he needs to."

"You're suggesting he has criminal alliances?"

"Stranger theories are possible."

Twain grinned another exaggerated grin. *Please, not another mind freak.* "You know, Stephanie, you get this expression on your face when you have conviction. It's absolutely irresistible."

His eyes looked absolutely crazy.

Drugged as he was, I didn't know what Twain had

in mind. He was a godly looking man, but infidelity was the last thing on my mind. Okay, maybe not the very last thing, but it certainly wasn't on my top ten list—what with psychotic suspects, missing persons, and a snow white skull bouncing about, it was better to keep the blinders on. I gave him a peck on the cheek. "Go home, my friend." His pupils were dilating before my eyes. "Come, I'll put you in a cab."

"I so enjoy helping you."

"You already have. Don't undo the good work you've done by having someone accuse you of acting unprofessionally."

I could see him weighing the gravity of my comment. "As you suggest, I'm ready to go."

I had an ulterior motive in mind. I wanted to slip out of the hospital before Liu tracked me down. I put Twain in a taxi and gave the driver the address. I wasn't taking any chances that Twain couldn't remember where he lived, looking the way he did. The cab had just pulled away when Ambler rolled up in front of me.

"Get in," he said.

"What's going on?"

"The Chinese ambassador is looking for you everywhere and we got a call from the FBI office in Suffolk. Another skull turned up—Zugg's already out there."

Skulls were becoming as prevalent as dandelions on a weed laden lawn. I had been wondering where our case was going to lead us. Our perp had been forced to abandon his old lair. So, if Zugg was right, Rat couldn't have realized his insane dream without help. The question in my mind was who would help a madman?

# Forty Nine

Ambler and I were standing in the Medical Examiner's office in Hauppauge, Long Island, watching the forensic photographer hover around Zugg as he irrigated the skull with water until the silt began to wash out of the porous surface. The camera's shutter snapped, accompanied by the strobe's flash—simultaneously, the strobe's discharged capacitor began to recharge, filling the air with a high-pitched buzz. Snap, flash, buzz. Snap, flash, buzz. The photographer took a succession of shots as Zugg began the painstaking task of freeing the decedent skeleton from the mud it was encased within.

A microphone was clipped to Zugg's collar, allowing him to record data as it was unearthed. "Judging by the porosity of the skull, I'd say these remains are at least three years old." He looked up at the photographer. "Concur?"

"I'm not sure," the photographer replied.

Zugg shook his head with disappointment. "Go

out on a limb for Pete's sake—you're not being graded."

"Two to four."

Zugg smiled at the photographer. "Ballsy."

Using a soft-haired brush and the irrigation tube, Zugg meticulously washed out the oral cavity as the photographer continued to chronicle his every movement. A dental explorer was used to remove grit from between the teeth. Using a mouth mirror, Zugg inspected the oral cavity. "The decedent has a gold crown on #13. This too is in keeping with the cadaver's suspected age. Precious metals are rarely used in contemporary dentistry—synthetic laminates over inert metal is generally used for cosmetic reasons and to lower the cost of the prosthesis."

Zugg worked at arm's length now, so that the photographer could position his camera directly over the oral cavity to shoot pictures of the teeth. Zugg pulled down the mandible so that the anterior aspect of the teeth could be photographed. A palatal reflector was used to chronicle the lingual surface of the teeth, including the aforementioned prosthetic premolar. Once again, the photographer snapped several pictures before stepping back. Zugg made note of the large metallic fillings that were in evidence. "There is crowding of the lower incisors, which may be the result of mesial drift." Zugg was through with his initial observation of the oral cavity. Subsequently, a forensic odontologist would complete the process Zugg had started. The teeth would be X-ray'd, dental work and anomalies in the teeth would be noted—finally the teeth would be matched to the dental records of heretofore unidentified victims. Dental records are usually well documented making for a high rate of success.

Zugg pulled off his gloves one at a time and strolled toward us. "What do you think?" I asked.

"The evidence is conclusive. He's dead."

His crack made me laugh. I was constantly assessing Zugg's appearance to determine his relative health.

His quip took me off guard. "I see that you're in a good mood."

"That's the oldest joke in the book, Chalice. I'm surprised you fell for it," he said. "I slept better the last couple of nights than I have in months. I think the case is helping to distract me."

"I'm glad."

"It's good to be useful. I've been spending too much time dwelling on my health problems."

"But seriously, do you have any initial ideas?"

"Well firstly, it's not Paul Liu's skull, that's for sure. This one's been out here for years."

"That's a relief. Anything else?"

"The victim was an Oriental male. The structure of the cheekbones and the flat nasal ridge indicate such."

"So, there's a good chance that this victim ties to our case. Kevin Lee, Paul Liu, our suspect, and this victim are all Asian."

"I would say so," Ambler said. "The question is what will we find when we start looking? The Pine Barrens cover a one hundred thousand acre maze of woods, swamps, and forest. There could be dozens of bodies out here."

"Sounds like a nightmare."

Ambler's statement frightened me to the core. I was not interested in our case escalating into the next John Wayne Gacy debacle, nor was I interested in having my name in the record books for apprehending the psychopathic murderer who had claimed the largest number of victims. The remains of twenty-eight young men and boys had been found in the forty foot crawl space beneath Gacy's house. That was not what I wanted, not at all—didn't want any piece of it. "Herbert, what you're saying is all well and good, but the burning question in my mind is not how much collateral damage we can dig up, but why here, and where is Paul Liu now? We're relatively sure that Rat had a coconspirator, someone who could help him with his fantasy skull transplant. Unfortunately, Rat isn't willing or is unable to tell us who his accomplice is."

"This skull may fill in some of the blanks," Zugg said. "We might have luck with the dental records. In addition, the FBI crime lab has highly advanced facial reconstruction programs. The computer is capable of producing a reasonable likeness in a matter of mere hours."

"That's our most direct angle," Ambler said. "If we can come up with the victim's likeness, we can go widespread in distribution and attempt to identify him—give his picture to the press if need be. I have a terrible feeling about all this. I feel like we're running out of time."

"I agree, but I certainly think there's more to be gotten out of Rat. Twain only spent a few minutes with him." There was no point telling anyone that Twain had examined our suspect while under the influence, it wouldn't have done anyone any good. Besides, even on his worst day, Nigel Twain was better than most on their best day. "I understand our suspect has his issues, but I can't help feeling he knows more than he's telling us."

"I'd like a crack at him as well," Zugg said. "Any chance you're heading back to the city?"

I turned to Ambler. "I can do more good back in the city, working with our suspect. Do you agree?"

"Yeah, you head back into the city with Damien and I'll stay out here to oversee the dredging of the swamp. There's a possibility we may find the victim's body when we start snooping around. We're setting up a mobile command post while we search The Pine Barrens."

"I know you're always up to a commune with nature—don't forget your bug spray."

Ambler scowled at me. I could see he'd have preferred to have said something uncomplimentary. In fact, it looked like he was biting his lip. "I'll arrange to have you driven back."

I was concerned about the task of finding clues in a place as vast as The Long Island Pine Barrens. Although Manhattan was significantly denser, I was much more comfortable investigating on my own turf. By comparison, The Pine Barrens was incredibly vast, and with such diverse topography, it represented a real and difficult challenge. I was torn; hoping that Ambler's work would prove fruitful, just not too successful. It would take the FBI significant time to cover the area, and as we all know, time was running out.

# Fifty

The mobile command center had been positioned some twenty yards from the swamp in which the last human skull had been found. Ambler roamed the grounds, kicking stones, as he composed his thoughts and waited for the special operating teams to arrive. Searching The Pine Barrens represented a significant challenge. He felt a hollow gnawing in his chest as he waded through the myriad of possible strategies for recovering evidence over such a formidable terrain.

He looked forward at the wall of towering trees in front of him, the dramatic countenance beyond which lay one hundred thousand acres of densely contiguous forest: forty-foot pitch pines and oaks, tidal wetlands, coastal ponds, maple swamps, and cranberry bogs. The victim's body and perhaps many others were hidden somewhere within this snarl of obstacles. He didn't have to wait very long.

Ambler looked up when he heard the dogs yelping and whining around the periphery of the white cedar swamp. Their handler was kneeling next to the dogs and rewarding them with treats. They chewed them happily and quieted down. The male crushed his bone in two powerful chomps and swallowed. The handler tossed him a second bone, which he caught in mid air. Two more powerful chomps and then he ran off to scratch his belly against the tall-growing sedge. He smiled as the sedge's stiff shafts grazed his funny bone.

Ambler waved the handler over.

The handler was rubbing the female's tummy. He scratched her behind the ear and then responded to Ambler's signal.

"Playing favorites?" Ambler asked. "You gave the male two treats; you only gave the female one."

"We're watching Lucy's weight. She's a little more sedentary than Ricky is."

"So what's going on?" Ambler asked.

"I'm sure your man has spent a lot of time in this area. Ricky and Lucy have been trained only to ask for rewards after they've made a significant discovery."

"I love the name choices."

The handler smiled. "I named them. I was a big fan of I Love Lucy."

Ambler smiled. "Me too. You see anything significant here?"

"Whatever has the dogs on alert seems to be coming from the swamp. There was one time, Lucy accurately indicated the bodies of two homicide victims that were submerged beneath a hundred feet of water in a Pennsylvania quarry. The water was so cold that it delayed putrefaction for days, which kept the bodies from floating to the surface." The handler swept his tongue behind his top lip and then spat on the ground. "I'm telling you these two dogs are uncanny. If they're telling us that there's someone in the swamp, there's someone in the swamp."

"Fine," Ambler said. "I'll give the order; we'll dredge the goddamn thing."

# Fifty One

It's amazing how quickly we made the trip back to Manhattan. We were walking into the lobby at Lenox Hill Hospital in under an hour. Zugg and I were eager to spend some serious time with Rat, but I could see that Zugg was losing steam. He excused himself and went to the men's room while I pulled out my Palm Treo. It was equipped with GPS, and I wanted to get my arms around The Pine Barrens' geography. I needed to understand just what exactly we were up against in terms of sheer size and complexity.

My location must've been poor because it took forever for the Palm to bring up The Pine Barrens' location. The phone rang while I was waiting. It was my dear friend Glenaster Tully from the Medical Examiner's office. I answered the call while the unit searched for the proper map.

"Tully, how are you?"

"Just fine, Chalice." Tully had only lived in New York for about half a dozen years and spoke with the heaviest of Jamaican accents. "What's my fine lady up to today?"

"Solving crime, jailing slime, same as any other day—you've got some news for me, my friend?"

Tully chuckled. I could picture his happy grin on the other end of the line. "Ya, *mon*, I do. It's about your John Doe. Cause of death was respiratory failure, but there's something I don't like."

"What's that?"

"Toxicology found opiates in his bloodstream, but you said he was in the hospital a couple of days—he should've come up clean."

"That does sound a little odd. Why would you give morphine to someone in a coma?"

"That's exactly what I mean, Chalice. The victim's lungs were healthy. I'm not so sure he didn't have a little help checking out of this world."

"So you're saying that he might have been murdered?"

"Don't know one hundred percent, Chalice. All I'm saying is something don't add up."

"I'll look into it. Was there anything else?"

"The victim was not capable of speech. His vocal cords were destroyed by caustic injections to the voice box. Someone wanted to make sure John Doe didn't make noise, not a peep."

Tully's news made my own throat ache. It all made me start to wonder. Was Rat capable of doing that too? Doe had been tortured, blinded, and had his vocal cords destroyed. Whoever did this was a monster. There was no other name that applied better. Alas, a lot still remained unexplained. "Good work, my friend. As always you've been a big help."

"Bring it home, Chalice. If anyone can do it, it's you, *mon*. I got faith in you. Take care."

I was picturing that wretched deformed man lying in his hospital bed. What were we dealing with here? Was he a victim or was it the other way around? The question would have to keep a little longer as I was startled by a loud thud which seemed to emanate from the men's room. I knew in my heart that it represented bad news. I jumped to my feet, jammed my Palm Treo into my pocket and raced into the men's room.

# Fifty Two

"How's he doing?" I wasn't used to seeing Zugg in a hospital gown. As sick as I knew he was, I hadn't really thought of him as an infirm. I'd thought of him as a struggling investigator, trying to make a contribution despite it all, one who was still able to stand on his own two feet, however briefly. Seeing him now, pale and unconscious in a hospital bed, gave me a real understanding of just how ill he really was. His Yankees cap was conspicuously missing, giving me ample time to study the surgical scar that traversed the top of his head.

About an hour had passed since I had found him unconscious in the men's room with a syringe dangling from his arm.

The attending doctor's name was Kahn. "He's in shock. I won't know what we're up against until we know what he injected himself with. Do you know what medications he was on?"

"I know he took Imtrex—he gets terrible

migraines. I saw him pass out after injecting himself once, but he came right back."

"We're having the contents of the syringe analyzed. I hope that's all it was. His scans didn't show a concussion. We have God to thank that he didn't hit his head when he fell."

I did the sign of the cross mentally. "Yes, thank God. Why would you think otherwise? I mean what else might he have injected himself with?"

"I'm not sure. Imitex makes sense. Glioma patients often suffer from headaches, nausea, and vomiting—seizures are possible. More worrisome is that glioma patients sometimes suffer with personality and mood swings. They have problems with judgment. Almost anything is possible when alterations take place in the gray matter. I'm trying to locate his medical records and contact the doctors who are familiar with his case. You wouldn't happen to know where his surgery was performed, would you?"

I shook my head. "I'll try to find out. Glioma is brain cancer?"

Kahn nodded. "Yes, it's one form of anaplastic malignancy".

I began getting choked up. I could still see him rising naked from the pond, having given himself his daily baptism. It was all starting to hit home, the full severity of Zugg's condition. "Are we in danger of losing him?"

Kahn put his hand on mine. "Not today." He smiled warmly. "Let's be optimistic, Detective. Does he have family we should notify?"

"I'm not sure if he has family. I'll find out."

"Well then it's good that you're here for him. I have to make my rounds, but the nurses can page me if there are any changes."

"Thanks, Doctor."

I pulled up a chair and began a vigil, watching over him. I didn't know if there was anyone else he could count on.

I really wanted my friends and loved ones around me: Ma, Ricky, and Gus. I was going for my phone to call Gus when I remembered that Dr. Kahn needed as much information about Zugg as possible. As I reached for my phone to call Ambler, I saw that the GPS system had finally located a map of The Pine Barrens. I'd forgotten that I had started a search just before finding Zugg passed out in the men's room. It was fortuitous that my Palm had completed its assignment. It had secured a very clear map of The Pine Barrens, complete with details of the major structures within it. One area in particular caught my interest. I took a closer look at the map and got an eerie feeling as to why our investigation had shifted from Manhattan to The Long Island Pine Barrens. I keyed Ambler's number and waited for him to answer.

# Fifty Three

"Chalice, what's up? We found a body." Ambler was staring at the remains being pulled out of the swamp; a skeletal arm dangling out of a cocoon constructed from a vinyl tarp. "They're pulling it out of the swamp now."

"Zugg's not doing well. He passed out giving himself an injection and went into shock. He's here at Lenox Hill. He's been admitted."

"Shit. What are the doctors doing for him?"

"They're trying to determine what he injected himself with. Do you know what medication he takes?"

"Imtrex."

"That's what I said, but the doctor wasn't sure. Do you know the name of the doctor that takes care of him?"

"No, he's very private about that stuff, but he's still getting Bureau benefits. I'll make a call and see what I can dig up."

"He's very sick, Herbert."

Ambler must've sensed the sadness in my voice. "You knew that, kid. I told you what he had."

"I know, but hearing it from you and hearing it from an oncologist are two separate things. He's unconscious."

"Steady, Sweetheart, he'll pull through. He's tougher than you give him credit for."

It had only been a few years since my dad had passed away. The pain and unhappiness was all coming back. "Please see what you can find out and call me back. The doctor needs to know what he's dealing with."

"I'll check into it and get right back to you."

"Oh, guess what else?"

"Surprise me, I know that's the way you want it."

"Pilgrim State Mental Hospital—it's located smack dab in the center of The Pine Barrens."

"Yeah, that's right. Its vacant now, isn't it? I mean the place was shut down years ago."

"No, not shut down, just scaled back. They still have thousands of inpatients and outpatients."

"And you think that figures into our case?"

"Let's see, we have a lunatic looking to swap skulls with Paul Liu and he needs someone equally insane to help with the procedure, not to mention that we just found another skull in their backyard—I don't know, I think Pilgrim State might be worth a look."

"Alright, you've made your point. I'll check on the progress of the facial reconstruction project and have the photos brought over to Pilgrim State as soon as they're ready."

"That's a good lad. Check into Zugg's records, will you, and please call me right back."

Ambler was chuckling on the other end. "God love you, you're a piece of work—later."

# Fifty Four

Melancholy wasn't big on my list of healthy personal traits, so I switched gears and refocused on the case to keep my mind busy. The conversation I'd had with Tully was coming back. Why had Doe been given morphine? It was time for me to track down Dr. Maiguay. I paged him several times without receiving an answer, so I took an elevator to ICU so I could look for myself. Maiguay, who had always been handy, was nowhere to be found. The evening nurse had just come on duty, so I figured I'd see if she knew how I could get a hold of him.

"Good evening." I flashed my shield. "I'm Detective Chalice. Can you tell me where I might find Dr. John Maiguay?"

"Did you try paging him?"

"Several times, no answer."

"He may be off, but let me try." I watched as the nurse looked up Maiguay's number and paged him.

"Let's give him a few minutes and see if responds. Is this about John Doe?"

"Yes... I'm sorry I didn't get your name."

"Adelaide Tucker. That poor man, he sure was a terrible mess. Who would do that to another person? Terrible, just terrible—maybe it's better the good Lord took him."

"Can you tell me why Dr. Maiguay might have prescribed morphine for someone in Doe's condition?"

"Morphine? I don't remember him prescribing morphine. He gave him a small does of Valium once, just enough to calm the poor thing down. He had a bad case of dream terror—got all agitated."

"How does a coma patient get dream terror?"

"Don't know. I suppose they still dream. At least that's what Dr. Maiguay thought it was. The man was moaning and shaking. Dr. Maiguay had to give him something to settle him down."

"Valium you said, but not morphine—you're sure?"

"Oh definitely. The Valium worked just fine, settled him down right away."

"Can you check the charts for me?"

"They're long gone. They go right to accounting and then audit and archive. You're best bet is talking to the doctor."

I looked at my watch. "He should have called by now."

A second nurse was on her way out. Adelaide flagged her down. "Diana, you see Dr. Maiguay today?"

Diana looked worn. "I think he's off. He hasn't been around all day."

My cell phone rang. It was Ambler, no doubt, calling me to provide an update on Zugg's medical information. Ma always said that a hospital was the unhealthiest place in the world. Of course she was talking about hospitals in terms of accidental deaths, and for being a cesspool for diseases you would never normally encounter in the course of your day to day life. Suddenly there was new wisdom in words. No disrespect to Lenox Hill, fine institution that it was, but it was time to convey Ambler's information to Dr. Kahn, and then get the hell out of the building.

# Fifty Five

I found Dr. Kahn leaning against the wall outside Zugg's room. He looked pale, as if he had just been informed as to the imminent demise of the earth's population as the result of a global pandemic.

"Are you alright, Doctor? I have a phone number for you and the name of Dr. Zugg's oncologist." I handed him the information on a slip of paper. He looked at it and put it in his pocket. I asked again, "Are you alright?"

"He's been self medicating."

"How bad? You're not talking about aspirin, are you?"

Kahn looked even paler than he had the moment before. "He's been injecting himself with neurotoxins."

I didn't know what Kahn was talking about and I needed clarification. The word toxin needed no translation. I was hoping that Zugg wasn't intentionally poisoning himself. I dragged him down the hall to the lounge. We sat down in chairs facing each other. "What exactly has he been doing?"

Kahn rubbed his chin. His skin looked clammy. "You have to understand—glioma can be extremely aggressive—in some cases, life expectancy can be as short as six to eight months. You can see why someone might try something drastic, something radical, especially someone like Dr. Zugg, with an advanced background in biochemistry. Coupled with the deviant behavior that sometimes comes about as a result of the tumor's placement in the brain—"

I was getting the vapors. I found myself struggling to fill my lungs with air. "Please, Doctor, what are you telling me?"

"The lab reported its findings. Dr. Zugg has been injecting himself with scorpion venom."

"Why?"

"Because he's desperate, because conventional therapy, stereotactic radiation has severe side effects. Even so, the chances for prolonging life are not good."

"But why Scorpion venom?" I pictured myself standing in front of Zugg's front door and being offered a scorpion cocktail. My, but the good Dr. Zugg had a droll sense of humor.

"A protein in scorpion venom bonds to the glioma tumors. There's research going on in which drugs or radioactive material is bound to the scorpion protein as a new treatment against brain cancer. It's very new, and very controversial—virtually unproven. No doubt Zugg has synthesized his own medication in a last ditch effort to eradicate his cancer."

"So he's not crazy?"

"He's experimenting on himself with poison strong enough to kill a horse. Literally. He has no idea of dosage, or side effects, or if the material he's injecting has any medical benefit at all. So as much as I'd like to say no, the answer is that Dr. Zugg is clearly not thinking rationally. Yes, I'd say he's crazy. He could have gone to South America where they're experimenting with scorpion venom and have years of clinical experience. No one in their right mind would do what he's doing. At least we have an idea of how to treat him. I've administered a dose of an anti-venom. We'll have to monitor his condition very closely."

Kahn looked as though he had been tested to the limit and no one understood why as well as I did. After a few minutes, Kahn went about his rounds. I stayed behind looking in on Zugg. Hard as I tried, I couldn't put myself in his shoes, but knowing the desperate mind as I did, I knew that almost anything was possible. Pushed too hard, we're all capable of a bizarre reaction. Desperation can open the door for almost anything, and having pre-knowledge of the potential consequences doesn't seem to keep us from making mistakes. That's why people fall victim to torture, abduction, and murder. That's why I have a job.

# Fifty Six

I caught a chopper ride back to The Pine Barrens. On the seat next to me was a case of computer simulated photos bearing the facially reconstructed likeness derived from the skull that had been recovered there. The rendering depicted a man of Oriental ethnicity, somewhere about forty years of age.

On my recommendation, Ambler had established an effective perimeter around the Pilgrim State Hospital. Set on seven hundred forty acres, the complex consisted of seventy-five buildings. While I was en route, and with darkness falling, Ambler and Lido were beginning the difficult process of planning the search.

But for whom?

Who was the man in the photo? Intuition was telling me that the answer would be found at Pilgrim State. Time was running out for Paul Liu. With Rat in custody, there was little need for Liu's skull. Did Liu know his abductor's identity? Had he seen his face? Possessing that knowledge would unquestionably prove fatal for him. I only hoped it wasn't too late.

The chopper had wireless connectivity, so I used the travel time to familiarize myself with the Pilgrim State Hospital by means of a notebook computer. As I said, the complex was vast. It was the largest psychiatric hospital ever built. At its peak, it had as many as sixteen thousand patients. It was opened by the state in 1931 to accommodate the increasing need to treat the mentally ill. Over time, the services they offered were available elsewhere, and so Pilgrim's population decreased, many of the buildings closed, and parcels of the land sold off. It currently housed about six hundred inpatients.

The web photo depicted the main building as an enormous edifice which was located at 998 Crooked Hill Road. The building transformed within my mind into a caricature insane asylum—something out of nineteenth century Europe. I could picture lunatics screaming from behind barred windows and patients dangling out windows, clinging to bed linens, attempting to make good their escape—the kind of place Dracula paid frequent visits to, and freed Renfield from.

I went on to read about the hospital's history and about its facilities and vision, but it was a blog about the Edgewood State Facility that really drew my attention.

"Edgewood State Hospital, a thirteen story haunted house, connected to Pilgrim State by underground tunnels: At one time, a containment facility for World War II war criminals and tuberculosis patients."

I found myself obsessing about Edgewood as the chopper descended toward the ground, my head filling with even more ghoulish visions than before. As I stepped from the chopper I felt certain I was in the right place, my mind exploring the unnatural darkness of the underground tunnels. What better place for a snake to hide than under a rock?

# Fifty Seven

Dr. David Hector, the facility's chief administrator met me on the building's steps. He was awkwardly tall and thin, at least six-foot-six. His head was angled down moderately, the result, I assumed, of some manner of neck trauma, or a really bad night's sleep. He greeted me and we went straight inside. Walking alongside Hector down the corridor to his office, I noticed that he walked oddly, drawing his knees high off the floor like a crane.

"I appreciate you taking the time to help me, Doctor. I know it's late."

"Please, there's many nights I stay far later than this. I'm happy to help. It's troubling to know that you believe the facility can help you with your homicide investigation."

"Multiple homicides actually. Evidence was found in The Pine Barrens that tied to a double homicide in Manhattan."

"But, Detective, The Pine Barrens is a huge piece

of property. Aside from Pilgrim State, the complex contains a state university, land under development, recreational facilities, waterways, residences—The Pine Barrens is far more than Long Island's largest natural land mass, it's an entire community."

We were in his office now. I closed the door and sat down. I had one of the computerized renderings in my hand. I placed it on Hector's desk so that he could take a crack at it. "Do you recognize the man depicted in this photo? I'm thinking he may have worked here."

Hector studied the photo. "My, but they're doing amazing things with computers these days; so lifelike and natural. This man isn't familiar to me, but I can't say that I'm one hundred percent familiar with everyone on the night staff—this place goes twenty-four/seven, you know. I know most of the current employees, but that doesn't mean he didn't work here before I arrived."

"And when was that?"

"About two and a half years ago. I was the director of the San Joaquin Psychiatric Health Facility in Stockton, California. I moved here when the job opened up. I couldn't deal with the man who ran the state's program—if you ask me, he needed more help than most of my patients." Hector smiled at his own remark. "I replaced Dr. Robert Marsh who ran this facility for almost twenty years."

"Do you know where we can reach him?"

"Oh yes, sure. Dr. Marsh lives in Sag Harbor, not too far from here. I'd be happy to give him a call—wonderful man."

"Thanks, that's a help. In the meantime, I presume you have photo IDs for everyone on staff?"

"Yes, of course."

"What about past staff?"

"Recent terminations are computerized. Older ones are archived."

"Paper files?"

"That's right. We have an archives room in the basement."

"We're going to need to see them."

"Of course. I'll have them brought up to the conference room. But I do have a request of my own."

"Of course, what is it?"

"I'm concerned about my patients. Having the police and FBI conducting an investigation is enough to unnerve anyone, let alone the psychiatrically challenged. I trust you've never been in a psychiatric hospital."

*That's right, never, and don't plan to be.* "No."

"The patients here need to be here. Many are unstable or can just barely hold their lives together. I can't risk having a psychiatric meltdown in my facility. It would be dangerous for the staff and patients. That FBI gentleman, Agent Ambler, he's all business, isn't he?"

I heard a patient's scream filter into Hector's office right through the wall. A woman was screaming, "Marie, Marie, I want my ice cream." Though I tried not to think about it, I knew that I was in an asylum. It was politically incorrect to use that terminology anymore, but we all understood the reference. "I understand your concerns, Doctor. I'll have a word with Agent Ambler—he's not as bad as he looks. I'm sure he'll do his best to keep the investigation unobtrusive."

"It's appreciated, thank you. Let me see if Dr. Marsh is available." Hector dialed his colleague and left a message for him at his home. "He's probably out to dinner." Hector leaned forward, feeling the need to whisper despite the fact that we were alone behind closed doors. "His wife isn't much of a cook. They had me over once—did you ever know anyone who could ruin spaghetti?"

In my family the term was pasta. Spaghetti was a word used by those who over boiled their noodles and doused them with jarred sauce. "I'm Italian—I've never had a bad dish of pasta." Well actually there was that one time, back in my college days. I was in Hays, Kansas driving back from the coast with some friends. We stopped for the night and the only place around was the motel restaurant. It was modeled after a Bavarian chalet, and went by the name Pancake Haus. My girlfriends and I thought we were going to pig out on waffles and ice cream, but all they were serving that night was spaghetti in tomato sauce or canned La Choy Chow Mein. It's a bad sign when a restaurant writes *tomato sauce* on the menu. So, if you ever find yourself driving down Route 70, don't stop in Hays, even if it's the middle of the night and you're downright starving—just keep on going.

"I appreciate your help, Dr. Hector. I'll go have a word with my colleagues, and if it's not too much trouble, I'd appreciate it if those old files could be made available to me right away."

"I'll take care of it. With any luck, Dr. Marsh will call right back—I told him it was important."

I was mentally preparing for a long night of strong coffee and bloodshot eyes, a night of laboring over dusty files hoping to find a photo that matched our computerized simulation, but then Lido knocked on the door. I introduced him to Hector. After a few minutes of polite conversation, Hector left us alone in his office so that he could arrange for the personnel records I had requested.

"Can you do me a favor?"

Lido nodded. "Sure. What?"

"Can you pull a few men to cross reference our simulation against hospital records?"

"That's it?"

"No, Dr. Hector's very concerned about his patients' wellbeing. He's afraid the police and FBI will scare the bejesus out of them and do them irreparable harm. We can't have that, now can we?"

"So, you want me to have a word with your buddy, Ambler?"

"If you would be so kind."

Lido shrugged. "Sure... So what are you going to do?"

"Ask me no questions, I'll tell you no lies."

"Oh, I don't like the sound of that. What are you thinking?"

My head filled with the dream I'd had the day before. Lido and I were once again in an insane asylum. The howling started off low as a whisper and built into a roaring crescendo. I leaned forward and planted one on him, pressing my lady parts firmly against him, hoping to distract him—a little slight of hand, or breast, never hurt a girl. Now you see me, now you don't. The good Lord bequeathed unto us those all important feminine wiles for a very good reason. I may have abused the privilege. In any case there was no time for an official ruling.

"Now promise me you won't do anything stupid."

"I promise I won't do anything stupid without checking with you first."

Lido smiled at me, one of those I'm on to you smiles. "Bull shit, wait two minutes, I'm coming with you."

# Fifty Eight

Okay, I don't know the nuts and bolts of the process, but a good endorphin rush really seems to get me going, and I was getting a hell of a rush and a sense that something exciting was at hand. I couldn't get Edgewood out of my mind. The blog I'd read refused to leave me alone.

"Edgewood State Hospital, a thirteen story haunted house, connected to Pilgrim State by underground tunnels: At one time a containment facility for World War II war criminals and tuberculosis patients."

I couldn't fight it any longer. I had a hunch about who I was after and though it was nothing conclusive, my sixth sense told me that Rat's coconspirator and Paul Liu were somewhere within this massive sarcophagus that was once Edgewood State Hospital.

I persuaded Hector to grant Lido and I access to the defunct building and turn on the power—though out of use for decades, the building remained structurally sound.

My plan was simple. We'd start on the top floor and forge downward, securing one floor at a time until a confrontation with our suspect became unavoidable—at least that's what I was hoping for. I had my automatic out and ready, my Para Ordnance 14.45 Light/Double Action with a high capacity fourteen round magazine. The *LDA* had a tuned single-action trigger pull. Straight out of the box, it was better than anything I had ever fired before. I had only used it in the field once before and it had saved my life. I had a feeling I'd need it again today.

The building was desolate and filthy, damp, and cold in the midst of spring. I summoned to conscious thought the timeline of care for the mentally ill at this facility as I recalled it from the computer research I had done. Insulin shock began in 1936. Electric shock therapy was introduced in 1940. Surgeons began performing prefrontal lobotomies in 1946. Drug-based treatment arrived in the 1950s, starting with Thorazine. It was at that point that the patient populations began to decline. Edgewood's useful life was curtailed in 1971 and had been left to decay ever since.

Indeed, there were many ghosts here. I could feel their presence and hear them whispering all around me. There was no denying the feeling I got walking down the abandoned corridors. It was as if the wronged were calling out to me demanding justice be done. Had the blog been accurate? Had this been the place where World War II war prisoners were incarcerated and experimented upon? I doubted I'd ever know. John Doe had been tortured before he died, or should I say, was murdered. Had Kevin Lee been tortured before he was murdered and beheaded? What had Paul Liu been forced to endure? I was hoping to put it all to rest this evening, here, in this tomb of a building that had been witness to so much pain.

"This place is a kick," Lido said, "Like something

out of a Boris Karloff movie."

"I know—could use a pair of curtains and coat of paint. Thank God I don't believe in werewolves."

We continued to clear the building, floor by floor, working our way down until finally the basement tunnel entrance stood before us. I pushed on the heavy steel door. It opened with a deafening creak.

# Fifty Nine

The sound of the creaking door reverberated through the underground tunnel, setting Paul Liu's heart to a rapid and desperate rate. He could feel his chest pounding against the concrete floor as he lay bound, gagged, and blindfolded, helpless and alone. *End this for me, end it for me now*, he repeated in his mind. It was his dire resolve. His last ditch effort to hang on. He'd been a prisoner so long, and wondered if there was any hope. He'd been completely isolated from the outside world, no telephone, no computer, nothing—no one to speak with, no idea if anything was going on. *Were the police getting close?* He only knew that his captor had become desperate. He could sense it in his voice, in the insults hurled at him as he was moved from the light into the darkness.

He'd learned to tighten his facial muscles so that scant rays of light would penetrate a crease in the blindfold, but there was no light here, no light at all.

The tunnel smelled musty and of animal urine. It

was nauseatingly strong and was with him whenever he was conscious. He could hear the rodents scampering by in the dark. They were everywhere. They ran around him and over him. He would writhe violently to scare them away, but they always came back. Eventually, he feared, they would not flee when he contorted his body. Eventually, they would have him for their dinner.

What Liu couldn't see was that piled against the wall of the tunnel were broken wooden articles, painted toy soldiers, bird houses, and pegboards. Back in the day when the hospital was operational, the inpatients prepared crafts and would sell them at a fair once a year in order to contribute revenues to the hospital. The fractured remains of their handicraft were a sad reminder of the contribution they had made to support the facility and the effort the individuals had made in an attempt to hold onto the last shred of their self respect.

He'd only been fed once since coming to the new location. As much as he despised his captor, he was grateful when he returned with water. Liu had begged for mercy in the few moments that his gag was removed, but his outpouring was only met with arrogance and insults, and the gag was back in place and tighter than before.

"You're useless, ugly, and useless."

He was the son of a very wealthy man, and wondered if a ransom had been requested and if it had been paid. But if it had been paid, why hadn't he been set free? Had there been a successive request for money? Did this monster have no intention of setting him free? Uncertainty was killing him slowly, but the will to live forced him to drink when his dignity told him to refuse. He thanked God for the cool liquid running down his throat, lubricating the parched tissue of his esophagus. That was seconds before he heard the piercing sound of the creaking door. A spark of hope crackled in the darkness of his mind. *Someone's coming,* he thought. *They're finally here.*

# Sixty

There was no light in the tunnel, none at all. Lido found the light switch and tried it, but the lights didn't come on. Good sense told me we should call for backup.

"What do you think?" Lido said.

"You mean what do I think about exploring an underground tunnel in the dark to search for a psychopath?"

"Yes, what do you think? Want to call for backup?"

"Probably should."

Lido pulled out his phone, "Amazing, I've got a signal." He phoned in our position and requested help.

"So what now? You want to wait around like a couple of scared kids or do you want to push on?" I clicked on my battery powered lantern. It was not a Maglite, but it would have to do. It was a utility lantern that probably had not been used in years. The light it emitted was weak and diffuse. To make matters worse, it flickered constantly.

"With resources like that...okay, let's move on. At least we'll go out together."

"You're such a romantic."

We slowly descended into the darkened tunnel that connected Pilgrim State Hospital to the Edgewood Mental Facility, the deteriorated facility that time had long since forgotten. Debris crunched under my feet as I walked.

After a moment, we came upon the skeleton of a large dog, its rib cage exposed beneath its dusty, matted pelt. A few steps later I heard water dripping. Above me, water seeped from a rusted supply pipe fitting. At my feet, the concrete walkway disappeared beneath the unintentionally formed manmade pool. I lifted my cuffs and carefully trudged through the stagnant water. With each step, I decided more and more that the stories I had read about Edgewood had been true.

Thirty feet into the tunnel, we came upon dozens of rusted mattress frames, stacked against the walls, which I assumed had once been the beds of tuberculosis patients. I had studied the building from the outside before entering it—thirteen stories of red brick. The building had a decidedly ominous appearance. By contrast, I'd read that the inner quarters had been bright and cheerful. I imagined the large wards filled with these beds. I could hear the telltale hacking of the patients echoing in my ears; patients fully aware of their short life expectancy. *So much sad history here*—I couldn't prevent the terrible images from flooding into my mind. World War II war criminals had purportedly been brought to Edgewood for experimental purposes. I wanted to understand what had truly taken place here without allowing my imagination to play havoc with the facts. I saw the faces of those that science had maligned and left broken. Experimentation had turned proud human beings into helpless, drooling zombies. They were the early lobotomy experiments, vestiges of semi-primitive medicine from an era when almost nothing was really known about the human brain.

*Stay focused.* Somewhere in this darkness might wait a desperate murderer, a mentally disturbed killer—I tightened my grip on the LDA and pushed forward.

Do you believe in psychic phenomena? I do, and in accordance with my eccentric beliefs, the lantern flickered and went dark.

"That's not good," Lido said.

I panicked for an instant, feeling ill equipped to handle an unexpected attack in the dark. I took comfort in the fact that I was not alone. "Backup will be here soon."

"I guess we should stay put until they get here."

"I suppose." I keyed my Palm Treo. It threw off enough light for me to see Lido.

"You sound disappointed."

"And you're not?" I heard a noise off in the distance and knew immediately that it wasn't the sound of a rodent or the old structure settling. It was the sound of the man we was looking for. I could see that Lido had heard it too. I nodded to him and he nodded back. All our years of training went out the window. We turned to pursue our perp.

# Sixty-One

With the phone off, the tunnel was once again completely black. I felt exposed in the darkness. I didn't know if the perp was carrying a weapon. I only knew that he was deranged and dangerous. In the dark, my hand brushed against the rusted iron members and springs that made up a bed frame. They were stacked several deep against the wall. Many rows of bed frames separated me from the man I was after. I moved quickly and quietly, taking cover behind the old frames.

I had never been in a situation like this and wasn't sure how to proceed. I could sense that Lido was close by and could just make out his shadow in the darkness. Don't ask me why, but I closed my eyes. With my eyes closed, my other senses grew dominant. I could sense those present in the tunnel, almost feel their heart's beating. I could sense a minor pulsing in the distance. I opened my eyes and saw the intermittent flash of a light emitting diode, an LED. It was a red LED barely noticeable, as red is the most difficult color to see in the absence of light. I could hear the sound of strained breathing, nervous breathing.

And then he spoke. “I have a knife against his throat. One move and he’ll die.”

“The tunnel is surrounded. There are dozens of law enforcement officers just outside, waiting for my signal,” Lido said.

I was listening for a response when it occurred to me, the man holding a knife to Paul Liu’s throat knew these tunnels inside and out. There might be several exits. In the dark, he might easily escape. I was considering my options when he forced my hand.

“Then all is lost.”

I heard a muted guttural scream, and knew I had to act. Holding the Palm Treo against my jacket to block the screen’s light, I retrieved a name from the address book. I pushed Send and dropped the phone into my jacket pocket. I put both hands on the LDA and focused the best I could on the flashing red diode. As I watched, the red LED turned to a bright turquoise and the message display illuminated. My eyes were well adjusted to the dark—for the brief second that the pager flashed, I could see a bound man with a knife being held to his throat. At that instant, I squeezed off a single round, aimed at the pager of Dr. John Maiguay.

# Sixty Two

The shot did not prove fatal.

I watched as the paramedics carried Maiguay to the ambulance on a stretcher. The single shot I had fired had shattered his ilium, just missing the femoral artery. Had I aimed a few inches higher, the .45 would have severed the superficially running blood vessel, and Maiguay would have lapsed into shock and bled out before the paramedics had reached them. My aim and the LDA had once again proven reliable. The round had pierced the pager first before continuing into Maiguay's body.

I was able to get my searchlight back on. I gave it a few whacks and the sputtering light came back on just enough to see Paul Liu lying gagged and bound on the tunnel floor, next to the injured man who had long pretended to be the deceased John Maiguay. I remembered the first time I'd met Maiguay, noting that his facial features were a blend of Asian and occidental. I remembered his mustache and the thin surgical scar it attempted to conceal, which I had thought to be the scar from a repaired cleft lip. Seeing Maiguay writhing in pain on the tunnel floor confirmed my initial observation. A palatal appliance had been dislodged when he hit the floor. I could hear his unnatural breathing as he gasped for air. With the appliance out of place, there was nothing to stop air from resonating between the oral and nasal cavity. As a result, his breathing sounded adenoid. He sounded just like Rat, the deformed man we'd found lurking behind the wall in the Nine Circles Restaurant. I suspected there was a connection between those two, a connection that far surpassed that of two psychopathic coconspirators. Paul Liu was safe, but many questions still remained unanswered.

Lido stayed back in the tunnel, waiting for backup to arrive while I helped Paul Liu get to his feet and walk to freedom.

An army of law enforcement officers rushed toward me the second they saw me emerge from Edgewood, struggling to support Paul Liu.

Liu was weak and frightened. I knew that a traumatic ordeal like the one he had been through would not be easily forgotten. He would however have the best care that money could buy. As I watched, a police chopper descended toward the ground. The first person out of the chopper was the Chinese ambassador, R. C. Liu. The dignitary broke into a wind sprint at the sight of his son. He threw his arms around Paul and wept without uttering a word. Emergency services were already on the scene. R. C. Liu reluctantly relinquished his son to their care. He turned to me as his son was being led toward the ambulance. He was attempting to become the rock again, to toughen himself up into the higher powered man the world knew him to be, but he couldn't. He walked slowly toward me, put his arms around me and continued to weep.

"Paul's okay now. Everything's going to be alright."

Liu pulled back for a second. He nodded and then hugged me again.

I saw the press running across the hospital's quadrangle. "The media is here."

Liu wiped away his tears and pulled himself back into shape before the first camera flashed. "This act of bravery will never be forgotten, Detective. You have made a friend for life." He straightened his suit and joined his son at the ambulance as darkness turned to artificial daylight from dozens of flashing camera strobes.

I watched the joyful reunion for a moment before noticing that I too was being observed. I had never met the woman staring at me, but knew her instantly. It was in her posture and the way she carried herself—the confidence in her smile. By the way, she was wearing an absolutely amazing man-tailored suit.

"Detective Chalice." She approached me with her hand extended. "Pamela Shearson." She had the poise of a seasoned politician. "I'm so glad to finally meet you."

Shearson and I had only talked on the phone. The case was going full tilt and I hadn't had the opportunity to stop by the house for a formal introduction. I felt a little shabby next to her. I was dirty and unkempt from searching the underground tunnels. "Amazing work, Detective—I read Sonellio's assessment of you three times because he praised you so highly—looks like every word of it was true. I have to admit, I was a little concerned with your MO, exploring defunct subway tunnels and rushing into obsolete mental facilities. You're a bit of a maverick, aren't you?"

"I just follow my instincts."

"How can I argue with success? Be more careful next time. I need you." Shearson brushed the soot off my shoulder and then buttoned her jacket. She turned toward where the media was devouring Paul and R. C. Liu. "I sense a photo op," she said. "Come on, Detective, let's get noticed." We took a few steps and then Shearson stopped. "Don't forget, you stand behind me. I don't want to be upstaged by your pretty face and big chest."

Ambler was nearby and obviously within earshot. I saw him smirk over Shearson's orders. The woman was the consummate political animal. As sweet as she had come off, I knew she was only interested in me for what I could do for her—make her look good and facilitate her meteoric rise to the top. She may have been one hell of a polished bullshit artist, but I was an NYPD detective. It was my job to assess personality and motive. She spilled the beans when she said, "I need you." I'd known others like her, affected personalities and lip service, empty promises and treachery. It would be a good long while before she'd earn my trust.

So I did as instructed and stood behind her while the press snapped our pictures.

# Sixty Three

"Nice shooting, Kid." Ambler threw his big paw over my shoulder. "I tell you, Chalice, you've got a brass pair. I thought that I was a tough guy, but you, you take the cake, running around in the tunnels beneath a defunct nut house. Man, what a great story this is going to make." Ambler stopped short and stung me with a stare, his demeanor doing an abrupt about face, "That was incredibly brave and incredibly stupid. You and Lido pull a hair-brained maneuver like that again and I'll strangle the two of you myself. The two of you went after a cold-blooded killer with a Five and Dime flashlight. Do you know how bad your odds were? You're lucky that you, Lido, and Paul Liu didn't all end up dead."

Ambler was not an overly emotional man, but I saw in his eyes that I had pushed him over the edge.

"I never want to be the one that has to tell Ma and Ricky that you were killed in the line of duty." He shook me by the shoulders. "This is no joke. I want your word you'll never do anything like that again."

"One day that sixth sense of yours is going to get that ass of yours in a situation you won't be able to extricate it from."

"I said I'm sorry."

"Okay, end of speech. Hector and Marsh are waiting for us inside. Marsh knows the true identity of our suspects."

It was time to put emotion on the back shelf. There were so many questions. I couldn't wait to sit down with Marsh and get the answers. My phone rang.

"I need you and Ambler back in the tunnel," Lido said.

"Why, what'd you find?"

"Stop asking questions and get down here. You won't believe it."

I began to run with Ambler chasing after me, relaying Lido's message along the way.

Edgewood had been transformed into a crime scene and the once cavernous, pitch black tunnel was now flowing with law enforcement personnel, and was adequately lit with emergency lighting systems. It was at the far end of the tunnel, where it articulated with Pilgrim State that we found Lido. He had a pair of bolt cutters in his hand. I wasn't sure what to expect from him, but he appeared to be jazzed over his discovery.

"Lido was beaming. "Check it out." A heavy metal chain and snapped padlock hung from a door handle. Lido pushed on the double doors and we walked into an old storage room not far from the tunnel entrance. Now you have to understand that this entire level had long since been abandoned. It was filthy and dilapidated—spider webs hanging from the ceiling were large enough to support a team of aerialists, I swear. But this storage room was neat and clean. It had been freshly painted a bright white, and the linoleum floor had been buffed to a clinically acceptable shine. Overhead lights had been replaced with modern operating room lamps and surgical instruments had been set out on trays. In the middle of the room were twin operating tables, surrounded by all manner of surgical gizmo and life support monitors. In short, anything and everything a madman could ever hope for—everything he might need in order to perform the surgical procedure Damien Zugg had imagined.

I have to admit, Dr. Frankenstein's laboratory had come to mind when Zugg first hypothesized as to the reason Paul Liu and Kevin Lee had been abducted. I had pictured massive Van de Graaff generators and operating tables being hoisted toward the night sky while lightning bolts flashed and werewolves bayed at the moon…but that was fiction. As difficult as it was to believe, at Edgewood Hospital, here in the middle of Long Island suburbia, reality had replaced fantasy.

"Ready for the best part?" Lido said.

Ambler and I shrugged. I couldn't imagine how he could top what we had just seen.

Lido approached a wall mounted X-ray viewer and flipped on the light. The illuminated x-ray clipped to the viewer was of Rat's deformed skull. Zugg had been right on the money.

# Sixty Four

Lido's sense of the macabre had not been sufficiently sated, so we left him below ground to nose around the operating room while Ambler and I hoofed it back up to Pilgrim State to debrief Dr. Marsh.

Marsh looked nothing like I expected. He had WASP-fro hair. How's that for a portmanteau? He was wearing plaid pants and was puffing on a pipe. Oddly, he reminded me of an aging porn star, reminiscent of the days when adult films were shot in 8mm.

Marsh and Hector were huddled over a pair of folders, reviewing notes, when Ambler and I arrived. We sat down at the conference room table and waited a moment while the good doctors completed their current stream of thought. This was my first contact with Marsh. I reached across the table and shook his hand.

Marsh turned the folders around so that we could examine the photos they contained. The first folder contained pictures of the man who had been posing as the late Dr. John Maiguay. The photos spanned several years chronicling him as he progressed from a young boy into a teenager. His cleft lip scar was clearly visible in the early photos, the one's taken before he developed facial hair. With the dark mustache in place, it was almost impossible to detect his birth defect. I recalled the first time I'd met him, the minutest hint of a scar just peeking out from behind his mustache and commenting to myself that only a very observant eye would notice it. He was the lucky one—the photos of Rat were impossible to bear.

Here too, the photographs had recorded his development as he progressed from a young boy into a teen. As Zugg had foretold, Rat's abnormalities were congenital. The early photos were the hardest to look at, the child's face with the enormous cyst on the forehead occluding his eye. It was more than I could handle. I closed the folders and pushed them back across the table.

"Their names are James and Terrance Ryan," Marsh said.

"Ryan?" Ambler queried, no doubt surprised as I was that the boys did not have Asian names.

"That's right, James and Terrance Ryan, twin brothers, the sons of Patrick and Mayra Ryan. Patrick Ryan was a veteran, born and raised on Long Island. As a vet, he had his military benefits to pay for the care of his boys."

"Which one is which?"

"James is the one that's been impersonating the deceased Dr. Maiguay. Terrance is the one with the extreme deformities."

"Then their mother was Asian?"

Marsh nodded.

My mind once again flashed back to my initial encounter with the man posing as Dr. Maiguay. I recalled thinking that his features were a curious blend of Oriental and occidental—now it made sense. "You seem to be very familiar with this case."

"Detective, I was employed here at Pilgrim State for almost thirty years. I started as a staff psychiatrist right out of medical school and worked here until I retired a few years back—in charge of the facility for the last twenty. You have no idea what I've seen over the years." Marsh took a moment to wet his lips. "I haven't come across a more difficult case study than the one involving Terrance and James. One of the most tragic stories I've ever encountered."

I honestly didn't know that I had the strength to hear Marsh's story, but I knew I had to. "I'm sure this is difficult for you, Doctor. We don't need all the gory details, a high level overview will suffice."

"That might be best," Marsh said.

It was getting very late and I was beginning to feel physically and emotionally spent. Whatever it was that had kept me going had run out. We had recovered Paul Liu and had two suspects in custody. It was only a macabre sense of curiosity that kept me in my chair while my queen sized sleigh bed and pillow cried out for me. I was dying for a good night's sleep and would be happy enough to wrap up the details in the morning—or so I thought.

Marsh took a moment while he packed more tobacco in his pipe. Thank God he didn't light up. "Ryan met his wife and married overseas—the Philippines I believe." He reviewed the folder before continuing. "Mother's name was Mayra de la Cruz." He shut the folder and looked me in the eye. "The Philippines is the Third World. Have you ever been to a Third World country, either of you?"

"I've been to Haiti," Ambler said. "It's not pretty, children running around naked, hungry people living in shacks. It's very bleak."

"That's right, inadequate nutrition, disease, lack of medical care—all adds up to a high level of birth defects. Do you understand where I'm going with this?"

We did, and I'm sure he could read in our eyes that we didn't need to know the gruesome details pertaining to Terrance Ryan's congenital birth defects.

"You can leave out the details concerning the

boy's physical deformities, Dr. Marsh," Ambler said. "We're more concerned with their behavior and anything that would help us to understand why they became deviant."

"These boys never had a chance. By the time they were brought here for care, they had already endured their mother's suicide and years of rejection and ridicule. Their father blamed them for their mother's suicide. He was a very traditional Irishman with strong opinions. He didn't make their lives easy."

I didn't want to assume, but could understand why Mayra de la Cruz had taken her own life—the pain she must have endured as a foreign woman trying to bring up two deformed children with no support from family or friends. All the same, I had to ask. "Do you know if the mother left a suicide note?"

"No," Marsh said. "I only know about the suicide because it was disclosed during the intake procedure."

"And their father is dead?"

"I can only assume so. He was in a bad way when he brought the boys here."

"Bad way?" Ambler asked.

"Out of work—I suspect he was a lush. He dropped the boys off and never came back. Despite our best efforts, the boys endured a living hell while they were here."

"How long was that?"

"Almost ten years as I remember. They were discharged when they reached their majority. They took advantage of outpatient services for a while after that—eventually we lost track of them."

"And Maiguay was a physician here?" Ambler asked.

"Yes, he worked in the infirmary for many years. The man had a good heart."

"How so?"

"Well, just the fact that he devoted so many years to this facility. The state doesn't pay all that well, you know. He passed up many lucrative offers, just so that he could take care of Pilgrim's resident population—he was one of the only kind souls the Ryan boys knew. Finally though, economics won out and he accepted a position at Lenox Hill in the city."

"How long ago was that?"

"Just before I retired, three to four years ago."

Ambler and I looked at each other, presumably arriving at a similar conclusion at the same time. The real John Maiguay never made it to his new job at Lenox Hill. Somehow James Ryan must have stayed close to Maiguay, learning enough medicine to pose as a physician and take his spot at Lenox Hill. The real John Maiguay, the devoted physician that cared so deeply for these unfortunate twins never made it out of The Pine Barrens, and was likely the twins' first victim.

"It's not hard to see why they turned out the way they did. Still, James must have been a brilliant child in order to pull off the elaborate scheme that he did."

"Oh yes, James was bright alright, extremely bright. Both boys had above average IQs, especially Terrance."

"But I thought he was mentally impaired," Ambler said.

"Terrance, mentally impaired? Why would you say that?" He flipped open one of the folders and began looking through it. "He was tested a number of times—consistently scored over one hundred sixty on the Wexler Adult Intelligence Scale."

"I knew it," Ambler shouted. "He's a goddamn faker."

"What do you mean he was faking it?" Hector asked.

"Terrance was psychologically evaluated shortly after he was apprehended. We were led to believe that he had very limited intelligence, likely as a result of his congenital deformities. We were told he had limited executive functioning."

"Not the Terrance I knew," Marsh said. "He was brilliant despite everything he was going through. If either of these boys was capable of committing a complex crime, it's Terrance. Despite his small size, he completely dominated James. He was physically abusive. He used to slice his brother's scalp with glass, beat him, and burn him, but smart enough not to leave any marks on the face or arms. He got away with it for years and James never turned him in."

"Why do you suppose that was, Dr. Marsh? Why do you suppose James put up with physical abuse? He was bigger, stronger—it just doesn't make a hell of a lot of sense," Ambler said.

"It makes all the sense in the world. You see, all the physical size in the world won't help you when you're intimidated, and in this case, the simple answer is that James was afraid of his brother."

"James was afraid of Terrance?"

"Oh certainly," Marsh said, "Almost everyone was." He took a pack of cigarettes out of one pocket and retrieved a lighter from the other. "Anyone mind if I smoke?"

I wasn't a fan of smoking, but I wasn't going stop him. We were finished with Marsh's debriefing. He lit the cigarette. The first whiff of it sent my mind flying. "I've got to go. Thank you for your time." As I left the room I wondered why I hadn't made the connection before.

# Sixty Five

John Doe, the apartment over the restaurant, and the tunnel staircase, they all reeked from cigarette smoke, and then it hit me, so did Ryan. I don't know why it hadn't dawned on me before, but it all hit home the moment Marsh lit his cigarette. Terrance Ryan, the man we knew as Rat, needed to be looked in on, and he needed it now.

Ambler had stayed behind to wrap things up. Gus was sitting next to me as the chopper lifted off and headed back to Manhattan.

I took the time to brief him on the meeting Ambler and I had taken with Marsh and Hector. Needless to say, I had his full and undivided attention.

"You have to wonder, why didn't they torture Paul Liu the way they tortured John Doe?"

"Because, Gus, he was the right one. In Paul Liu, they'd had found their holy grail, the one human being that could be used to repair Terrance Ryan's congenitally deformed skull. It was their prize and they needed to keep it, keep Paul Liu in good condition until they could perform the surgery."

There was a lot that I had to presume, but presume I would for I needed to make all the pieces fit within my mind before I reached Lenox Hill. Marsh had stated that the twins had been discharged from Pilgrim State upon reaching their majority. He also said that they had been outpatients for a short time, but soon after, disappeared. The word, disappear, meant different things to different people. To a man like Marsh, it meant that they stopped making appointments and coming to the hospital. To me, it meant that they had simply dropped out of sight.

I would never be able to imagine what life was and had been like for someone like Terrance Ryan. His deformities had forced him to retreat underground, to shun society and lurk within Manhattan's shadows and the tunnels that connected Pilgrim State and Edgewood Hospitals. He must have learned early in life to intimidate and to use his intellect to his best advantage, in order to survive against the never ending pain he was forced to endure as a result of his appearance. Torture and manipulation had become the tools he relied on for survival.

The promise of a new day must exist in the human mind in order for an individual to go on day after day. There must be hope, and to create hope, Terrance had fantasized about and attempted to carry out his warped plan to alter his appearance by replacing his congenitally deformed skull with a healthy one. I could only imagine that his plan was years in the making, learning medicine, learning surgery, dreaming, scheming—in his sick mind, somehow it all made sense. As for his brother James, he was either equally deranged, or so completely dominated by Terrance, that he could not escape his brother's evil.

The trip back was over in the blink of an eye. As Lido and I stepped from the chopper, the whomp of the chopper blades subsided, and for a brief moment I was acutely aware of how quiet and serene the city was in the middle of the night. For a few brief seconds, all was still. There were no cries for help, no alarms, and no gunshots. Manhattan was peaceful and serene, bathed in the tranquility of night. And then, just as quickly, status quo returned.

The automatic doors slid open. Lido and I raced into Lenox Hill's emergency room. The quiet was gone, medical personnel were rushing about, a stricken older man was moaning, a woman was sobbing—the world was back to normal.

We took the elevator to the floor where the psychiatric patients were housed, identified ourselves, and rushed to Terrance Ryan's room, Rat's room.

It was empty.

# Sixty Six

"This is bad."

The policeman who had been assigned to watch Ryan was lying face down on the floor with a hypodermic needle sticking out of his neck. The sharps container had been ripped off the wall and torn apart. The needles are supposed to be broken off before the syringes are disposed of, but someone had gotten lazy. Lido helped the officer up and he started to come around.

I was eye level with the bed. One of the leather restraints that should have secured Terrance Ryan was saliva soaked and had been gnawed through. I couldn't imagine that he had been flexible enough to bend over and chew through the leather restraint, but in that instant I knew that was exactly what had happened.

"What hit me?" the officer said. He leaned forward and rubbed the back of his head.

"Don't move," Lido said. "There's a hypodermic needle sticking out of your neck."

The officer winced.

"Any idea how long you've been out?"

He shook his head.

"Stay with him. I'm going to take a look around." There was no need to buzz for a nurse. I heard footsteps racing down the corridor.

"No hero shit, right?" Lido said.

"I'll be right back."

I dashed out of the room and scanned up and down the hallway—nothing. I began going door to door, from one patient room to the next, checking every bed to make sure Ryan wasn't in one of them, playing possum. I finally came upon an on-call room and yanked the door open. A man was lying face down on the floor, clad only in boxers. He had a pulse, so I left him and raced back to Lido.

A doctor was already attending to the police officer. The hypodermic was out of his neck and the doctor was dressing the injection site. A nurse was assisting.

"There's a man unconscious in the on-call room down the hall. We need to mobilize security. The man who was in this room is a suspect in a murder investigation and is trying to escape. I need all the exits sealed immediately."

"Help them," the doctor said. "I've got this."

The nurse raced out of the room.

"We'd better hit the ground floor. I've got no idea how fast hospital security moves."

The doctor was shaking his head. "Unless it's time for a coffee break, you're on your own."

We raced to the elevator, pacing, while we waited for it to hit our floor. We jumped in and began planning strategy. "He may be gone already. It's New York City. If he's hit the street, he can vanish in a hundred directions."

I could see that words were stuck in Lido's mouth. We went three floors down before he spoke. "Unfortunately, we have to split up. I'll take the main entrance and coordinate sealing off the building with hospital personnel."

"I've already called it in. I'll cover Emergency."

He grabbed me and kissed me before the doors opened. It was unexpected, but not unwelcome. I felt myself slipping away. We were both so tired. I wanted to rest in his arms and leave the world's problems behind me, but in the next instant, the doors parted, and we reluctantly split up.

When I hit Emergency, it was no different than the way I had left it. The old man was still moaning and the woman was still sobbing. I could see an ambulance pull up just outside. Within a moment, the ER doors burst open. A pair of paramedics rushed in pushing a gurney. Emergency room physicians rushed over to them. The place was in pandemonium.

I checked everyone in the room. I wasn't sure how Ryan would be dressed, but there was no camouflaging his face, and for that reason, I considered it an unlikely route of escape. Ryan would seek an exit that would afford as little attention as possible. I tried to think as he would. I knew that he was most comfortable below ground. Lenox Hill had a basement, probably a hell of a basement, filled with supplies, emergency equipment and generators, but that would only provide him a place to hide—egress to street level would be difficult.

I was standing in the center of the ER's entrance, turning in a circle, trying to will the answer into my head, when from the corner of my eye, I noticed that outside, the doors on the back of the ambulance opened and closed. I hit the street.

# Sixty Seven

Less than a minute had passed from the time the paramedics had rushed into the ER. Unless I was mistaken, they hadn't left the building. If Ryan was already outside the building, it didn't make sense that he would remain nearby, knowing that we would be looking for him. Still, something told me not to ignore what I'd seen.

As I drew the LDA from my shoulder harness, I realized that I was pulling a recently fired weapon. It felt different in my hands as I gripped it, as if it were still warm from being discharged, although that was not the case. I had no desire to fire it again, but knew that I wouldn't hesitate to use it on Ryan. In quadrants of my mind, I held pictures of his victims, John Doe, Kevin Lee, and the real Dr. John Maiguay. All three were heinous and violent atrocities. Doe had been abducted and maliciously tortured. Lee had been murdered and used as a study for Ryan's insane surgical procedure. John Maiguay had befriended Ryan, and lost his life as a result.

I was outside the ambulance when I heard a muffled voice coming from within. It was not anything I expected to hear. Once again, the voice was muffled, but what I thought I heard was, "Do you take Jesus Christ as your Lord and savior?" It struck me as so bewildering, but at the same moment I understood. I heard it again, "Do you take Jesus Christ as your Lord and savior?" The possibility was so extremely remote and yet I was one hundred percent sure. I opened the ambulance door.

Terrance Ryan was on the floor, pressed into the corner of the ambulance bay. He was dressed in short sleeve hospital scrubs. Damien Zugg was still in his hospital gown. Without his cap, I could clearly see the horseshoe shaped scar on his head. He had Ryan pinned in place with his foot against Ryan's throat. He was a large man and had little trouble keeping Ryan underfoot. The IV start was still in Ryan's arm. Zugg was holding a syringe. The syringe's needle was already inserted into Ryan's IV line.

"Damien, what the hell are you doing?"

Zugg looked at me, but didn't see me, and I could tell by the look in his eyes that he was off. All the medications had taken their toll on him, the pain killers and the scorpion venom. And there was the cancer, the glioma tumors growing within his brain, eating away at him, changing him irreversibly.

"I offer him salvation," Zugg said.

"I've no interest in salvation," Ryan said. His voice was still adenoid. I could still hear his wind resonating where it didn't belong, producing an unnerving wheeze, but this was no longer the voice of a child. It was the voice of furious contempt, the voice of an intelligent man who hated the world and every perfect soul that dwelled upon it. "I want everyone to suffer."

"Damien, you and I both know this is not the way we serve justice. Let me take him in."

Zugg was still looking and not seeing me. "His hatred is his only true deformity."

"We both know that, Damien, and we both know this is not the way law enforcement officers administer justice. Don't do this—you've served so many years—don't let it end this way."

"Do it! Do it!" Ryan wheezed. "We'll burn together."

Zugg looked down at him, "Walk toward the light. The good Lord will overlook your contempt."

I didn't know what was in the syringe that Zugg had prepared. I didn't know whether Ryan's death would be instantaneous, or if Zugg had planned to administer death as an agonizingly slow retribution to this creature that was foul in appearance and foul of heart. I did know one thing for certain—Damien Zugg was going to squeeze that plunger and end the creature's life. The LDA was still in my hands, but pointed at the ground. There was something I was supposed to be saying, something about dropping the syringe or I'll fire. But Zugg was going to squeeze the plunger with or without a bullet in him.

May God forgive me.

I holstered the LDA, made the sign of the cross and stepped from the back of the ambulance.

It wasn't until the doors were closed that I once again heard Zugg's muffled voice.

"And you shall dwell in the house of the Lord forever and ever. Lord hear our prayer."

# Sixty Eight

Terrance Ryan, the man who had lived his life anonymously, planning one day to walk the streets of New York City normal in appearance, but mentally insane, was found dead in the back of a NYCEMS ambulance. Cause of death would be determined to be myocardial infarction.

My best guess was that Zugg had administered small consecutive doses of potassium chloride through Ryan's IV. An elevated potassium level will stop the human heart. The problem is that if done in one quick dose, elevated electrolyte levels are detectable during autopsy. By administering small doses once every ten seconds or so, Zugg was able to bring on cardiac standstill and allow the body time to metabolize the poison, making it undetectable in postmortem testing. By the time Ryan's body was autopsied, all electrolyte levels were once again within normal range. Zugg was not reported missing from his room, and the lethal syringe was never recovered.

Only God, Zugg, and I, knew the way it actually went down, and it is something I would have to wrestle with all the remaining days of my life. One day we will all have to answer for our time on earth. Zugg would likely stand before his maker many years before me—but not today. I prayed that the book of Damien Zugg's life on earth still had many chapters unwritten.

The sun was coming up over New York City as Lido and I walked back to my apartment, arm in arm. The sky was clear, and the morning air was refreshing. It gave us just enough strength to stagger the path home.

My cell phone rang just as we were mere yards from my doorstep. I didn't recognize the number. Exhausted as I was, my first thought was to ignore it, but once again, something, call it instinct, told me answer. The voice on the other end of the line belonged to Dr. Bock, the physician that had given me my departmental physical exam. He was calling to give the results of my lab work.

The breath caught in my lungs.

Lido undoubtedly saw the look on my face. "What's the matter?" I held him at bay until Bock was completely finished.

I mentioned to you before that I pray each night for my loved ones and friends. I pray for the memory of my father, and for Ma and Ricky, and Ambler of course. Gus would always be in my prayers, and I prayed for those like Sonellio and Zugg, the ones that needed a little extra help.

Tonight I would add one more.

Made in the USA
Charleston, SC
27 May 2011